BOOKS BY FREDERICK BUSCH

FICTION

Absent Friends　1989
Sometimes I Live in the Country　1986
Too Late American Boyhood Blues　1984
Invisible Mending　1984
Take This Man　1981
Rounds　1979
Hardwater Country　1979
The Mutual Friend　1978
Domestic Particulars　1976
Manual Labor　1974
Breathing Trouble　1973
I Wanted a Year Without Fall　1971

NONFICTION

When People Publish　1986
Hawkes　1973

Absent Friends

Frederick Busch

ABSENT FRIENDS

Alfred A. Knopf *New York 1989*

THIS IS A BORZOI BOOK
PUBLISHED BY ALFRED A. KNOPF, INC.

Thanks to the editors of the following magazines where some of the stories first appeared, sometimes in altered form: *Crazyhorse*, "Greetings from a Far-Flung Place"; *The Georgia Review*, "Dog Song"; *Gulf Coast*, "Name the Name"; *The Iowa Review*, "North"; *Memphis State Review*, "Naked"; *New Directions Anthology*, #50, (1986), "Comrades," *New Directions Anthology*, #52 (1988), "In Foreign Tongues" (both published by New Directions Publishing Corporation); *The New Yorker*, "Orbits"; *The Ohio Review*, "Gravity"; *The Quarterly*, 8, "Ralph the Duck"; *Tikkun*, "One More Wave of Fear."

LIBRARY OF CONGRESS CATALOGING-IN-PUBLICATION DATA

Busch, Frederick.
    Absent friends / Frederick Busch.—1st ed.
        p.   cm.
    ISBN 0-394-57426-5
    I. Title.
PS3552.U814A64 1989
813'.54—dc 19   88-13411
                          CIP

Manufactured in the United States of America
First Edition

For Reynolds Price

A solemn consideration, when I enter a great city by night, that every one of those darkly clustered houses encloses its own secret; that every room in every one of them encloses its own secret; that every beating heart in the hundreds of thousands of breasts there, is, in some of its imaginings, a secret to the heart nearest it! Something of the awfulness, even of Death itself, is referable to this.

CHARLES DICKENS, *A Tale of Two Cities*

Contents

Absent Friends

From the New World

N ORMAN'S P.O.V.: The blue-white spin of heavy snow in the afternoon, the metronome of their windshield wipers, and only the high banks of ice and slush, only Tess and Norman tunneling upstate. ROLL CREDITS. "They came up here before everybody else decided to," he said, waving at New York State, a hundred miles from Manhattan, and years away from himself.

"Not anymore," Tess said.

"What, not anymore?"

"You can't *go* anyplace that everyone doesn't go to."

He turned off the two-lane on which they'd driven from the Taconic Parkway, and now they were climbing to the ridge where he and his parents had lived, and then his parents, and then his father alone. It was the week when temperatures in the East fell to zero and below, and no one went out if they could help it except to work, or to save the dying, or to serve the remaining purposes of the dead. On the West Side of Manhattan the wind-chill factor brought the temperature to twenty-two below; out here, it would drop to forty below zero tonight, and there were snow squalls. "Maybe Maine," Norman said.

"What's left in Maine? Nuclear plants on the coast, a navy installation inside every cove, and the lakes are polluted. What about the paper companies in the woods? What woods? All that's left is L. L. Bean, they still pay the postage."

"You are not cheering me up, Tess. This road isn't plowed."

"Yes, you can see the piles on the side."

"Not today. Not this afternoon. Not now."

She put her hand on his leg and patted it. "There must still be parts of Maine," she offered him. "We could go out there this summer."

They were at the side of the road, or where it might have been. A whiteout caught them, and he stopped. They slewed when he braked, and Norman said, "We might have to walk from here."

Tess pointed to the loafers she wore.

"Well, I told you to wear boots."

"I thought that was because you were jumpy. You know. About this."

"No," he said, and he heard the cruel relish on his voice, "it was because of that." He jabbed his thumb at the moving snow that appeared to lie on the air about them.

"It'll clear," Tess said.

"I'm not waiting. We'll die of carbon whatchamacallit."

"Monoxide," she said.

4

"Thank you."

He released the brake, put the car in gear, and pressed the accelerator. They moved, and he said, "Thank you, Lord."

"Who always says that?"

"Tony Cummings."

"The boom guy?"

"He always says, after a good shoot, 'Thank you, Jesus.' "

"And you changed it to 'Lord'?"

"I'm not converted, Tess. Just grateful."

"There's the house," she said. "Thank you, Lord Jesus."

The squall was blowing off as they crested the low hill onto which the narrow, snow-clogged road turned sharply. A low gray sky was lighted from a distant, silver source inside its boil and plunge. The wide, white two-story house with its snow-covered roof stood against the moving sky like something painted, a set. "Don't talk about movies," Norman said, pulling up the handbrake.

"I didn't."

"*I* did."

With his eyes still closed, he leaned toward her, in the car that grew cold, under windows that had already begun to fog from their breathing, and he burrowed onto her shoulder and into her neck. He did it like a boy, he knew. Hands on his lap, eyes turned into his skull: there to be nursed. She kissed his lips. Her lips were soft and cold. Then she patted his head with a mitten she'd drawn on.

"Men," Norman said, resting his head on her shoulder.

"Men," she intoned, "are dogs."

Then she gently pushed him away. She reached behind his seat and pulled up a pair of boots. "I do listen," she said.

He sighed. "What a theatrical sigh," he said. "So let's

go bury them. No. We did that. Let's go bury me."

"Self-pitying flatulence."

"Whom, then, shall we bury?"

"When will Anna be here? Is there a possibility of reprieve? Would you mind it if your sister died too? Today? No. An awful joke. In terrible taste."

"And not a joke," he said.

"Well, barely one."

"She'll come tonight, after work. I promised her I'd cook for her."

"She must be relieved. She always thinks I always try to poison her."

"But you don't?"

"Not always."

They sat in the cold car, and then Tess took a breath, and then Norman did. Tess opened her door, crying out at the shock of the cold, and began to high-step through snowdrifts to the side door of the house. Norman picked up canvas bags and leather suitcases and, like a parody of bellman, he followed her. She fumbled with the key and dropped it in the snow, searched for it, brushed at it, worked it into the lock, and let them in.

It was icy and silent. Norman breathed deeply and knew he was disappointed. Whatever he had expected to smell—the flesh of a parent, familiar cooking, paint or wax or cleanser he associated with their life—with his—was absent. He smelled coldness, and Tess's clothing, her hair and perfume, cold ashes from the Franklin stove. Norman set the bags down. He reached for the switch to the ice-melting coils on the roof. He flicked it up, then saw that he had done so.

6

She giggled. "Never mind," she said.

"What?"

"I had this terrific urge to shout out, at the top of my lungs, *We're ho-ome*."

Norman put his hands around his mouth, and he bayed—through the dark kitchen, out one door at the living room, out the other to the dining room, and beyond it to guest rooms and office, extra bathroom, the stairs that went to his parents' bedroom, the room in which he'd lived as a boy and later sneaked his lovemaking with Tess. He cried, "I'm *home*!"

Windows moved in the storm, and the house creaked, as if it leaned in the wind. His voice died at once, a stone fallen through a dark pond. Tess patted his buttocks, then stooped to retrieve the bags. Norman shook his head and shaped his tone to banter.

"Latchkey child," he said. "What a way to raise a kid."

"Make a fire," Tess said. "Please make a big, hot fire." She reached for a switch and turned on the overhead light, an electrified barn lantern. "Do you know where the thermostat is? Or will they have turned off the furnace?"

"Not in this weather. If they had, there'd be frost all over the inside. It's on, but very low, just to keep the pipes from bursting."

Tess went to the sink and ran a tap. "There's hot water."

"And there's heat. In the living room, inside wall, on the right, when you go in. The thermostat?"

"Oh, yes. Near that goddamned decoy that poor man made for her."

"Which she pointed out was inaccurately painted. Of course, he'd only been making them for thirty years."

"Make a fire, Norman. I've decided, I think, to forgive her the decoy."

Tess went to the living room, and Norman opened the flue of the Franklin stove. There was plenty of kindling, firewood and newspaper. As he crumpled paper and made a cross-hatched structure of kindling on it, he heard the furnace kick on, then shut off. "Norman," Tess called.

"What?"

"Call that you're home again."

"What?"

"Say you're home."

"Why?"

"Say it."

He said, in almost a monotone, "I'm home."

"Did you say it?"

"Yes. I did."

"Say it louder."

As he struck a match against the fender of the stove and watched the paper catch, he stood and closed the fire screen. He turned toward the living room and called, "I'm home!"

The furnace thumped on again—she must have turned it up when he spoke. He heard it chug away, and there were corresponding tinklings in the low radiators in the kitchen and the rooms nearby as more hot water pushed through the baseboard pipe and the metal plates along it expanded. "Welcome home!" Tess called. "It's possible."

He was about to go to the living room to thank her when he began to cough and tear at the eyes. "Thank you, *Jesus*," he howled.

"What?" Tess called.

8

"Stay where you are," Norman said. "If you do, you might be able to breathe." Holding his breath, and working at the knob, he shoved it back; he had pulled it forward. "I thought I *opened* the goddamned flue."

She was in the kitchen now, talking with her fingers clamped on the end of her long brown, wickedly curving nose. "Bud ub course you closed it."

"But of course."

Tess said, "Norman, fuck it. You can do this thing anyway. Standing on your head. Screw the omens and portents."

"We'll just smoke the bastards out," he said.

He started to walk the first floor rooms. He imagined himself to be sauntering. "They're smaller than I remember them," he said. "Isn't that what people always tell you when they go home? That it looks smaller? It does."

But Tess wasn't there as Norman made his circle through connecting doors—out the left-hand door of the smoky kitchen and through the long living room with its eight mullioned windows on three sides, and then through the door (the huge fireplace took up the living room's interior wall and was bracketed by doors), and into the dining room, and through it into the hallway that connected two small downstairs rooms. When he was there, shivering in the unlighted narrow hallway across the house from Tess, he looked behind him and around, as if he couldn't remember what he'd just seen: the sofas in their busy bright slipcovers, the delicate curving furniture, the long cherry dining table, the Oriental rugs, the paintings and prints he always had seen. From a telephone stand in the hall, he picked up the phone and listened for the dial tone. He checked his watch.

9

Tess, behind him, said, "It's one o'clock on the Coast. Nobody's back from lunch."

"I gave them this number."

"But nobody stayed away from lunch to call you up and rescue you. Some friends."

"These aren't friends I'm expecting to hear from. One's my ex-partner and one's a writer."

"I don't know which one's worse."

"The writer. He thinks I'm corrupting him."

"Oh. Eddie Brownstein."

"The Virgin of the Apple IIe. I *made* him develop his novel into a script."

"And forced him to take your money."

Norman nodded. He brushed at his mustache.

"You shaved it off," Tess reminded him.

"Would you call that a castration wish?"

"Who told you that?"

"Who else?"

"Serota tells you whatever he thinks you don't need to hear. That's why you broke with him."

"He tells me he's the one broke up the partnership. I'm a nice fella, but I'm unreliable."

"That means he wants something you won't give him."

Norman nodded, and he gestured with his head toward the other side of the house, its warmth. Tess looked down the hall quizzically. Norman shook his head. "No," he said. "I haven't been in there. I'll go later." She looked at him and then she shrugged, then smiled. "I will," he said. He started to walk. Over his shoulder, he told her, "Serota wants me to sell him my share of *Benito Cereno*."

"He's too busy to call Herman Melville?"

"Don't you remember? Ten years ago, we paid that kid, Stoddard, to do a script?"

"Oh. Right. That was a bad script."

"Well, I'd read his stories, they were all about the black-white thing, they were very moving, the kid was hot, it seemed smart."

"It's a very literary script," she said, walking through the dining room with a hand on his shoulder, as if he led her.

"But it's got a couple of touches."

"And what does Serota propose?"

"He thinks he can get Mailer to rework the screenplay. He thinks Greg Peck will do the captain. What's his name."

"Isn't that a schmo role? The hero-schmo who doesn't understand?"

"At the end he understands. He whacks a few bad guys with his sword. The part Serota loves, he's working on convincing Michael J. Fox to play the Spanish captain the slaves take prisoner."

"Never," Tess said.

"I know."

"So sell him the Stoddard script that doesn't work so Mailer, whom he can't afford, won't write it, so Peck, who won't do it, can play opposite Michael J. Fox, who can't act that role and anyway he would never, ever try."

Standing in the kitchen now, hands in his pockets, bouncing on the balls of his toes in front of the Franklin stove, Norman said, "Yeah. But I hate to see Serota getting what he wants."

The kitchen was warm, and the windows were dark. It

felt like night. Tess began unpacking what they'd brought, mostly food and drink, and Norman moved through the kitchen, finding silverware in a drawer he hadn't known to look in and glasses in a cupboard opposite the one he'd guessed. He shook his head, and Tess—he looked up to see her watching him—said, "You haven't been here for a very long time."

"Are you nursing me?"

She thumped a bottle onto the counter. "Would you like me to start getting tough?"

He shook his head.

"Then just look sheepish, and behave yourself, and let me take care of you the best way I can."

"I'm all right," Norman said.

"That's right. What are you making for your sister? There's all this *stuff* you packed."

"Huh?"

"You promised Anna you would cook?"

"Oh. Right. Right. I thought I could marinate the London broil in a teriyaki sauce and, I don't know, bake some potatoes."

"Here's the soya. And you better get the potatoes in, first, before you make the marinade."

She tossed him a potato. He failed to catch it. As he stooped to retrieve it, he saw a piece of paper, two or three inches wide, and about as long, on the base of a pine dry sink his parents had used as a liquor cabinet. He held the potato in one hand and the paper—it was a gummed paper for memos from a pad of such slips—in the other. When he straightened, he didn't read the little page, but looked toward Tess.

But she was opening the refrigerator, her back was to Norman. She said, "Some neighbor's cleaned it up, or picked it over. All there is is ice."

He looked at the page. It was blank. He turned it over. The other side was blank. He slapped the page onto the potato, but it fell off and onto the floor. He scuffed it back under the dry sink.

"All the usual clues," he said.

At the refrigerator, Tess turned. "What?"

"Nothing. I was just being theatrical again," Norman said.

Tess closed the refrigerator door and leaned against it. Her face was tender, her shoulders were slumped. She said, "You go be what you need to."

Norman asked, "Are we done with the hard parts yet?"

The meat was in a casserole dish, covered with soy, sherry, oil, garlic, ginger, and orange rind. The potatoes baked. Norman and Tess sat in front of the Franklin stove and drank Glenfiddich straight.

Tess said, "I guess we should go upstairs and see about making beds and heating rooms."

"Soon," he said. "Later." He said, "Sometime. Eventually."

"On the other hand, we're not the hosts," she said. "Anna and Alexandra can help us, and we can do it just before we go to sleep. Or we can all sleep down here. On the floor."

"A good old-fashioned Tauber-family sleepout."

"Lockout would be all right with me." Tess checked the wall clock. "Anna should be pulling up soon. In a black coach behind two black horses with red eyes. Driven by a hunchbacked assistant to an evil doctor. Accompanied by the shrieks of her victims and the baying of hounds."

"She probably can't wait to see us, either."

"She can't wait to see whether we're stealing anything that's her rightful legacy. By virtue of your being the prodigal shithead independent son, and her being the dutiful daughter."

He unscrewed the cap of the Glenfiddich.

"Oh, no, you don't. You want me drunk."

"I want *me* drunk."

"We're both already halfway there. We're tired. We're stressy."

"Stressy is a word?"

"Fuck you, Norman. Don't correct my vocabulary." She cocked her head. "Did I get that right?"

He held the laugh in with tight lips, but it came out his nose as a piggy sort of snort. Tess opened her mouth and howled. The telephone rang. As they looked at each other, it stopped.

When it rang again, Tess answered it. The phone was on a wall, near a pantry closet across the room. She listened, she murmured, she shook her head, and then she hung up.

"Lhommedieux," she said. "The real estate guy."

"What'd he offer this time?"

"A quarter of a million."

"And you said?"

"To call tomorrow. When the Beast of Brooklyn's here. *He* can listen to her declamations about cash flow."

"She does need it."

"She could *not* need it, and she'd still be whining. Your sister has never understood the concept of *enough*."

"If he's offering a quarter now, he'll come up."

"He can't build whatever it's called, Crappy Acres, whatever, without this piece."

"Well, he could. There'd just be a hole in it."

"Screw Crappy Acres. Screw him. And screw your sister."

Tess kissed him on the neck, under his ear, and he closed his eyes and smelled her. She smelled like berries. She smelled like the cold cellar of a stone house.

The back door rattled and thumped.

"Anna," Norman said.

He put his glass down and went to the back door. He flicked the outside light on, noting as he did that he'd remembered where the switch was. "There's nobody here," he said.

"Doesn't the female lead say, 'I guess it was the wind'? And the guy agrees? And they turn away from the door, and then the ravening creature bursts through the doorway and everybody screams."

"I guess it was the wind," Norman said.

"No, I'm supposed to say it. I guess it was the wind."

"And I agree."

They watched each other watch the door. They shook their heads simultaneously. "No ravening creatures," Tess said.

Norman said, "We haven't been upstairs yet. There might be creatures upstairs."

Tess said, "We haven't been down the hall."

"Nobody's lived upstairs for years," Norman reminded

15

her. "I think it's mostly storage, now. Anna's the only one who came here after Mom died."

"So you think the creature's down the hall, Norman?"

He nodded.

"In your father's bedroom?"

"I saw the tracks his wheelchair cut into the carpeting. Coming from the hallway into the dining room. Going from the dining room into his office. Bedroom. Whatever you call it. It *used* to be his office. When I was a kid, it was his office. I think it's ironic. Funny. Not funny. He ends up in his office. It's where he mostly lived, anyway. Psychically, I mean. He loved his work. He was more comfortable with it, with his clients, than with Mom. Than with Anna or me. I hate the way that sounds—the rich kid complains his old man didn't love him well enough."

Tess said, "You are not a kid. And he *didn't* love you well enough. He did a lousy job at it. And that's why you left. You were right to."

He shrugged.

"Just as you're right to say the creature's down the hall. In his room."

He said, "Probably."

"Just as you're right to want to go down there *now*, before Anna comes and stirs so much silt up, you'll never be able to see."

"You think?"

"Yes."

"Now?"

"Yes."

He poured more Glenfiddich. "Dutch courage," he said.

"We don't need it."

"But we could take some with us."

Tess said, "We should take the whole bottle."

They went out the right-hand kitchen door, through the long dining room with its formal chairs and dark paintings, creamy paint, thick moldings. It was the darkest room in the house, and they had mourned their way through grim holiday meals in this room. Norman was sure they'd eaten party suppers and other celebrations there, but all he could remember was Thanksgiving. It was the assimilated Jew's national holiday, when national will and Protestant history and the yearning for communal ratification came together. Then, his mother sulked, and his father drank too much Pommard, and he and Anna fought as youngsters, got drunk as college students, and talked a brittle, boring litany of vocational adventures, just before he came home with Tess, and then left.

He was forgetting what he saw as he saw it—the tones of paintings, patterns in rugs, the sound of the *crack* of a hardwood plank as he walked over it, turning slowly into the hallway and looking down in the parchment-colored light of a converted gas lamp to see the grooves his father's wheelchair had cut into the green and tan and maroon carpet. He was drained of sensations and what thoughts insisted into him, as if he were a perforated bucket, like the rusted tin colander on scroll-shaped legs his mother had found in the packed-earth cellar and had used for washing vegetables. He would forget the colander he had just remembered, he

17

thought. He would lose this house and family as certainly as he had left it long before because he couldn't have it if he kept himself.

Tess, in the darkness at his back, in what felt like another in a series of outposts they had come to in coming here, whispered, "Do you want to go ahead in?"

"I didn't know I'd stopped."

Her hand was on his neck, lying on it; she didn't push or pull. She said, "You stopped."

"What would your mother have done?"

Tess's laugh was brief, light. "Mama? She'd have told us about ghosts. She'd have carried something of his up into the attic and made an offering, maybe. That kind of Mexican slow-motion delirium. Unless Daddy was home. Then she'd have sat down and listened to Ben Webster with him while he got his column ready. But she'd have kept her leg tapping, that way she does. And not in time to Ben Webster. She'd have been thinking about ghosts."

"That's the trouble with mixed marriages," Norman said.

Tess said, "Oh, I know."

"So have I stalled a pretty long time?"

"How long's enough?"

"Enough," he said. "Here we go."

Norman turned the glass knob of the heavy old door and it swung in gently, riding smoothly on the hinges. The light switch was cut into the side of the ceiling-high bookcase that extended to the doorway's edge. When he prodded it, a desk lamp and a reading lamp came on. He walked in. Tess came in behind him, but she didn't touch him. He could feel her. The room was painted a Colonial light blue, and the two windows behind the bow-legged table his father had used as a desk were decorated with maroon velvet curtains tied back into scallops. The paintings and prints, of Lincoln and Washington, Ulysses Grant, looked down their wall at a wing chair and a dark wooden table.

Gesturing at them, Norman said, "The usual Jews."

The books were about history. He suspected that he knew most of them and could find a lot of them by letting his hand remember where to reach. There were no filing cabinets; his father had kept his files at his office on Pine Street, in New York, had paid his bills at home as they came in, and had sent his documents to the office, even after his retirement, for storage by the firm. There was a closet. Its door would have to be opened. There were a few documents on the desk, held there by a paperweight. They would have to be examined.

The red leather chair with its matching ottoman, arranged as a client's chair near the desk, was the one he had sat on whenever he could, stretching out his boy's legs and sighing as his father did, after work, when Norman took care to sit elsewhere. On Thursday or Friday nights, he remembered, his father brought home *Life*. When Norman was small, he sat on his father's lap as his father sat in the red leather chair, and his father read an ad to him. It was about Elsie Borden and her husband Elmer, he thought he remembered. It appeared to him now as a drawing, a cartoon. And he sat on his father's lap and smelled his day's rich breath, and then they went in to dinner and he listened to the radio or went to bed. He must have been small. He couldn't remember whether he'd been able to read. He couldn't recall what his bedtime had been.

The wheelchair was closed and leaning against the wall

near the wing chairs. The wall looked wrong to him. Norman traced the wheel marks on the blue-and-red rug. The desk chair was a straight-backed dining room chair with a cushion covered in the dark velvet of the drapes. Norman moved it from the wall near the window, placed it behind the desk, and sat there.

"Want to sit down?" he asked Tess.

She stood before him, lean and tall, narrow-shouldered and narrower-waisted, wearing baggy tan slacks and a dark blue cotton sweater. She sat in the leather chair and let her long legs stretch to the ottoman. She'd changed back to loafers, he saw. Her color, in this dark room, seemed light, no longer mahogany, as it usually looked in daylight or in a bright room, but closer to the pitch of knots in a varnished board of pine. Tess was darkly bright.

Norman looked down to the surface of the desk. Under the dust, its good wood shone. There was a cheap insurance company calendar showing December, with nothing noted on any date. There was a small plastic cube that held wallet-sized photographs: his mother squinting at the sky as if it were dangerous; Anna at her high school graduation; Alexandra at hers; Axiom, the German shepherd they'd put down after he bit two of Norman's boyhood friends; and a black-and-white picture of Norman saluting the camera, wearing his three-year-old's approximation of an army uniform, puffing out his chest as he had seen his daddy do on his return from the campaign for Sicily.

"Well," Norman said. "I wasn't forgotten."

He held up the cube. Tess, though, was sitting back in the soft chair, and her eyes were closed. "Oh, you were not forgotten," she said.

"Did we ever discuss whether your father and my father might have been in the same place during the war?"

"We did. You thought he would have been in one of the all-black detachments, and I told you he was part of a Texas cook's company that had blacks, Mexicans, and, according to Daddy, three Filipinos, a Nisei Japanese, and a seven-fingered white man. My father was in Italy, too. We did talk to him about it."

"The Yugoslavian border. I remember that. In the mountains. My father never got that far. He got sent to North Africa, later on."

"Someone on my family tree might have served him his dinner. Or who *knows* what else."

The paperweight was a heavy brass reproduction of the investment company's logo. It held down a letter from the American Association of Retired Persons and a letter from Alexandra. The letter from Alexandra was under the letter from the AARP. And that was under a letter in a business-size envelope, his father's gray-white personal letterhead. On the back of the envelope was embossed ABRAHAM TAUBER and the address. On the front of the envelope, in the spidery late version of the firm hand he remembered, scratched in black ink with the Mont Blanc Meisterstück Anna had told him she wanted for Alexandra—Norman guessed it was in the table's single drawer—was his name.

He felt his stomach roll. He looked up: Tess was asleep, her head to the side, her mouth open, her hands folded in her lap. She breathed deeply as she slept. And he remembered the other indictments from his father. He was certain that he held a bill of particulars in its heavy envelope. *You were afraid you couldn't remember, Tauber. Don't you wish?*

Don't you wish? He wanted to say those words loudly enough to waken Tess, so that she might blink, and look up, and say, *What?* So that he could tell her how Abraham Tauber, given to writing long lists of his children's malfeasances, especially Norman's, had left behind a final, lengthy itemization of how his son had failed and failed and failed him.

He set the envelope on the desk. The room grew warmer as the furnace did its work. The surface of the desk felt cold, though, and so did his back, which was to the windows. He stood, and on his toes he walked around the desk to the closet. Tess didn't waken. The letter glowed on the dark maple desk. He turned the crystal knob of the closet and pulled. His father's smell poured onto him, its fleshness and expensive sweet soaps and sweated suits and silk of ties and sportcoat linings, the thick leather of his excellent shoes. The smell was stale and grand, merely skin and only perfumes, but so familiar and so intimate as to frighten him. He pushed the door closed too hard.

Tess, waking, said, "What? Are you all right?"

"I'm sorry," he said. "I got scared."

"There's no one hanging in there?"

Norman shook his head.

"Then we're safe," Tess said. "Almost."

"Almost. He left me a letter."

"Oh, lord."

"I wish he hadn't done that."

"Did you read it?"

"No."

"No. Will you?"

"No," he said. "I don't know."

Tess said, "No."

"You think I shouldn't?"

"I was only praying," Tess said, "not giving advice."

They were upstairs, on the theory that not even the silent second floor could be scarier than Abraham Tauber's office. It wasn't, yet. The top floor, shaped like a big U divided by interior walls, had a wing on the living room side and a wing on the office side. Of the five bedrooms, none was wrecked, though all were dusty and cold, and several had piles of taped cartons in them. Norman opened the radiators in one of the guest rooms while Tess found cold damp sheets and made up one of its narrow beds. "I don't care *how* uncomfortable it is. I am not sleeping by myself tonight," she said.

"I should bleed these pipes," Norman said.

"What if actual blood comes out?"

"What do you mean, *what if*?"

Tess said, "Norman."

He straightened in response to her tone. She looked across the twin bed.

She said, "Where did your father sleep?"

"Downstairs. In his office. He did it for years."

"Yes. On what?"

"On the daybed. Oh."

"That's right," she said. "Where was it?"

"Against the wall to the left of the closet."

"Where the wing chair is, and the little table?"

"That never quite registered," he said.

"It didn't with me, until now. Is anything else gone?"

"Is anything else gone. Yeah. Me." He laughed shrilly, and saw from her serious expression how hysterical he must sound. He closed his eyes. When he opened them, he said, "A picture from the photo cube, the plastic thing, on his desk. Him and Mom, a thousand years ago. In Paris. On the Ile de la Cité. Young, in love, all of that. With his wide-brimmed hat over his eyes. A Jewish Gary Cooper with a ditto Gene Tierney *manquée*. I think the bookshelves in the living room looked a little gap-toothed. So did the shelves in his office, I think. There were *pictures* gone, Tess. Am I right, the last time we were here, there was a sculpture of a dog or cat on the floor—it looked up? Must have been a dog, right? Looking at the moon?"

"Baying at their daughter-in-law."

"Well, that, too. Jesus, it's cold. The heat's beginning to get up here, but it's colder'n hell. And there's stuff missing."

"Anna's the executor. Executrix. She could take stuff, if she wanted, right? Maybe I mean executioner."

"I don't know about legally, but I imagine so. I know she *would* if she decided she was right."

"You mean if she wanted something," Tess said, folding a sheet over a crocheted afghan in bold primary colors that Norman had seen on one bed or another in his parents' house all his life.

"I think that's what I mean."

The radiator thumped and the pipes that led to it started to clank. Tess said, "What's his name comes through the door next, right? He tells us—Marley. He tells us about greed?"

They stood silently in the small, apple-green room, its walls lined with cartons and garment bags and piles of magazines and newspapers. A photograph of Albert Schweitzer, a mad musician's glint in his eye, hung over one bed; over the other was a mannered painting of a birch in winter, its limbs as sinuous as serpents on the move, its browns muddy, its whites untinted.

"I'm recognizing stuff when I see it, of course," Norman said. "I'm amazed at what I remember—after it jumps up and waves at me. What's scary," he said, and he watched Tess nod, as though she had already guessed, "is what I don't remember. And what that means, unless I stumble on it, or somebody tells me about it, is I'll probably keep on forgetting it. Why not? So I've lost it. It's gone. Unless Anna remembers it, and when in hell would I ever see *her*? I not only don't have it anymore—I can't get it back."

"That's probably why people save most things," Tess said, pointing to the magazines and papers, the clothes. "Out of the fear of maybe missing it. Not because it matters. Are you going to sell the house?"

"Are we?"

She said, "You and Anna. Not me. I'm the coal-black bitch came in and stole your genes away."

"You *wish* you were coal-black. You always wanted to be exotic."

"You know."

"Anna will finally decide, I guess. She'll pretend to consult me. Maybe she will. I'm not deciding with her until I talk to you."

"Fair enough, if that's what you want."

"You just don't like helping Anna."

"I want to respect their wish to keep separate from me."

"Even after death," he said.

"Of course."

"They'd never be that fair to you."

Outside, they heard tires whining, grinding against the ice beneath the snow. They nodded at each other: Anna.

"They never were," Tess said.

They went downstairs toward the kitchen door. Tess dropped back as Norman walked slowly through the kitchen from the hallway stairs. "You think Anna took the daybed?"

"Who else? I'm calling Francie," she said.

"Now? Good timing."

"You bet your ass, good timing," she said. She was at the wall phone near the pantry, dialing for Northfield, Minnesota, where Francisco was a tall, swanky café-au-lait history major in his junior year.

Anna's headlights flared at the kitchen windows as she parked near their car, and then the windows went dark. Soon there were feet stamping and voices burring, and the door was struck hard. "Sanctuary!" Anna cried.

"Save me," Tess murmured at the phone. But then she had Francisco, and she was grinning and talking and showing Norman all the innocent wide eyes she could muster. So he went to the door and opened it, and in they came, Anna stamping snow from her boots and hooting about cold and driving and exhaustion, Alex striding softly, wordlessly, in behind her.

They embraced, then looked toward Tess, who smiled, all Louis Armstrong teeth, and pointed to the phone and mouthed *My baby.* Anna signified her joy and sympathy for Tess by nodding very hard several times and rolling up her eyes and grinning back. Then Anna took her coat off and, picking up Alex's, then Tess's and Norman's, which they'd draped on a kitchen chair, she carried them all to the closet just outside the left-hand door to the living room.

Norman walked a few steps behind, as if to keep her company. He said, "I forgot all about that closet."

Alex, tall and severely thin, looking almost frail in black miniskirt, black tights, black turtleneck, black shoes, pulled at his arm from in back. When he turned to her, she stood on her toes and embraced him, hard. "Hi, Uncle Norman," she whispered. "I hope you're all right."

Tears came to his eyes, and he had difficulty in speaking. "Hi, kid," he said. "Thank you. We'll talk, all right? I want to hear about you."

He felt her nod. Then Anna returned.

"Doesn't she look *awful*? She's been dieting. She looks anorexic, I keep telling her. She looks like someone in the *camps*. But watch: tonight she'll eat what *you* make. From me, she takes nothing."

"I'll give you my recipe, then," Norman said. "How've you been, Anna?"

"For an older woman with a daughter who keeps an apartment on 48th Street and Eighth Avenue—"

"That's Hell's Kitchen," Norman said.

Alex smiled. Her teeth were small and perfect. Her hair— frosted blonder, Norman thought—hung in soft tendrils about her face, covering her high forehead. Thin and pale, she still was beautiful, he thought; she looked like his mother in the photo that was gone. "Now they call it Clinton," Alex said. "Theatrical people live there."

"I didn't know you were in the business," he said. "Can I help?"

Alex opened her enormous, heavy-looking leather bag

and took out cigarettes and matches. She tapped a filtered cigarette out and stuck it in her mouth, then lit it. She snapped the match out. Seeing no ashtray, she dropped it into her bag. She shook her head. "I'm theatrical in how I *act*—you know. I mean, I'm as much of a showboat as anybody else. But I'm not doing theater. I'm in the same racket."

"You still like it?"

"After I do their design work, I get to use their presses and run my own. I'm a business, Uncle Norm. Margins, Limited. You like it?"

"You doing all right?"

"I'm not starving. No matter what she says. I got a subcontract, this month, from a girlfriend who does posters for the Met. The Metropolitan Museum?"

"I'm familiar with the institution. And I think that's wonderful."

She nodded. "And it only took four years of RISD and two at Hunter, and last year I made almost fifteen thousand dollars. Before taxes."

"I think you're wonderful," he said, feeling his throat tighten again.

"Not just brave?" Alex said.

"Wonderful, smart, beautiful, and would you marry my son, please?"

"Illegal!" Anna cried. "First cousins can't marry!"

"Saved by the law," Alex said, low.

"Don't you call me a racist," Anna said.

Norman heard Tess say, "Bye, baby," and then hang up. "Now," Tess said from the other side of the kitchen, "who's the racist, did you say?"

The telephone rang. Norman almost stepped on Anna as he strode toward it. "For me," he said. "From the Coast. I'm expecting some calls, I'm afraid." He watched Tess embrace Alex, who hugged her back. He saw Anna put her hands on Tess's waist, as if to hold her away; but Anna looked up at Tess and gave her a giant smile. Tess touched Anna's jet hair—he thought it had been brown at the funeral—and Norman saw Anna almost flinch. Alex rolled her eyes in disgust. Tess went to the refrigerator for ice, and then Norman turned toward the door that went to the dining room, listening to the clink of bottles, the chugging of whiskey and gin over ice, and the high, nasal, somber tones of Eddie Brownstein, who was talking about standards.

Norman said, "Eddie, I agree. I also didn't want to develop a script where people learned things by overhearing them. And you are absolutely right to loathe that method of discovery. And of *course* it's a gimmick for getting information across. Eddie. Wait. That's why I hired *you*. So that I could have a script by a quality writer who wouldn't rely on—what do they call it in pro football? Gadget plays? Gadget plays. Then that's what I mean: gadget plays. I understand that your experience is narrative, and that you come more recently to the art of dramatizing. No, your novels are, indeed, dramatic. I mean a different kind of drama. Like the difference between, you know, theatrical and theatrical. No! Of course, I don't mean you're being theatrical. Nor are your books melodramatic. Jesus, kid, you really want a fight, don't you? Listen. Eddie, listen up for one minute. All we have to do is figure out a way the father learns what his wife tells his kid. That's all we're doing, all right? It's a problem.

It's a—treat it as a math problem is all. We either find the solution, or we do something else to eliminate the problem
from needing to be solved. All right? Eddie: I would like
you to telephone me within the next few hours. Not late, all
right? It's, it's six at night here. Okay? I want you to call
me by six, your time, and tell me you feel okay about the
project. That's all I need. As for the problem itself, we'll
work on that by phone and at conferences, if we need them.
Ed? Think about the boy seeking out the father and telling
him, on purpose, what the mother said. Yeah, but maybe he
does want them together again. All right? Yes. You'll call
me. Bye, Ed."

"That was Ed," Tess said, walking to the telephone and
handing him a wine glass with Glenfiddich in it.

Anna raised what looked like a huge martini on the rocks
and silently toasted them. Norman, leaning against the wall
near the phone, raised his glass in return. "Yes," he said, "that
was Ed. He's being writerly tonight. This afternoon."

"Imagine living in two times at the same time," Anna said.

"I love your dress," Tess said to her. Anna looked down
at her bright lavender print.

"It's old," Anna said.

"But pretty," Norman said.

Tess smiled at him. Anna drank some martini. "Well,
thank you *both*," she said loudly. "Aren't we full of compli-
ments?"

"I'm full of cold," Alex said.

Norman went to the Franklin stove and stirred the coals,
added more wood. Tess offered a sweater from her luggage,
but Alex chose to sit closer to the stove and to sip at ver-

mouth. Norman took the marinating meat from the refrigerator, scraped the orange and ginger and garlic from it, set it
on a broiling rack he found in the drawer of the stove, and
checked the potatoes.

"Tess will make the salad," he announced. "I will roll the
baked potatoes out like, well, like hot potatoes, after broiling
the, well, London broil. I will expect each of you to drink
several swigs of this fairly fancy Côtes de Beaune I lugged
from Astor Wines and Spirits, all the way here, for love of
family—"

"Of wine," Anna said, in a tone you could call light.

"That, more than ever," Norman answered her.

He turned to the slab of beef, and, after some silent
seconds—he heard Tess whacking away at celery with a
knife more suited to the London broil—Alex asked, "How's
Francie?"

Tess didn't answer. She was still, Norman knew, slicing
into Anna's comment. Norman said, "Great. He's happy, he
loves it at Carleton. He thinks he wants to go to law school."

"That would have made your father happy," Tess had
to say. "Knowing Francie was going into a profession."

Anna, eventually, said, "Yes."

During the meal, which Alexandra told them, every ten
minutes or so, was delicious, and during which Anna performed a contemporary miracle, Tess later said, by eating too
much yet keeping her lips pursed, they held Conversations.
They batted a subject lightly, like a shuttlecock plonked
with delicate strokes, and they smiled a good deal—Anna,

Tess said, between pursings—and they stayed away from color. Although, in bed that night, Tess insisted that Anna's reference to the Harry Belafonte appearance in Forest Hills for AIDS research fund raising had to qualify as color. ("Then what about dark streets and dangerous neighborhoods?" Norman asked. "And nighttime? And *opposites*? She talked about light. She wished for sunshine. She mentioned, for heaven's sake, she mentioned *snow*!" "She's not only a bitch, and a racist," Tess answered, "she's a ferrety and subtle racist bitch.") So they entered into (sometimes timidly, sometimes backwards, sometimes as if by accident, and sometimes in a loud rush) Conversations: the possible senility of their President and commander in chief; the impossibility of theocracy (Norman), and the respondent concern that he might have in mind someplace like Israel (Anna); Mrs. Thatcher's stern will; the rise of trade unions and fall of industry; the fall of trade unions and rise of merchant banking; their father's final days with visiting nurses and medical social workers and even a good country doctor who drove out twice a week and had still not sent his bill. "Oh, he sent it. I took care of it already," Anna said. "Somebody had to." Alexandra talked about her little apartment and cheap French restaurants, and Tess talked about bistros she and Norman still pined for. Anna saw their French restaurants and raised them two lives: "What was the name of that place they always loved? On the Right Bank?" Norman saw her lives and bumped her two more: "You mean the place in that picture of them on his desk?" Tess checked: "It's not there now, is it?" Alexandra folded. Anna showed her hand: "I took it home. I didn't think anyone would mind.

It means a great deal to me, you know." Norman's "Yes, apparently" and Tess's "Norman loves it too" were not enough. As Norman cleared the table, as Anna raked her winnings in, Alexandra went to the sink to start washing the dishes. She and Tess stayed behind as Norman gestured to Anna, and they carried coffee in big white mugs to Abraham Tauber's room.

Anna put her mug on the correspondence on the desk. She sat down behind the desk. Norman sat in the red leather chair. He pointed at the wing chair against the far wall: "I didn't even realize his daybed was gone. Not for a long time."

She sipped her coffee and made a face.

"We brought up coffee," Norman said. "Beans from Zabar's. We ground them this morning. I hope it doesn't taste too strong."

"Just right," Anna said.

"So you took the sofa?"

"I didn't know it meant anything to you."

"And the picture."

"I was surprised to learn you remembered it."

"And—what? Books. And some artwork. Anything else?"

"I could prepare a list," she said, "if you need an accounting." She smiled at Norman as she always smiled at Tess, he thought—so broadly, with such cold eyes.

"No, Anna. I don't think I need an accounting, thanks. I was just wondering."

"I was wondering too, Norman."

"What about?"

"How you could come here now."

"West Side Highway to the Hawthorne Circle is how, then up the Taconic. It's easy."

She grimaced into the coffee again, then nodded over it and set it down. "I guess it is easy, since you're here. And I guess it wasn't ever easier before," she said, "and that's why you were never here before."

"Not never, Anna."

"Never in all those years."

"But you were here," he said. "You were here with them."

She said, "I had obligations. There were people that I loved, and they required my attention."

"Anna," he said, setting his cup on the carpet, "do you love me?"

She stared at him as if she were a child, trying hard to look at the center of the sun. Her lashes began to flutter, and her long, sad face began to move—her lips pinched in, her nostrils widened, and tears sprang to her light blue— faded blue, he suddenly realized—eyes: Abraham Tauber's light, bright eyes.

"Why do you smile when I cry?"

"Anna," he said, "I wasn't laughing at you, or enjoying what you're going through. I saw Dad's—I saw his eyes in yours, all at once. You looked like him."

"He became so frail," she said. "His back bent over and his neck was so thin. His hands—"

He nodded. All he meant to show her was that he'd seen old men. But, as he nodded, he felt his shoulders droop and his neck protrude. He moved to sit on the edge of the easy chair, back erect and feet planted flat.

Their silence went on. Anna blew her nose in a tiny white

34

handkerchief she pulled from the sleeve of her dress. Norman said, "That real estate man, Lhommedieux, a real operator. He called up."

"He wasn't supposed to call you! He knows that! I'm the executrix! I inherit the house!"

"You've read the will."

"Yes. He left it on the desk for me. I get everything. You are—it says you're supposed to get a certain sum of cash."

"I don't need cash."

"He wanted you to have it."

"How is the sum determined? I have no intention of accepting it. Or if that complicates your bookkeeping, I will take it and then give it away."

"He wrote down how much. It's in the will."

"And?"

"And the lawyer will tell you."

"And you won't?"

She studied the surface of her coffee. He watched her move the mug. She shook her head and sighed. "You'll hate it, whatever it is. It'll feel like a message. I don't think he meant it as a message. I think he thought of it as honorable."

"All right," Norman said. "How much is my honor worth?"

"Two K. Is that how they say it in Los Angeles?"

"Two thousand dollars?"

She nodded.

"You can take care of somebody's kid in a hospice for two thousand dollars for a while."

"And he left—you saw this, if you saw the picture cube."

"His letter? I didn't read it."

"I don't know what it says, Norman."

"I thought you might have helped him type it or something."

"It's handwritten," she said. Then she pawed at the air, shook her head. "I didn't read it. I just looked at your name on the envelope. He wrote it by hand."

"You can have it if you want. A souvenir."

"Won't you read it?"

He leaned forward and picked up his coffee mug. He rocked farther, and he stood. "Anna, I don't know. I don't want to. All my life, all my adult life," he said, looking across the desk across which he had looked in chagrin so often, "he read me bills of particulars. As if I were one of the people who worked for him at the brokerage. As if I were an employee. A criminal in court, even. You did this. You did that. You spoke harshly to your mother. You didn't embrace me when I got out of my car to visit your home. Or: You introduced me to your new wife in a hostile manner. You've conditioned your son to be suspicious of me. Well." He listened to the high and youthful complaint of his voice as it echoed in that room filled with echoes. He heard them colliding, the great Franz Kafka Family Billiard Game. "Well, well." He breathed deeply and forced his voice into someplace lower than his tongue. "Listen to that, eh? You think you're all right and then—"

Anna nodded. He read real sympathy on her face. "And then you're not all right," she said.

He said, to his sister's face, to his father's eyes, "I am not at all sure that I can read that letter. If I leave it unread, I no doubt miss a lot of life's passing parade. With maybe me, stuffed and mounted, brightly costumed effigy, as part of it. On the other hand, there's always the other hand: that my father wanted, finally, to talk to me. And did. Or didn't, and just railed. It's like that Stockton story, about what comes out of the cave, or doorway, whatever: the lady or the tiger."

"I never heard of that," Anna said.

"Many years ago," Norman said, "I read the Classic Comic."

She touched the envelope, centered it under the logo of their father's firm, and stood. They looked at each other across their father's desk. "You're going to always blame it on your wife."

"I blame nothing on Tess."

"I know that. I said it wrong. You surely love that woman."

"Surely do."

"I meant, you'll always think it happened, whatever happened, between you and Daddy, because of who you married."

"He did a fantastic imitation of that."

"He was a *liberal*, Norman! He gave to Kennedy, Eugene McCarthy, even. He gave to the NAACP!"

"That will always be a source of satisfaction to me, and especially to Tess, I'm sure."

"Don't be smug with me, Norman. You don't just marry a Negro woman and expect your family to be the same. Some people might *pretend* to be the same. But in our family, with Mommy and Daddy, the truth was told. Feelings were not hidden very long, and the truth was always told."

37

"Something always was, anyway," Norman said, "and I'm sure they felt better after they told it. But truth? Our family hasn't done *truth*, whatever that is, for some time. We couldn't relay the weather report from the radio news without making it an occasion for giving pain or stating the extent of our psychic injuries, Anna. I don't want to have this discussion with you anymore. Or again. You see, that's why I'm not reading the letter. Why I haven't read it. Let me just say that my family offered me a choice: her or them. Maybe I knew they would. Maybe I offered it to them. It was the right choice, all around. I will never think we were wrong. Any of us."

She sat down again, as if her legs were weak. And he could watch her require of her legs, as he had just required of his voice, obedience. She received it, and she stood slowly and slowly pushed at the envelope on the desk. Then she nodded, and she walked around the desk, and in a wide arc so that she would not pass too close to him, and toward the door. That's where she stopped, and turned, and said, "The answer is yes."

"What's the question, Anna?"

"You asked me, before, if I loved you. So: yes. You really wanted an answer? Yes."

Eddie Brownstein telephoned to say that a child might want his father back so much, he would betray the confidence of his mother who had comforted him. In this case, Brownstein told Norman, treason was love. "But love's not treason, Eddie? Never mind. We don't want to be smart or philosophical or even wise. We want to be logical, we want to be interesting, we want someone to see what's at stake, to believe that it *is* at stake, and to care. Your idea of having the child come right from the mother to the father is a wonderful one. If you have the pages soon, send them. Otherwise, I'll call you on the Coast. I think we'll probably be there soon, I don't know when yet. But I'll call. Good work, Eddie."

And Serota telephoned to ask about buying Norman's interest in a story written a hundred and thirty years before. Norman said, "I'm going to say no. I understand your disappointment. I do this out of a sense of obligation to the author. I really don't think Melville would have cast Michael J. Fox. And I'm really not sorry. No."

Lhommedieux telephoned to say that he would telephone in the morning. Tess said, "Yes, my husband and his sister understand how much you're offering, and that they should act quickly because the development would be glad to build *around* the house and forget this headache they're causing you. You'll be dealing with my sister-in-law, as I understand it, and I wish you all the luck in the world. Because while I simply don't believe you, my sister-in-law doesn't even trust *herself*."

And then the black cold night in the house with its furnace turned down by the programmed thermostat. And the lights at last going off in the room down the hall from theirs, and then the sound of Anna, thrashing against the sheets and comforter and giving up her militant consciousness at last, at last sleeping, humming high in her head—Norman saw the sigh as somehow coming from the region of the bridge of her nose—and sounding as if she were content. And the longer rustle of bedclothes and bedsprings and headboard from the room across the hall from Anna's, where Alexandra read magazines, turning their pages with a sulky slap-and-rattle, then pausing as she read, or looked for something to read, and then the unhappy explosion of paper, and then the pause. And, eventually, she too going silent, although Norman couldn't hear her breathe, and then only Tess, who waited until her in-laws were silent before she spoke, and with whom he began to review the night, and who, as he tried to tell her something of Anna's dare, affront, or declaration in his father's room, also fell asleep, exhausted by a day with the Tauber family in what, Norman thought, you might call mourning, but which wasn't too horribly different from how they had been, and how they'd affected her, before estrangement and death relieved them, a little, of one another.

There he was, then, finally, alone in his aloneness, sitting in the darkness of his family's house, hearing it breathe, hearing the sighs, the little moans of its tentative repose. It was haunting itself. It was also haunting him. And, in a way, wasn't *he* its ghost?

INT. TAUBER HOUSE/NORMAN'S BEDROOM—LATE NIGHT

Norman looks at Tess, asleep. He touches one brown arm. She turns, rapidly, and buries herself under the covers. Her bottom pushes back, questing, until it touches his thigh. She immediately breathes deeply, is motionless.

Norman sidles from the bed. He rummages in the darkness until he finds a crewneck sweater which—we will SEE THIS *later—he puts on inside out.*

He sits on the floor and, by touch, slides into unlaced running shoes.

He LEAVES THE ROOM.

INT. TAUBER HOUSE/SECOND-FLOOR HALLWAY—LATE NIGHT

Norman DESCENDS THE STAIRS.

FROM BELOW:

Norman, as he ARRIVES NEAR FIRST FLOOR.

NORMAN'S P.O.V.:

In darkness, WE SEE *the objects of his parents' life and his.* Certain objects GIVE OFF A GLOW, *as if* LIGHTED FROM WITHIN.

CLOSEUP:

Norman's face, as HE RESPONDS.

NORMAN'S P.O.V.:

We are ENTERING THE KITCHEN. *It is bleak-looking and small.* LIGHTING MAKES IT COLD, *and* WE CAN FEEL *that the room—a house's heart—will* RECEDE, *soon, from Norman's life.*

Refrigerator SUDDENLY BEGINS TO HUM AND VIBRATE.

Norman JUMPS.

CLOSEUP:

His startled face.

TRACKING SHOT:

Norman, as he SEIZES *a glass and Glenfiddich, and* WALKS SWIFTLY *out the right-hand doorway through the living room.*

He WHISTLES *tunelessly, softly, like a frightened kid.*

Norman TURNS *at the doorway to the corridor. He* PAUSES. *Then he* WALKS, TURNS RIGHT, PROCEEDS *to his father's room.*

FROM BEHIND NORMAN:

He PAUSES *in the doorway,* HOLDS *there, as if about to knock, and then* WALKS IN.

HOLD THE SHOT: *it is as if the darkness swallows him.*

INT. TAUBER OFFICE—LATE NIGHT

Norman SITS *in the red leather chair. He* RESTS *the Glenfiddich on the desk after* POURING *himself a generous measure. He* DRINKS, SIGHS.

NORMAN

Whoops, I should have toasted you. Guys in this scene always do.

He RAISES *the glass,* HOLDS *his hand aloft.*

CLOSEUP:

His face, as he TRIES TO DECIDE *what to say.*

NORMAN (CONTINUING)

They say, *Absent friends.* Then they break the glass in the fireplace. Or they lift the glass (*a Clark Gable smirk on his face*) and they say, *Well, old man . . .* Or they—it depends on the picture—they could cry. Or just take a belt of the goddamned Scotch.

MEDIUM SHOT:

He DROPS HIS HAND *and then* SIPS. *He* LEANS *his head against the back of the chair.*

NORMAN (CONTINUING)

You should never cast yourself.

From behind him, Alexandra said, "Norman? Can I come in, Norm? I didn't mean to scare you."

"That's okay," he said. "I was scaring myself, anyway."

"Do you think anybody's sleeping?" She lifted the glass from his hand, sniffed, made a snorting noise, but took a drink anyway. "Brr," she said. "That's awful. But warm."

"Tess is," he said.

"I think my mother is, too. So how come we're not allowed to?"

"*Somebody* has to have the nervous breakdowns. You want some more?"

She shook her head, then struck a match and lit a cigarette. "Mm," she said.

43

"You sound so happy with it, maybe I'll start again. I could use a little innocent vice."

"Is suicide a little innocent vice?" She held the cigarette up.

"As long as suicide's the only vice you're doing at the moment, what the hell."

He sipped. She smoked, sitting on the wing chair with her legs drawn up under the hem of her long plaid bathrobe.

The letter, under the light of the desk lamp, lay centered on the desk. Anna must have moved it before she went to bed. He leaned forward to see if she had opened it, but couldn't tell.

"Mom told me about the letter. She saw it when we came up for the furniture and things."

"If you lack for mail," Norman said, "you're welcome to it, Alex."

"I don't know what I'd do if Mom did something like that to me."

"She could do it."

She looked up.

"I'm sorry," he said.

She shook her head. Her fine hair spun out. "No," she said, "I was thinking about that. I guess I can really see that. I've been working really hard at being friends with her. New York's lonely enough anyway, and I could use the company. But also, I hear all these people I work with, people I run into, these women, they all talk all about how their mother is their *friend*. It's like they all took the same course. It's like I missed class that day, or something. So I decided to work on that. I'd love to have a terrific, comfortable feeling like that."

44

"But you can't?"

"Maybe it's me."

"This family has never been wonderful at the graceful small pleasures."

"The Swiss Family Nutcake," Alex said.

Norman poured more whiskey. Alex stood her cigarette on its filter on the edge of a bookcase. "It'll burn out," she said. "Don't worry about the wood."

"I promise not to," he said.

"I wish I could see you and Tess. When you're in New York. I know you're busy and all—"

"We're lazy. And I guess I was never sure how Anna would react, and you. We lost track a little, didn't we? But we'll see each other. And when Francisco is home, if we're east, maybe you'd take him around town or something? He's a sweet boy."

"I can get him into those cocktail parties they do in the lobby of the Met, after hours, for fund raising."

"He'd love it. He's an elitist pig. Maybe you could visit us on the Coast sometime. We could figure out the airfare. Get you all tan and full of abalone."

"I love having family," Alex said. She was silent for the length of the lighting of another cigarette. Blowing out the smoke, she said, "I miss that."

"It's a lonely business," Norman said, nodding his head.

"What?"

"It."

"Oh," she said. "*That* it."

He nodded.

"Yes, it is," she said.

"I almost looked forward to sitting around with your

mother, each of us holding a clipboard or a pad, you know, and trying not to fight about who gets the antique Spanish blanket chest at the far end of the living room—"

"Sorry," Alex said.

"She got it already?"

She said, "Mom thought it couldn't possibly go with what she says is your very severe decor in New York. And she figured you wouldn't want to bother shipping it to the Coast."

"As I said," Norman said, "I was *almost* looking forward to it. For the company. Family companionship. I wonder how much I'm going to need to squabble. She may have saved me the trouble already."

"Actually, Mom has a list. Of what she figures is more or less up for grabs."

"I understand. The old Black and Decker drill. The sponge mops. The imitation Shaker furniture in the upstairs hall."

Alex shrugged. She looked at him, and then she looked down. She stood another cigarette on the end of its filter and soon she'd lit another one.

He said, "What, Alex?"

"Maybe you *had* to say good-bye to them. Maybe everybody's separated already, and the separateness is the way it's *supposed* to be."

"It's tough now in New York. And at work. Right? It's a rough ride for you?"

She blinked and smoked, slumping against the wing chair. "And maybe," she finally said, "people like you and Tess— when it works, maybe *that's* the accident. The exception. The terrific piece of luck. Maybe the rest, all the shit and

46

lying and misery, all those hours. Maybe that's just, I don't know, *normal*."

"Listen, kid, it's going to be—"

"So don't open it, Norm."

"No?"

"Don't open it."

And now everyone was in a room, at two or three or four in the morning—he chose not to check the time; he didn't want to be anchored to anything—except Norman. He was in foyers and entryways, halls, corridors. He drifted in the house that once had been theirs, when he was one of them. He'd left the glass and bottle in his father's room. His hands swung empty as, in the darkness he could see through now, he walked the connective tissue of the house—downstairs hall to front-door foyer off the living room, back stairs off the bathroom near his father's room upstairs to the narrow hallway on the second floor that went to the unused wing. In that wing—he was in the wide, fir-floored, dark-stained hall of it—he and Anna had slept; in addition to their rooms there was a small bathroom with rust stains on the enamel of the tub and sink, and a smell of sickness that had been there when they arrived; and there was a kind of family room or den between their bedrooms, which had served as no-man's-land, a place where they might dump their toys no longer wanted and clothing too small, and where they had *sometimes* played as friends. It was there, he suddenly remembered, standing in silence, breathing shallowly, that the day-

47

bed had originally been. It had been taken downstairs long after his mother's death and the onset of his father's atherosclerosis and diabetes and whatever else had invaded his body once the way was opened, and the man in a rage of despair. There had been old furniture, and the daybed, a television set (too vulgar for display downstairs), a record player he and Anna had fought about, and *Fun for a Rainy Day* and crossword puzzle books and board games and a New York Giants pennant that his father had brought him from the Polo Grounds when his father and a client had gone to see Sal Maglie pitch. To get into that family room unused by his family, but always occupied by its children, you had to walk from his room through a tiny corridor the size of a closet; to get to Anna's room, with its windows overlooking the enormous maple at the side of the house, where her car and theirs were now parked, you continued through the family room; the bathroom was off another door in the family room, and then there was this giant hallway serving nothing but a linen cupboard and the back stairs. And he stood there, remembering corners and doorknobs, the wide views from windows. And he *saw* himself, as he'd seen himself walking downstairs before, pale and tentative, haunted, alarmed, the restless spirit of that house and its lives. He saw himself as he had before, a name in a script, player on a set— alone and yet surrounded by the apparatus out of sight, all of it silent, in abeyance, waiting to assert control. He wanted to require of a writer under contract to him that directions be written in the script: *He dismisses it with a wave of his long, expressive fingers, and he wakes his beautiful wife, and they leave. They don't look back.* But he was not in control

48

here, he thought. He was a character in this, no independent producer tonight.

And therefore Norman Tauber reached out and opened the door to his childhood room and walked in.

It was empty. Its darkness was no darker than that of the rest of the house. His bed, with its headboard stuck with decals from the forties of army division emblems and American flags and bombers and tanks, was gone. His high oak bureau with the brass pulls that rattled when he walked—they used to trigger his mother's wrath when he sneaked home late from dates—was gone. His closet, he knew without opening it, was empty, and the desk was gone he had used from elementary-school days; the old itchy dark blue club chair was gone, which he'd been given when his father's firm had redecorated.

"Have a seat, son," he whispered in the room. He sat on the floor and leaned against the wall beside the doorway. He did so because he refused to permit himself to lean into the closet, to look along the baseboards, for clues, spoor, sign, verification that Norman Tauber, once upon a time, had lived in this room. "So I was wrong," he said, and then he was silent. But the thought continued. The room downstairs wasn't the worst. This one was the worst. This one had been waiting all day to be the worst.

He didn't sleep. He didn't think he slept. So, afterward, he didn't think he'd dreamed. This could, therefore, qualify as visitation. He was certain, later, that he'd heard himself say firmly, "I do not believe in you."

The house slept, although he couldn't hear their snores and whispered breathing from the other wing, and the wind

49

did shake some panes and cause some floors to shift. His buttocks grew cold, his ankles felt the drafts, and his back, against the wall against which he had stood, once, as tall as he now sat, became stiff. And he either slept, and dreamed it, or sat, with his eyes open in his room—the room they'd stripped in acknowledgment of his dying from them—and saw what someone might call ghosts.

It was the Thanksgiving of the awful storms, and the ice wouldn't melt. All the coils—one above the back kitchen door, one above the front door they so rarely used, one over Anna's bedroom window, and one over his parents'—all were on a single circuit, and all that electrical flow was jamming itself and heating the wire, blowing the fuses they used in those days in that old house, once, twice, three times in a row. So they'd closed the coils down, ice was building over the doors and windows to threaten the sills and shingles, the wood of the house, Thanksgiving vacation, their—this was his mother's expression, the pitch of her voice—their very lives.

His mother said over the kitchen wall phone to the electrician's wife, "You know how sorry I am to call him to the telephone on Thanksgiving. I wouldn't call unless—"

She listened. In a kitchen steamy with apple pie, the bite of mace and balm of sage, she said, "Yes. Unless it was *very* important. A—yes: a matter of life—"

And she listened again, and then said, "Yes, I understand."

She said, "Yes, I do." She said, "Yes. And you'll ask him to call just as *soon* as he comes in? You'll tell him how urgent it is? And do you think he'll come?"

She listened, and she closed her eyes. "But why *not*?" Her eyes were rolling, now, as if she might faint. "The *fuses* are blowing out. He wired them, and they're blowing out. We can't melt the ice on our *eaves!*"

Then his mother said, "I understand. Of course."

She hung up and said, "I can't understand this. I just can't under*stand* these people!"

Norman heard his father's voice from the dining room, where he was opening wine. "This is the country. They move at their own schedule. You wanted country life. Welcome to country life."

"These people never understand what *emergency* means," his mother said. "You know where? I mean, do you know what he's doing? What do you think he's doing? He's shooting deer. In this weather. You can't even *see* in it, and he's outside, murdering deer. You'd think—"

"You'd think we lived in the country," his father said. "You'd think I drove down the Taconic to work every day at six o'clock in the morning. You'd think these people didn't understand they had to change their lives because we wanted to cast aside the choking confines of urban life. You'd think they didn't know we didn't know it gets tough out here sometimes."

"Why are you so *sarcastic* with me?" his mother cried. She was tall and thin and her red dress was wrapped in a white, lacy apron. She looked to Norman like someone pretending to enjoy cooking. She stood at the telephone as if she were expecting their electrician to call.

"Because I'm a realist, goddamnit," his father said. "If we have problems, then we have them. Ice is ice. Nobody dies of ice."

"Says you," Norman's mother said. "What do you know? You grew up in the Bronx."

Snow came, thick and wet, and it slapped the windows like insects thrashing into lamps. The slapping was soft and continuous, and the snow clung, and everything grew white. Inside, they looked at the windows, and there was soon only the heavy, ceaseless motion, the accumulating blankness. Norman and his father and mother, all dressed up and waiting, spoke in rooms cluttered with replicas. The chairs and side tables and candle stands and dry sinks were authentic and antique, but they were purchased after his mother had seen them in the larger, glossier magazines; each room was an imitation of a colored photograph.

Then Anna came downstairs. Norman heard her footsteps as she weaved her way along an upstairs hall past objects that stood out from the wall. He heard her bounce on the wooden stairs, then heard things made of glass rattle on their glass shelves as Anna came through the back hall, past their mother, to the kitchen, where their father read his *New York Times* in front of the cold Franklin stove. Norman yawned wide yawns, like a nervous dog.

His father put the paper onto Norman's lap as Anna came in. He stood as Anna came near, and his large hands went out, as if he wanted to touch her, or as if she had brought him something he ought to receive.

His father said, "Did we wake up Alexandra?"

Anna kissed her father's nose and pushed him back into his seat. He willingly surrendered. Anna said, "Nope. I told her to sleep from one to three, and it's only two. She does what her mama tells her."

Their father said, "That's more than *my* children do."

Norman said to her, "He's lucky we do what we do at all for him."

52

Anna asked, "And what'd he tell us the last time he tried telling us what to do?"

"Let's see," Norman said, "I was supposed to take good care. And not get back to campus late. And—oh, yeah: study hard. I was supposed to study hard. Whereas *you* were supposed to take care of Alexandra *and* yourself, and call him in New York, or *anytime* at home, if you needed him. We were all supposed to keep in touch. And vote a straight Republican ticket."

Their mother said, not joking, "Isn't anyone supposed to listen to me?"

Anna said, "And everyone's supposed to listen to you."

"There won't be anything to listen to. Or about. If this keeps up."

Anna said, "If what keeps up," but didn't want an answer, her tone made clear.

"I can't cook without electricity, can I? And all the electricity is broken in this house."

Their father put his hand out to her, as he had to Anna, and their mother seemed to grow angrier. She walked to the sink and slammed things made of metal.

Anna said, "Listen, Ma."

"You can't talk this away, Anna."

"Do I talk things away, Ma?"

"I didn't say that."

"It sounded like it to me. Could you be speaking of my bastard child, Alexandra? Do I talk her away? Have I ever tried to?"

Their mother warbled, "*Every*thing's broken here. The house is broken, the family is broken."

Norman said, "Let's make like Pilgrims. Why not? It's

Thanksgiving. Let's cook dinner on the Franklin stove."

Anna said, "Let's cook a Franklin on it."

"With all the stuffing," Anna said. "I'll make the stuffing. You know, kite keys, printer's ink, one Early to Bed, one Early to Rise. Serve on a bed of wild rice."

Norman said, "A rice of wild bed."

Anna said, "Let me tell you about *that* one."

"Go ahead," their mother said.

"I apologize for that," Anna said.

"And meanwhile," their mother said, "look at the stove." And there was the wide shiny Franklin stove on its platform of bricks, and there was the brick hearth behind it; but, connecting the two—the wide black pipe Norman had taken for granted—there was nothing. Where the pipe should have entered the wall was a square of cardboard held onto the bricks with silver duct tape, a bandage on a wound in the kitchen wall.

"I didn't notice that," their father said.

"Of course you didn't," she said. "I had to have it taken out while you were in the city." His father filled his face with air, his cheeks bulged, then he let the air hiss out. "I was home alone, as usual. And every time I lit a fire, the smoke poured in until I choked. *He* came home from work"—she pointed at their father—"he was late, and I thought we'd have a drink in front of the fire and give him a chance to relax. He came home from work right after all the smoke had come pouring in, and I thought I was going to *die*, and he looked around and grinned like a dope and said, 'I *love* that! It smells like a campfire!' Of course, I had to call the man and have him come over and take the pipe away. He has to bring new pipe. What could break next?"

54

They said nothing. Norman's mother, her lips pressed tightly together, her narrow face clenched like a hand, stood at the sink and cut food into small pieces. On the counter beside her, the pale shiny turkey lay naked and swollen in its pan.

Norman asked, "What's *cold* Franklin taste like?" Anna laughed, and their father did, after a fashion: he spread his lips and showed his teeth and urged them on to laughter so that his wife might laugh too. Upstairs, Alexandra's crib rattled, and they heard her cry herself awake.

Their mother dropped her knife. She said, "The baby! Was that the baby? The baby's crying!"

Anna said, "It isn't *the* baby. It isn't a category. It's Alexandra, and she's waking up."

"Don't," their father said. "Anna. Don't be argumentative. Please."

Their mother said, "Excuse me," and picked up her knife.

Norman asked, "Anna, how come she always cries when she wakes up?"

Anna gestured with both arms—she seemed to be trying to include everything in one motion—and she said, "*Ha!*" as she left the kitchen.

To his father, Norman said, "Some sister I got."

His mother asked, "Does he visit them?"

"What?"

"You certainly know what I mean," she said. "The man who—the father. Alexandra's father. Does he visit them?"

"I don't know, Mom. I don't ask."

"Good," his father said.

His mother turned away and his father closed his eyes and rocked in his chair. The flesh beneath his father's eyes looked dark and tender. And when his mother turned from the sink to study their silence, Norman saw how hollowed and staring her eyes were. He brought his father's *Times* up in front of his face, and he shut his own eyes.

Then Anna came with her daughter, swaddled in so many colored wools that she was sweaty. Although Anna didn't offer, their mother took Alex from her and held her, bent around her. Anna held on to her baby's right hand. Norman tried to reach a conclusion about his family's need to hold.

His mother leaned her head into Alexandra and then drew it back, darted down, then retreated, darted in and back, saying, "A-boo. A-boo. A-boo." Anna, holding her daughter's hand, turned her head away. Norman squeezed his hands together.

Their father said, "I could build a fire in the living room fireplace."

Norman said, "You could cook the Franklin in there."

But his father wasn't joking anymore. He was fleeing, or establishing order. He scowled at his son, and then—Norman could see the expression receive its orders—his father forced his face to clear. He nodded.

Their mother, though, was the one to go into the living room. She pulled Alexandra away, and she left them in the kitchen. Anna said, "Why must she do that! Take Alex like that. Tear her away from me. I don't understand her."

"No," their father said.

"I—Daddy, I don't understand *you*—for understanding her."

He nodded.

56

"She thinks I'm a whore who got knocked up." Norman looked at his father, whose face was blank. "Some kind of a whore."

Their father said, "You're not. You're a complicated person. A complicated woman. Like her."

"Like *her*?"

"You're very complicated people, you and your mother. And him, of course." He pointed, with his chin, at Norman. "You're tough to see into. Pin down."

Norman said, before he knew he was finding the courage to say it, "And you?"

"Me?"

"What about you?"

"You tell me," their father said.

"A regular father," Anna said.

Norman said, "I don't know."

He and his father looked at each other, directly and easily, each knowing, Norman thought, that there just might be nothing more to say.

Anna said, "No, how'm I like her, Daddy?"

Their father said, "Because this morning, early this morning, when I was roaming around the house—"

"The local ghost," Anna said to Norman. "Who needs any sleep? Right?"

He meant to nod, but he didn't move. He looked at his father.

"I looked in on you," their father said to Anna. "Little Alexandra was humming and burbling in her sleep, and you were breathing very softly—very *happily*, I would have said."

57

Norman wondered what he looked like to anyone while he slept.

"And I went back to our bedroom and your mother was awake. I'm afraid I wakened her. And she asked me if I thought that you and she were alike. If that's why you fought so much. I told her, 'Yes. Absolutely.' And she asked, 'Like *her*?' Exactly the way you just did."

"And that's why she steals my baby?" Anna asked.

And their mother, back in the kitchen now, said, flatly, coldly, "Please take your baby back, Anna."

Anna looked up. Her face was red. Their father stopped rocking. Norman yawned. "I'm sorry if I hurt your feelings," Anna said.

Their mother said, "So am I. I don't think that matters much, however. Do you?"

Norman said, "It all matters."

"Quiet," his father said.

His mother said, "What matters is that you and your baby feel secure."

Their father said, "Let's not let this get out of hand."

Norman said, "Before I shut up—"

"I really meant it," their father said.

Alexandra cried, and Anna went to her. Their mother handed the baby over to Anna, and their hands looked tangled in their usual knots. How could you tell if their mother was giving Alex up or taking Anna toward her?

Norman said, "Why can't—"

But their father said, "Now, *hush*!"

Norman, closing his eyes so that he wouldn't see his father's face, said, "Why don't you guys listen to me!"

Their mother said, "Why don't we? Why don't we *talk* to each other? We don't need to fight."

"Perhaps we do," their father said. "We seem to do so much of it. Perhaps we really want to."

"What'll we win, I wonder." Norman looked up: he had the conviction that he'd said something wonderful.

Anna said, mostly into Alexandra's face, "There isn't too much more I want."

"Don't be smug," their father said, talking gently and looking at his wife's stricken face. "It just begins now."

Norman asked, "What?"

Their mother said, "You'll find out." She turned her face toward their father. "Don't be in a hurry."

"Like me, you mean?" Anna asked.

"I was talking to Norman."

"Oh. I wondered."

And their father, his wounded eyes closing for an instant, his face hardening—his attention once more focusing inside his skin—said, "Now it all begins."

Norman asked—and, sitting now with his back against the wall of his emptied childhood room, he heard it as a whine—"Daddy, *what?*"

He saw his father stand and reach to the gawky boy and touch his shoulders, and then slide his hands from shoulders to arms to forearms, then ribs. He stood in front of his son, holding his ribs, as if detaining the boy from departure, retaining him from danger; and then, with a delicate reluctance curling his fingers, his father let go. He saw his father step back. He saw him, but not with nonchalance or carelessness, shrug. It was helplessness, Norman thought.

59

Norman, on the floor of his room, almost nodded. But he was leaning his head against the wall, and though he felt the impulse to nod, the icy unseen wall compelled his stillness, and he made no motion in reply to what he'd dreamed, or thought, or remembered, maybe seen.

He pried his sneakers off, and tried to slide into the bed without waking Tess. But he saw her eyes in the darkness, open, alert. "What?"

"Drifting," he said. "Walking to and fro. The usual."

"Nothing here's the usual."

"No," he said. He huddled against her, butted her chest and reached for her back, pulled her against him as he shivered.

"Let's go," Tess said.

"We're supposed to divvy the loot. All that good child-hood treasure."

"Yeah. That's why I said we should go. What do you want from here? Really want to take away and keep where you can see it all the time?"

He held on to Tess, and he shook. She rubbed at his back and shoulders as if she had pulled him choking from the sea. He said nothing.

Tess said, "And therefore?"

"Let's go," he said.

Tess got out of bed and turned on a light. The cartons and magazines jumped away from the wall, and their shadow loomed cold. First Tess dressed, and then she brought Norman a flannel shirt, woolen socks, heavy corduroys. "Put the shirt on over the sweater and the pajama tops. You can fix yourself up later. It's almost five. Let's just blow the joint."

"Anna will be confused."

"Anna," Tess said.

Norman giggled. "I was going to say, 'She once was my sister.' I worshiped her. I'd forgotten how much I used to love her."

"That shows you," Tess said, "how chewed up and spat out and stepped on on the sidewalk that word can be."

They were whispering, and jamming clothes into canvas duffel bags and suitcases. "I'll wear my sneakers," Norman said. "To hell with the snow."

"To hell with it all," Tess said.

She put a plaid blanket over his shoulders, man saved from drowning, and she led him down the stairs. They hushed each other and stiffened as stairs creaked, and in the kitchen they laughed with hands over one another's mouths until they had tears in their eyes.

Norman gasped, "A note? Hoo! A thank-you note?"

They sniggered and chuckled and held their mouths shut.

"*His* note," Tess whispered. The *his* hissed through the kitchen, and Norman couldn't laugh any more. "If we ever talk about this to Francie or anyone, this'll be the point of telling it. You see? The note."

"The McGuffin," Norman said.

"Except the son of a bitch put real dynamite inside of it."

"You think it'll be that bad?"

"Oh, baby," she said, low in her throat. "Why else would he have *left* it?"

"He never talked that well. Maybe he couldn't say it. Maybe he *had* to write it."

"He *sold* stuff. That's nothing *but* talk."

"But not to your own kid."

"Who he disowned."

"Oh, no. Don't forget—"

"That's right," she recited, "a special sum of cash."

"No: certain. A *certain* sum of cash."

"What do you think he said by saying *that?*"

"So we leave it on the desk for Alex."

"Why Alex?"

"She'll find it and swipe it, and she'll bring it to me someday, thinking I might have wanted it."

"Well," Tess said. "Then we'll have to do it better." She tiptoed out of the kitchen through the door that would take her to the corridor off the dining room that went to his father's room, and desk, and final message. Norman carried their bags out to the ice-covered car. His footsteps squeaking on the frozen snow, his toes growing numb, and then his fingers, he scraped at the ice on their windshield. And then Tess came out. She tried to look casually at him—in itself, a signal of her tension, since she could look casually at nothing—and she smiled a smile and patted her pocket. She got inside the car.

Norman put his hand up: wait. He went to the side door and, inside, at the kitchen entrance, he swept his hand down along the wall, and flicked off the switch to the heating coils on the roof.

The moon hung, full and heavy-looking, brilliant in a night the storm had blown clear. The snow in moonlight shone blue-white, like a baby's eye, or a new tooth. He stood at the driver's-side door of his car and looked at the house. It was white on the white of the snow. He opened his door and held his hand out. He didn't look in. "Please?" he said. And when Tess put the envelope on his palm—it felt light, as if his father had written it on tissue paper, or as if its contents were few—Norman closed the door gently and walked back to what had once been gardens at the side of the house. His hands were so cold in the morning's cold winds that he hardly felt the letter by the time he stood, his back to the car and to the house, and wondered what he must look like from above. He wondered how, if this were a crane shot, his tall figure, not much more than a shadow if the angle was right, would appear, holding what could be made, with proper lighting, to look like nothing at all. A shadowy man on a blue-white ground beside a blue-white house with a roof made bluish white by heavy snow under moonlight, holding up what might be a message in an envelope: it could, if you shot it that way, *not* be the message from the dead. It could disappear.

His hands were so numbed that he had to watch them to confirm what they did. His fingers set the envelope on the frozen crust of the snow. He squinted and, in the darkness of dawn, the envelope disappeared. He was wondering what the letter said, and how, as his clawed right hand pushed the envelope down, and it broke through the top layer, then easily sank in. Anna would call the man who used to plow for them, and he, or his son, or someone he recommended, would come with his truck and plow and would slam these banks and billows into mounds, and they would freeze again, and melt, and, later in the year, the letter would simply disappear into the earth somehow.

Then Tess was beside him. "What if it melts?" she said. "I mean, it *will* melt. It could be there in the spring." She knelt on the snow and plunged her bare hands into it, and fished the letter up. Then she turned to sit, like a child, with one leg folded beneath her and one straight out. She held up the envelope, folded it in half, and pushed it into the pocket of her thigh-length jacket. "I'll hold it," she said. "We can burn it at home. Or throw it away in a gas station. Never mind. I'll get rid of it later on."

"You'll get rid of the letter. She'll get rid of the house."

Tess said, "In fifteen minutes. This morning, in fact. I guarantee it. You know Anna."

He said, "They'll tear it down and put up three in its place. Bungalows. Condominiums. And the furniture will go in her house. The best stuff will. The rest of the stuff, what I grew up with—"

"Baby, you will be an orphan," Tess said.

"Am now," he said.

"Are now."

"Would you give me the letter again?"

She brought it from her pocket at once. The ink had run from the snow's moisture, and the paper was damp, it felt thicker. He tore the letter in half. He tore the halves in half. Then he plucked at the pieces, tore the edges that yielded, and he threw them all, in a backhanded sowing motion, into the air. From above, if he were filmed, he thought, the fragments would flare in the moonlight and then be lost against the snow.

A windowpane rattled. Something flew up into moon-light on heavy wings from the bare black maple in the door-yard behind them. Tess and Norman looked back, and up, and they waved their unthinking, automatic answer to Anna, who crouched in the window of her childhood bedroom, and waved a slow white hand to her brother and his wife. Good-bye, she waved. Good-bye.

Ralph the Duck

I WOKE UP at 5:25 because the dog was vomiting. I carried seventy-five pounds of heaving golden retriever to the door and poured him onto the silver, moonlit snow. "Good boy," I said because he'd done his only trick. Outside he retched, and I went back up, passing the sofa on which Fanny lay. I tiptoed with enough weight on my toes to let her know how considerate I was while she was deserting me. She blinked her eyes. I swear I heard her blink her eyes. Whenever I tell her that I hear her blink her eyes, she tells me I'm lying; but I can hear the damp slap of lash after I have made her weep.

In bed and warm again, noting the red digital numbers (5:29) and certain that I wouldn't sleep, I didn't. I read a book about men who kill each other for pay or for their honor. I forget which, and so did they. It was 5:45, the alarm would buzz at 6:00, and I would make a pot of coffee and start the wood stove; I would call Fanny and pour her coffee into her mug; I would apologize because I always did, and then she would forgive me if I hadn't been too awful—I didn't think I'd been that bad—and we would stagger through the day, exhausted but pretty sure we were all right, and we'd sleep that night, probably after sex, and then we'd waken in the same bed to the alarm at 6:00, or the dog, if he'd returned to the frozen deer carcass he'd been eating in the forest on our land. He loved what made him sick. The alarm went off, I got into jeans and woolen socks and a sweatshirt, and I went downstairs to let the dog in. He'd be hungry, of course.

I was the oldest college student in America, I thought. But of course I wasn't. There were always ancient women with parchment for skin who graduated at seventy-nine from places like Barnard and the University of Georgia. I was only forty-two, and I hardly qualified as a student. I patrolled the college at night in a Bronco with a leaky exhaust system, and I went from room to room in the classroom buildings, kicking out students who were studying or humping in chairs—they'd do it *anywhere*—and answering emergency calls with my little blue light winking on top of the truck. I didn't carry a gun or a billy, but I had a flashlight that took six batteries and I'd used it twice on some of my over-privileged northeastern-playboy part-time classmates. On Tuesdays and Thursdays I would waken at 6:00 with my wife, and I'd do my homework, and work around the house, and go to school at 11:30 to sit there for an hour and a half

while thirty-five stomachs growled with hunger and boredom, and this guy gave instruction about books. Because I
was on the staff, the college let me take a course for nothing
every term. I was getting educated, in a kind of slow-motion
way—it would have taken me something like fifteen or sixteen years to graduate, and I would no doubt get an F in gym
and have to repeat—and there were times when I respected
myself for it. Fanny often did, and that was fair incentive.

I am not unintelligent. *You are not an unintelligent writer*,
my professor wrote on my paper about Nathaniel Hawthorne. We had to read short stories, I and the other students,
and then we had to write little essays about them. I told how
I saw Kafka and Hawthorne in a similar light, and I was not
unintelligent, he said. He ran into me at dusk one time, when
I answered a call about a dead battery and found out it was
him. I jumped his Buick from the Bronco's battery, and he
was looking me over, I could tell, while I clamped onto the
terminals and cranked it up. He was a tall, handsome guy
who never wore a suit. He wore khakis and sweaters, loafers
or sneaks, and he was always talking to the female students
with the brightest hair and best builds. But he couldn't get
a Buick going on an ice-cold night, and he didn't know
enough to look for cells going bad. I told him he was going
to need a new battery and he looked me over the way men
sometimes do with other men who fix their cars for them.

"Vietnam?"

I said, "Too old."

"Not at the beginning. Not if you were an adviser. So-
called. Or one of the Phoenix Project fellas?"

I was wearing a watch cap made of navy wool and an old
Marine fatigue jacket. Slick characters like my professor

like it if you're a killer or at least a onetime middleweight fighter. I smiled like I knew something. "Take it easy," I said, and I went back to the truck to swing around the cemetery at the top of the campus. They'd been known to screw in down-filled sleeping bags on horizontal stones up there, and the dean of students didn't want anybody dying of frostbite while joined at the hip to a matriculating fellow resident of our northeastern camp for the overindulged.

He blinked his high beams at me as I went. "You are not an unintelligent driver," I said.

Fanny had left me a bowl of something made with sausages and sauerkraut and potatoes, and the dog hadn't eaten too much more than his fair share. He watched me eat his leftovers and then make myself a king-sized drink composed of sourmash whiskey and ice. In our back room, which is on the northern end of the house, and cold for sitting in that close to dawn, I sat and watched the texture of the sky change. It was going to snow, and I wanted to see the storm come up the valley. I woke up that way, sitting in the rocker with its loose right arm, holding a watery drink, and thinking right away of the girl I'd convinced to go back inside. She'd been standing outside her dormitory, looking up at a window that was dark in the midst of all those lighted panes—they never turned a light off, and often let the faucets run half the night—crying onto her bathrobe. She was barefoot in shoe-pacs, the brown ones so many of them wore unlaced, and for all I know she was naked under the robe. She was beautiful, I thought, and she was somebody's redheaded daughter, standing in a quadrangle how many miles from home and weeping.

"He doesn't love anyone," the kid told me. "He doesn't love his wife—I mean his ex-wife. And he doesn't love the ex-wife before that, or the one before that. And you know what? He doesn't love me. I don't know anyone who *does*!"

"It isn't your fault if he isn't smart enough to love you," I said, steering her toward the truck.

She stopped. She turned. "You know him?"

I couldn't help it. I hugged her hard, and she let me, and then she stepped back, and of course I let her go. "Don't you *touch* me! Is this sexual harassment? Do you know the rules? Isn't this sexual harassment?"

"I'm sorry," I said at the door to the truck. "But I think I have to be able to give you a grade before it counts as harassment."

She got in. I told her we were driving to the dean of students' house. She smelled like marijuana and something very sweet, maybe one of those coffee-with-cream liqueurs you don't buy unless you hate to drink.

As the heat of the truck struck her, she started going kind of clay-gray-green, and I reached across her to open the window.

"You touched my breast!" she said.

"It's the smallest one I've touched all night, I'm afraid."

She leaned out the window and gave her rendition of my dog.

But in my rocker, waking up, at whatever time in the morning in my silent house, I thought of her as someone's child. Which made me think of ours, of course. I went for more ice, and I started on a wet breakfast. At the door of the dean of students' house, she'd turned her chalky face to me and asked, "What grade would you give me, then?"

It was a week composed of two teachers locked out of their offices late at night, a Toyota with a flat and no spare, an attempted rape on a senior girl walking home from the library, a major fight outside a fraternity house (broken wrist and significant concussion), and variations on breaking-and-entering. I was scolded by the director of nonacademic services for embracing a student who was drunk; I told him to keep his job, but he called me back because I was right to hug her, he said, and also wrong, but what the hell, and he'd promised to admonish me, and now he had, and would I please stay. I thought of the fringe benefits—graduation in only sixteen years—so I went back to work.

My professor assigned a story called "A Rose for Emily," and I wrote him a paper about the mechanics of corpse fucking, and how, since she clearly couldn't screw her dead boyfriend, she was keeping his rotten body in bed because she truly loved him. I called the paper "True Love." He gave me a B and wrote *See me, pls.* In his office after class, his feet up on his desk, he trimmed a cigar with a giant folding knife he kept in his drawer.

"You got to clean the hole out," he said, "or they don't draw."

"I don't smoke," I said.

"Bad habit. Real *habit*, though. I started in smoking 'em in Georgia, in the service. My C.O. smoked 'em. We collaborated on a brothel inspection one time, and we ended up smoking these with a couple of women—" He waggled his eyebrows at me, now that his malehood was established.

"Were the women smoking them too?"

He snorted laughter through his nose while the greasy smoke came curling off his thin, dry lips. "They were pretty smoky, I'll tell ya!" Then he propped his feet—he was wearing cowboy boots that day—and he sat forward. "It's a little hard to explain. But—hell. You just don't say *fuck* when you write an essay for a college prof. Okay?" Like a scoutmaster with a kid he'd caught in the outhouse jerking off: "All right? You don't wanna do that."

"Did it shock you?"

"Fuck, no, it didn't shock me. I just told you. It violates certain proprieties."

"But if I'm writing it to you, like a letter—"

"You're writing it for posterity. For some mythical reader someplace, not just me. You're making a *statement*."

"Right. My statement said how hard it must be for a woman to fuck with a corpse."

"And a point worth making. I said so. Here."

"But you said I shouldn't say it."

"No. Listen. Just because you're talking about fucking, you don't have to say *fuck*. Does that make it any clearer?"

"No."

"I wish you'd lied to me just now," he said.

I nodded. I did too.

"Where'd you do your service?" he asked.

"Baltimore. Baltimore, Maryland."

"What's in Baltimore?"

"Railroads. I liaised on freight runs of army matériel. I

killed a couple of bums on the rod with my bare hands, though."

He snorted again, but I could see how disappointed he was. He'd been banking on my having been a murderer. Interesting guy in one of my classes, he must have told some terrific woman at an overpriced meal: I just *know* the guy was a rubout specialist in the Nam, he had to have said. I figured I should come to work wearing my fatigue jacket and a red bandanna tied around my head. Say "Man" to him a couple of times, hang a fist in the air for grief and solidarity, and look terribly worn, exhausted by experiences he was fairly certain that he envied me. His dungarees were ironed, I noticed.

On Saturday we went back to the campus because Fanny wanted to see a movie called *The Seven Samurai*. I fell asleep, and I'm afraid I snored. She let me sleep until the auditorium was almost empty. Then she kissed me awake. "Who was screaming in my dream?" I asked her.

"Kurosawa," she said.

"Who?"

"Ask your professor friend."

I looked around, but he wasn't there. "Not an un-weird man," I said.

We went home and cleaned up after the dog and put him out. We drank a little Spanish brandy and went upstairs and made love. I was fairly premature, you might say, but one way and another by the time we fell asleep we were glad to be there with each other, and glad that it was Sunday coming up the valley toward us, and nobody with it. The dog was howling at another dog someplace, or at the moon, or maybe just his moon-thrown shadow on the snow. I did not strangle him when I opened the back door and he limped happily past me and stumbled up the stairs. I followed him into our bedroom and groaned for just being satisfied as I got into bed. You'll notice I didn't say fuck.

He stopped me in the hall after class on a Thursday, and asked me How's it goin, just one of the kickers drinking sour beer and eating pickled eggs and watching the tube in a country bar. How's it goin. I nodded. I wanted a grade from the man, and I did want to learn about expressing myself. I nodded and made what I thought was a smile. He'd let his mustache grow out and his hair grow longer. He was starting to wear dark shirts with lighter ties. I thought he looked like someone in *The Godfather*. He still wore those light little loafers or his high-heeled cowboy boots. His corduroy pants looked baggy. I guess he wanted them to look that way. He motioned me to the wall of the hallway, and he looked up and said, "How about the Baltimore stuff?"

I said, "Yeah?"

"Was that really true?" He was almost blinking, he wanted so much for me to be a damaged Vietnam vet just looking for a bell tower to climb into and start firing from. The college didn't have a bell tower you could get up into, though I'd once spent an ugly hour chasing a drunken ATO down from the roof of the observatory. "You were just clocking through boxcars in Baltimore?"

I said, "Nah."

"I thought so!" He gave a kind of sigh.

"I killed people," I said.

"You know, I could have sworn you did," he said.

I nodded, and he nodded back. I'd made him so happy.

The assignment was to write something to influence some-body. He called it Rhetoric and Persuasion. We read an essay by George Orwell and "A Modest Proposal" by Jona-than Swift. I liked the Orwell better, but I wasn't comfort-able with it. He talked about "niggers," and I felt him saying it two ways.

I wrote "Ralph the Duck."

Once upon a time, there was a duck named Ralph who didn't have any feathers on either wing. So when the cold wind blew, Ralph said, Brr, and shivered and shook.

What's the matter? Ralph's mommy asked.

I'm *cold*, Ralph said.

Oh, the mommy said. Here. I'll keep you warm.

So she spread her big, feathery wings, and hugged Ralph tight, and when the cold wind blew, Ralph was warm and snuggly, and fell fast asleep.

The next Thursday, he was wearing canvas pants and hiking boots. He mentioned kind of casually to some of the girls in the class how whenever there was a storm he wore his Lake District walking outfit. He had a big, hairy sweater

75

on. I kept waiting for him to make a noise like a mountain goat. But the girls seemed to like it. His boots made a creaky squeak on the linoleum of the hall when he caught up with me after class.

"As I told you," he said, "it isn't unappealing. It's just—not a college theme."

"Right," I said. "Okay. You want me to do it over?"

"No," he said. "Not at all. The D will remain your grade. But I'll read something else if you want to write it."

"This'll be fine," I said.

"Did you understand the assignment?"

"Write something to influence someone—Rhetoric and Persuasion."

We were at his office door and the redheaded kid who had gotten sick in my truck was waiting for him. She looked at me like one of us was in the wrong place, which struck me as accurate enough. He was interested in getting into his office with the redhead, but he remembered to turn around and flash me a grin he seemed to think he was known for.

Instead of going on shift a few hours after class, the way I'm supposed to, I told my supervisor I was sick, and I went home. Fanny was frightened when I came in, because I don't get sick and I don't miss work. She looked at my face and she grew sad. I kissed her hello and went upstairs to change. I always used to change my clothes when I was a kid, as soon as I came home from school. I put on jeans and a flannel shirt and thick wool socks, and I made myself a dark drink of sourmash. Fanny poured herself some wine and came into the cold northern room a few minutes later. I was sitting in the rocker, looking over the valley. The wind was lining up a lot of rows of cloud so that the sky looked like a baked trout when you lift the skin off. "It'll snow," I said to her.

She sat on the old sofa and waited. After a while, she said, "I wonder why they always call it a mackerel sky?"

"Good eating, mackerel," I said.

Fanny said, "Shit! You're never that laconic unless you feel crazy. What's wrong? Who'd you punch out at the playground?"

"We had to write a composition," I said.

"Did he like it?"

"He gave me a D."

"Well, you're familiar enough with D's. I never saw you get this low over a grade."

"I wrote about Ralph the Duck."

She said, "You did?" She said, "Honey." She came over and stood beside the rocker and leaned into me and hugged my head and neck. "Honey," she said. "Honey."

It was the worst of the winter's storms, and one of the worst in years. That afternoon they closed the college, which they almost never do. But the roads were jammed with snow over ice, and now it was freezing rain on top of that, and the only people working at the school that night were the operator who took emergency calls and me. Everyone else had gone home except the students, and most of them were inside. The ones who weren't were drunk, and I kept on sending them in and telling them to act like grown-ups. A number of them said they were, and I really couldn't argue.

I had the bright beams on, the defroster set high, the little blue light winking, and a thermos of sourmash and hot coffee that I sipped from every time I had to get out of the truck or every time I realized how cold all that wetness was out there.

About eight o'clock, as the rain was turning back to snow and the cold was worse, the roads impossible, just as I was done helping a county sander on the edge of the campus pull a panel truck out of a snowbank, I got the emergency call from the college operator. We had a student missing. The roommates thought the kid was headed for the quarry. This meant I had to get the Bronco up on a narrow road above the campus, above the old cemetery, into all kinds of woods and rough track that I figured would be choked with ice and snow. Any kid up there would really have to want to be there, and I couldn't go in on foot, because you'd only want to be there on account of drugs, booze, or craziness, and either way I'd be needing blankets and heat, and then a fast ride down to the hospital in town. So I dropped into four-wheel drive to get me up the hill above the campus, bucking snow and sliding on ice, putting all the heater's warmth up onto the windshield because I couldn't see much more than swarming snow. My feet were still cold from the tow job, and it didn't seem to matter that I had on heavy socks and insulated boots I'd coated with waterproofing. I shivered, and I thought of Ralph the Duck.

I had to grind the rest of the way, from the cemetery, in four-wheel low, and in spite of the cold I was smoking my gearbox by the time I was close enough to the quarry—they really did take a lot of the rocks for the campus buildings from there—to see I'd have to make my way on foot to where she was. It was a kind of scooped-out shape, maybe four or five stories high, where she stood—well, wobbled is more like it. She was as chalky as she'd been the last time, and her red hair didn't catch the light anymore. It just lay on her like something that had died on top of her head. She was in a white nightgown that was plastered to her body. She had her arms crossed as if she wanted to be warm. She swayed, kind of, in front of the big, dark, scooped-out rock face, where the trees and brush had been cleared for trucks and earthmovers. She looked tiny against all the darkness. From where I stood, I could see the snow driving down in front of the lights I'd left on, but I couldn't see it near her. All it looked like around her was dark. She was shaking with the cold, and she was crying.

I had a blanket with me, and I shoved it down the front of my coat to keep it dry for her, and because I was so cold. I waved. I stood in the lights and I waved. I don't know what she saw—a big shadow, maybe. I surely didn't reassure her, because when she saw me she backed up, until she was near the face of the quarry. She couldn't go any farther.

I called, "Hello! I brought a blanket. Are you cold? I thought you might want a blanket."

Her roommates had told the operator about pills, so I didn't bring her the coffee laced with mash. I figured I didn't have all that much time, anyway, to get her down and pumped out. The booze with whatever pills she'd taken would made her die that much faster.

I hated that word. Die. It made me furious with her. I heard myself seething when I breathed. I pulled my scarf and collar up above my mouth. I didn't want her to see how close I might come to wanting to kill her because she wanted to die.

I called, "Remember me?"

I was closer now. I could see the purple mottling of her skin. I didn't know if it was cold or dying. It probably didn't matter much to distinguish between them right now, I thought. That made me smile. I felt the smile, and I pulled the scarf down so she could look at it. She didn't seem awfully reassured.

"You're the sexual harassment guy," she said. She said it very slowly. Her lips were clumsy. It was like looking at a ventriloquist's dummy.

"I gave you an A," I said.

"When?"

"It's a joke," I said. "You don't want me making jokes. You want me to give you a nice warm blanket, though. And then you want me to take you home."

She leaned against the rock face when I approached. I pulled the blanket out, then zipped my jacket back up. The snow had stopped, I realized, and that wasn't really a very good sign. It felt like an arctic cold descending in its place. I held the blanket out to her, but she only looked at it.

"You'll just have to turn me in," I said. "I'm gonna hug you again."

She screamed, "No more! I don't want any more hugs!"

But she kept her arms on her chest, and I wrapped the blanket around her and stuffed a piece into each of her tight, small fists. I didn't know what to do for her feet. Finally, I got down on my haunches in front of her. She crouched down too, protecting herself.

"No," I said. "No. You're fine."

I took off the woolen mittens I'd been wearing. Mittens keep you warmer than gloves because they trap your hand's heat around the fingers and palms at once. Fanny had knitted them for me. I put a mitten as far onto each of her feet as I could. She let me. She was going to collapse, I thought.

"Now, let's go home," I said. "Let's get you better."

With her funny, stiff lips, she said, "I've been very self-indulgent and weird and I'm sorry. But I'd really like to die." She sounded so reasonable that I found myself nodding in agreement as she spoke.

"You can't just die," I said.

"Aren't I dying already? I took all of them, and then"— she giggled like a child, which of course is what she was—"I borrowed different ones from other people's rooms. See, this isn't some teenage cry for like *help*. Understand? I'm seriously interested in death and I have to like stay out here a little longer and fall asleep. All right?"

"You can't do that," I said. "You ever hear of Vietnam?"

"I saw that movie," she said. "With the opera in it? *Apocalypse*? Whatever."

"I was there!" I said. "I killed people! I helped to kill them! And when they die, you see their bones later on. You dream about their bones and blood on the ends of the splintered ones, and this kind of mucous stuff coming out of their eyes. You probably heard of guys having dreams like that, didn't you? Whacked-out Vietnam vets? That's me, see? So I'm telling you, I know about dead people and their eyeballs and everything falling out. And people keep dreaming about the dead people they knew, see? You can't make people dream about you like that! It isn't fair!"

"You dream about me?" She was ready to go. She was ready to fall down, and I was going to lift her up and get her to the truck.

"I will," I said. "If you die."

"I want you to," she said. Her lips were hardly moving now. Her eyes were closed. "I want you all to."

I dropped my shoulder and put it into her waist and picked her up and carried her down to the Bronco. She was talking, but not a lot, and her voice leaked down my back. I jammed her into the truck and wrapped the blanket around her better and then put another one down around her feet. I strapped her in with the seat belt. She was shaking, and her eyes were closed and her mouth open. She was breathing. I checked that twice, once when I strapped her in, and then again when I strapped myself in and backed up hard into a sapling and took it down. I got us into first gear, held the clutch in, leaned over to listen for breathing, heard it—shallow panting, like a kid asleep on your lap for a nap—and then I put the gear in and howled down the hillside on what I thought might be the road.

We passed the cemetery. I told her that was a good sign. She didn't respond. I found myself panting too, as if we were breathing for each other. It made me dizzy, but I couldn't stop. We passed the highest dorm, and I dropped the truck into four-wheel high. The cab smelled like burnt oil and hot metal. We were past the chapel now, and the observatory, the president's house, then the bookstore. I had the blue light winking and the V-6 roaring, and I drove on the edge of out-of-control, sensing the skids just before I slid into them, and getting back out of them as I needed to.

I took a little fender off once, and a bit of the corner of a classroom building, but I worked us back on course, and all I needed to do now was negotiate the sharp left turn around the Administration Building past the library, then floor it for the straight run to the town's main street and then the hospital.

I was panting into the mike, and the operator kept saying, "Say again?"

I made myself slow down some, and I said we'd need stomach pumping, and to get the names of the pills from her friends in the dorm, and I'd be there in less than five or we were crumpled up someplace and dead.

"Roger," the radio said. "Roger all that." My throat tightened and tears came into my eyes. They were helping us, they'd told me: Roger.

I said to the girl, whose head was slumped and whose face looked too blue all through its whiteness, "You know, I had a girl once. My wife, Fanny. She and I had a small girl one time."

I reached over and touched her cheek. It was cold. The truck swerved, and I got my hands on the wheel. I'd made the turn past the Ad Building using just my left. "I can do it in the dark," I sang to no tune I'd ever learned. "I can do it with one hand." I said to her, "We had a girl child, very small. Now, I do *not* want you dying."

I came to the campus gates doing fifty on the ice and snow, smoking the engine, grinding the clutch, and I bounced off a wrought iron fence to give me the curve going left that I needed. On a pool table, it would have been a bank shot worth applause. The town cop picked me up and got out ahead of me and let the street have all the lights and noise it could want. We banged up to the emergency room entrance and I was out and at the other door before the cop on duty, Elmo St. John, could loosen his seat belt. I loosened hers, and I carried her into the lobby of the ER. They had a gurney, and doctors, and they took her away from me. I tried to talk to them, but they made me sit down and do my shaking on a dirty sofa decorated with drawings of little spinning wheels. Somebody brought me hot coffee, I think it was Elmo, but I couldn't hold it.

"They won't," he kept saying to me. "They won't."

"What?"

"You just been sitting there for a minute and a half like St. Vitus dancing, telling me, 'Don't let her die. Don't let her die.'"

"Oh."

"You all *right*?"

"How about the kid?"

"They'll tell us soon."

"She better be all right."

"That's right."

"She—somebody's gonna have to tell me plenty if she isn't."

"That's right."

"She better not die this time," I guess I said.

Fanny came downstairs to look for me. I was at the northern windows, looking through the mullions down the

84

valley to the faint red line along the mounds and little peaks of the ridge beyond the valley. The sun was going to come up, and I was looking for it.

Fanny stood behind me. I could hear her. I could smell her hair and the sleep on her. The crimson line widened, and I squinted at it. I heard the dog limp in behind her, catching up. He panted and I knew why his panting sounded familiar. She put her hands on my shoulders and arms. I made muscles to impress her with, and then I let them go, and let my head drop down until my chin was on my chest.

"I didn't think you'd be able to sleep after that," Fanny said.

"I brought enough adrenaline home to run a football team."

"But you hate being a hero, huh? You're hiding in here because somebody's going to call, or come over, and want to talk to you—her parents for shooting sure, sooner or later. Or is that supposed to be part of the service up at the playground? Saving their suicidal daughters. Almost dying to find them in the woods and driving too fast for *any* weather, much less what we had last night. Getting their babies home. The bastards." She was crying. I knew she would be, sooner or later. I could hear the soft sound of her lashes. She sniffed and I could feel her arm move as she felt for the tissues on the coffee table.

"I have them over here," I said. "On the windowsill."

"Yes." She blew her nose, and the dog thumped his tail. He seemed to think it one of Fanny's finer tricks, and he had wagged for her for thirteen years whenever she'd done it. "Well, you're going to have to talk to them."

85

"I will," I said. "I will." The sun was in our sky now, climbing. We had built the room so we could watch it climb. "I think that jackass with the smile, my prof? She showed up a lot at his office, the last few weeks. He called her 'my advisee,' you know? The way those guys sound about what they're achieving by getting up and shaving and going to work and saying the same thing every day? Every year? Well, she was his advisee, I bet. He was shoving home the old advice."

"She'll be okay," Fanny said. "Her parents will take her home and love her up and get her some help." She began to cry again, then she stopped. She blew her nose, and the dog's tail thumped. She kept a hand between my shoulder and my neck. "So tell me what you'll tell a waiting world. How'd you talk her out?"

"Well, I didn't, really. I got up close and picked her up and carried her is all."

"You didn't say *any*thing?"

"Sure I did. Kid's standing in the snow outside of a lot of pills, you're gonna say something."

"So what'd you *say*?"

"I told her stories," I said. "I did Rhetoric and Persuasion."

Fanny said, "Then you go in early on Thursday, you go in half an hour early, and you get that guy to jack up your grade."

86

🏵 Comrades

W E B E G A N to feel better after we had wrecked the cobalt-blue pitcher on our hardwood kitchen floor and, like bad children bent on not being caught, our mouths open with fatigue, we had kneeled together to pick up shards. That night, we drank coffee together, grinding dark beans and pouring heavy cream into a small brown pottery jug. We sat in our denims while birch burned in the airtight stove. We agreed that what surprised us most was our feeling of ease. To be sure, her knee was black and blue, my forearm was yellow with bruising; there would be scabs above my ear and on her biceps. But, drinking coffee and talking sensibly, we agreed that we hated the pitcher from Mexico, given us by friends in Greenwich Village long ago. We also agreed that such a symbol of marriage, and that's what it clearly had become, would need to be broken, now that we had so violently concurred—and here we gave a sort of corporate laugh—that we ought to be divorced.

In the week afterward, we spoke briskly and were kind. We felt compact and healthy, and we didn't weep upon each other, or at each other, or in places where one was overheard. We called each other *Love* a lot, as in "Pasta with bacon and pinto beans for dinner, Love."

I worked for a mildly left-wing journal of politics and the arts, and Berry often called me *Comrade*. I once had detested hearing her say it, although I'd understood the tensions it derived from—for when we were to be married, her most intimate confession to her parents, and my most threatening trait, was that I was a registered Liberal. *Comrade*, in the second week after our agreement to divorce, replaced *Love*. Each time she said it, we smiled.

After twelve days, we had planned everything but the details of our journey from Wilton, Connecticut, to Athens, Ohio, where our daughter was a college freshman. We agreed that we should not summon her home. We agreed that we should travel to her together. We agreed that we should stay with her a while and then drive her back with us to Wilton if she wished us to. And then with no verbal agreement, but with a sudden strong sense of necessity, we postponed the trip. For it became very clear that Berry had to see her mother first.

That was where we went on the second weekend after our glad decision to divorce. We had grown more fatigued by the Thursday of that week, and Berry had called me *Comrade* less and *Love* not at all. I told her, over coffee before the Saturday drive from Wilton to Montpelier, Vermont, that I was worried about us.

"You're worried about yourself, Bob," she said. She was in a russet corduroy suit and loafers with little heels, and she looked like someone a man should be happy to know.

"No, Ber," I said. "I'm serious."

"Don't you think *I* am? You're afraid of what my mother will be like. You're afraid of what we'll tell her about us and what she might say."

"Ber, your mother isn't going to care. She isn't going to know."

"My mother isn't the issue, Bob."

"There is no issue. Did you notice I was wearing corduroy also?"

I was in my brown wide-wale sportcoat and khakis, good Saturday clothes for anyplace, and surely for a nursing home in Montpelier. She shook her head. She pulled at the square bottom of my brown knit tie. I made my teeth show, as if the tie were connected to a switch that she had tugged. Berry laughed. She had forgotten, I'd have sworn, everything, for just the duration of that knot-tightening. So I said, "Comrade: it was you."

"What?"

"Really. That I was worried about."

"All right," she said.

I said, "You sometimes don't look happy anymore. I mean, as happy as you did last week. All things being equal."

Berry said, "Elegance is not my strongest suit. Neither is fakery. Neither is pretense. You put them all together, you get what we got last week. All things being equal. You get *folie à deux*."

I said, "No, not yet. We'll order later."

"*What?*"

89

"It was a very bad joke. It was a menu joke. A waiter joke. It wasn't a joke. Never mind."

Berry nodded. The lines remained at the bridge of her nose and at either corner of her mouth. She smiled the smile I had just finished smiling in response to a tug on my brown knit tie. She shrugged, still smiling. I, smiling back, shrugged too.

And as I started the car, I wondered how we could have endured the last two weeks, and how our daughter would endure the other weeks, and why we were bent on driving together toward what was just more separateness. I drove us that way nevertheless.

Everybody's parent's old-age home is probably pretty much the same, I thought, when we arrived. I wondered if that meant that everybody's parent is pretty much the same. Or, I wondered, does it mean that oldness is the same for everyone. And, therefore, I thought, youth can't be so awfully individual either. I actually grew afraid as we walked up the steps. For there had to be *something* different, at some time or other. Most specifically, there had to be a happy divorce. So why not ours? I heard the answer, and in Berry's voice, inside my thoughts: Because we all are the same, Comrade. I thought of Barbara, our daughter, in her freshman dorm. I thought of the new side porch in Wilton, and of two storm windows I'd ordered.

It was early afternoon. The temperature in the home was comfortable, though slightly warm for me. Everybody's parent's old-age home is kept at approximately the same temperature. Berry walked a few steps ahead of me. I used to love her long stride. I should say that I still do. A stride is easy to love. She was ahead of me, and then she was bending above her mother. Everybody's bending above an aged parent is the same, no doubt, and we are all comrades in the having to bend, and in the boredom we share at having to hear about each other's bending. Berry bent, and so, at last, did I.

Berry knew what to say. Her mother was bulky under her pink quilted housecoat. Her face shone with medicines and cleanliness and seventy-six years come to something of a halt. Her brown eyes matched Berry's suit, I noticed. I reminded myself not to say that. She hated my noticing smallnesses when faced with large events. Their eyes were precisely the same color, and they matched Berry's suit. Berry said, "Hello. My name is Berry. I've come to visit you."

I said, "Hello. My name is Bob. I've come to visit you too."

The sweet smile shone, as it always did at such moments. I thought of a tug on my tie and my face's lighting up. Berry's mother said, "Hello. You've come to see me? Isn't that nice?"

"And we've brought you some gifts," Berry said.

I started to raise a box for her to see—it contained a pair of fleece-lined slippers, and it was prettily wrapped—when Berry's mother said, looking at her wrist on which there was no watch, "Oh, dear." She said it urgently. "Oh, dear," she said again. "You know, I have *got* to get back to work. I really must run. You're going to *have* to excuse me."

Berry said, "Mommy."

Her mother looked up quizzically. Perhaps the quizzical looking up of one's faraway mother is also like the looking up of everyone else's. But she did look up. Her face was sweet, her expression charming. She seemed prepared to be enlightened, and then to get away toward work.

All Berry said was "But Mommy."

"Hello," her mother said. "I have to get back."

A nurse, I realized, had been standing behind us all that time. Her gray-gold hair was up in a knot and her hands were folded before her as grade-school teachers, when I was a child, used to fold their hands. She smiled, she shrugged just a little, and then she nodded when I pointed down the corridor into which Berry's mother had slowly walked, looking at her wrist as if a watch were strapped around it. Berry followed her mother and I followed Berry. We walked past a number of other people's parents, and we found Berry's mother in the solarium, where she sat in a very large red leather and chromium chair, her back erect, as she had taught Berry always to sit, and her face as vacant of expression as Berry's now was filled. The tall windows behind Berry's mother were smudgeless, and their perfect cleanliness suggested that the windows had never been used. I wondered who ever looked in, from the outside of nursing home windows. Real sun came through them, but on the tan linoleum floor and the red chairs and the people who sat as if they were too small for them, the light looked artificial, and the solarium seemed an antique picture postcard, tinted into life.

"Love," I said to Berry. She looked up. She was furious with something. I realized that it might be me. I said, "Comrade. She's gone again. She doesn't remember. She can't. She isn't doing it on purpose. She would love you if she knew. She would love you if she could."

Berry, bent above her mother, as everyone else at some time must be bent, continued to look up. It must have hurt her back to crouch that way. She said, "Spare me, Comrade, the running commentary. Would you?" As if someone had pulled on a brown knit necktie, she smiled.

Berry looked down. I walked to them and bent down too. I said, "Hello. I'm Bob. I've come to visit you."

Berry said, "Hello. I'm Berry. I've come to visit you too."

I said, "We brought some gifts for you. Look."

Berry's mother, looking up and smiling, like everyone's mother who looks up to smile, said, "Oh. You've come to see me? Isn't that nice?"

"And we've brought you some gifts," I said, like all of their sons-in-law or all of their sons.

She laid her hand on the gay wrapping paper. The knuckles were swollen, and two of the clean white fingers with their frayed tips were permanently bent. Sometimes she made you forget that her body was also, in several ways, afflicted. Sometimes you thought only about her mind, and how far inside it she was hidden. She said, "Oh, dear."

Berry, in a lower voice than I'd heard that afternoon, though in a voice I had heard a great deal before our happy agreement to divorce, said, "You have to go back to work."

Her mother looked at the wrist that bore no watch. "I have to get back to work," her mother said.

Berry said, "Me too."

The nurse with gray-gold hair was with us. She took the gifts for Berry's mother and told us that the doctor would see us. He did. We asked the questions and he answered them. I suppose everyone asks questions like those. Everyone probably hears those answers. And everyone, then, goes down the corridor and through the lobby and into, in our case, a bright autumn afternoon in Vermont.

In the car, Berry said, "So there she is again."

"She's just the way we expected her to be."

"Really?"

"Well—you know."

"No," Berry said. "What if I expected her to say, *Hi, kid! What's cookin'?* That's what she used to say to me. I'd come home or I'd call her up, and she'd say, *Hi, kid! What's cookin'?*"

"I know. But she can't, Berry. It's natural to be angry at somebody you love who really gets sick. Especially a parent. But she really can't."

"Thanks, Comrade Doktor. But what if she won't? You know? What if she *won't?*"

"You aren't serious."

"No? What if she *will* not? What if she *wants* to hide away? And forget about us all. What about *that?*"

"And forget about *you* is what you mean, Ber."

"Yes," she said. "Forget about me."

You wouldn't have known, if you had been watching us, that soon we would drive to Ohio and tell our daughter about our divorce. Everyone driving a car very fast on a highway in fast-moving traffic looks like everyone else. I turned to Berry to say so. She looked like her mother. I turned back to look at the road. I drove and I drove and I drove until the sirens behind me, then the lights in the mirror, told me it was time to pause a while and look like other fugitives, slumped and pale, gripping the motionless wheel at the side of the road.

Orbits

Is visiting old parents like visiting old friends? Ginger and Charlie were talking about her mother and father while hot, wet wind poured into the car and took the sound of their voices away from one another. They kept calling, "What?" The radio was playing Haydn. They were driving up a hill and were at last in the shade for a while, were dropping into tired silence, when the station changed. Ginger looked at Charlie, but his hands were on the wheel and not the tuner. It was something in the air—radio waves or great explosions on the surface of the sun—or a secret hand in a secret place turning the dial invisibly from Haydn to an instant of rock and roll and to a voice that spat cruel syllables and then back to Haydn again, but with hissings, electrical squeaks.

Ginger said, "I'm turning it off."

They drove without speaking. Charlie waited for the radiator or the battery or all of the tires to explode. Nothing happened. He took the proper turns, and they were there when they'd said they would be.

Charlie had for twenty-five years thought of Ginger's mother as someone who strode. Now she walked slowly, with a kind of sideways hitch in her pace. She had broken a leg two years before, and though she was recovered, she also wasn't. While she had moved about, she'd been safe, he thought. But because she'd been pinned to a chair for some months, whatever it was that one fled had caught her. Her thin lips twisted as if the leg, or her sense of what Charlie was seeing, gave her pain. Ginger's father, once a tall, athletic man, now was curving at the shoulders and walked with uncertainty, as if his balance were afflicted. The hardening arteries that isolated his heart were also affecting his feet: a man filled with blood could still not get enough where it was needed, and he walked as if his feet were tender, bruised. It seemed as though a wind were blowing at him, at both of them, and that each time it gusted they were almost knocked down.

They all hugged. Ginger and Charlie reported on their daughters; one was in a dance camp for the summer, the other was a waitress at a bar near Provincetown. Ginger's father said, in his deepest professional voice—he had been a labor negotiator—that he still didn't like the idea of Sue Ellen's working in a saloon.

"It's a respectable resort, Daddy," Ginger said when they sat on the porch and drank tall drinks. Insects buzzed at the screen. The leaves hung limp on the maples. Her father

opened the collar of his dark knitted sports shirt. He rubbed
at the V of his pale chest as if to wipe away the heat. Charlie
knew that batteries in a pacemaker underneath the chest were
beating this man's heart.

Ginger's mother said, "He thinks Sue Ellen's twelve years
old."

"Add seven," Charlie said. "Actually, add about twenty-
five. I'm not thinking about *any*thing. I'm trusting her. She's
a great kid. Trust is—"

"I can't wait for it," Ginger said.

"Overrated," Charlie said.

"I always trusted *Ginger*," her mother said.

"Yes," Charlie said, "but you learned your lesson, didn't
you?"

They were laughing now, at what wasn't funny, at what
was only another way of naming what scared them, and they
were not talking about her parents' health or their growing
burden: this large Colonial house and its twenty acres; the
garden, which demanded tending; the lawn, which Charlie
would mow in the morning—the general maintenance, kept
up only by hiring strangers, at whose mercy they more and
more were. They drank their drinks, they told each other
news. Ginger and her mother left, refusing offers to help
with making dinner. Ginger's father watched Charlie pour
more gin, and he accepted soda water with lemon, and they
sat and listened to catbirds shriek. They talked about Aida,
the younger girl, who did tap, ballet, modern, and even ball-
room dancing at the camp in the Berkshires. Charlie spoke
of missing Aida but also of his pleasure at being alone with
Ginger for a summer. Ginger's father, in turn, spoke of how

they still sometimes realized all over again that Ginger didn't live with them. He said it gently, then shook his head, as if to signal how absurd he thought himself to be.

"Fathers," Charlie said.

"The softest, most demanding species of man," his wife's father said. "Nothing's worse." He adjusted a cushion at his back. Charlie watched his father-in-law's biceps and fore-arms under the pale skin. There was good muscle, but the skin was softening. He looked at its scabs and bruises, moles and spots and furrows, puckers.

"You did a good job," Charlie said.

"You're kind to say it. I did try to shut up a great deal."

"I wish I could learn to do that."

"Well, you will. The girls won't listen to you, and Ginger'll grow weary of hearing you say what nobody needs to hear, and you'll become a quiet man. Surprise. People will talk about how quiet you've become."

"You know," Charlie said, "nothing's *wrong*. I'm loving how they're growing up. Ginger and I are fine. There isn't anything really *wrong*."

Her father, who had more hair on top of his head than Charlie did, smoothed it over, pushed it into place, and folded his hands in his lap. The lap disappears, too, Charlie noticed: you become a stick figure drawn by a kid. Her father said, "Don't worry about it, Charlie. I'm making you nervous. Old people seem to have that effect, sometimes."

"*No*," Charlie said. He shook his head. He imitated the hair-pat gesture, but rubbed only fuzz and scalp. He said, and he heard the conviction in his voice as he said it, "No."

They ate a cold poached fish, and Ginger and Charlie

drank Sancerre, while her parents drank only water. It was a lovely wine, and Charlie drank a lot of it—almost enough to make him smack his lips and comment on the generosity of a man who, unable to drink because of his health, would provide a first-class wine for those who could enjoy it. Instead, Charlie held his glass up and beamed at the wine. His father-in-law nodded and grinned. Charlie watched Ginger's mother's face twist during the meal. Her lips almost curled. It came and went, as the voice breaking into the rock and roll breaking into the Haydn had come and gone. For dessert they ate fresh fruit. Ginger cracked nuts for everybody. She had done this, always, as a young girl, her father pointed out. Eating none, she distributed nutmeat to all. Charlie decided suddenly that her mother was suffering physically because of thoughts that danced like electrical charges through her. Her daughter, whose presence she sought, was reminding her of what she had lost and had to lose. When they spoke of the girls away for the summer, or of Ginger's going off to school so many years before, or of Ginger's second, and very difficult, pregnancy, the language set the impulse off, and a mother lost her child to time, and therefore herself, and the fact shot from her memory and hummed beneath her white hair like the insects at the porch.

There was no change of subject possible. They spoke of absent daughters, absent friends, the ailments of Presidents, and policies of nations. Ginger cracked nuts, as if she were the little child of these seventy-six-year-olds, surrounded by the house that they once had run but that now, with its demands for paint and new plumbing, its dampness in the basement, squirrels in the eaves, was running them. Around them, the grass rose to challenge their tenure, and the moths, as darkness came on, beat with big wings at the screens on the kitchen windows. Charlie watched the face of his wife's mother as it was assaulted by what he hadn't thought to possess any longer, much less to brandish: youth.

Inside, television reception was very poor. The Carol Burnett rerun broke into dots and a now familiar hissing. Public Broadcasting was a purple haze that sounded like a waterfall. They went back out to the porch. Ginger's mother reported on dead associates and distant relatives, a local sewage-tax scandal, and residential-zoning conflicts. Her father commented on Saudi Arabians who had purchased large parcels of land nearby.

They sat for a while, and then Ginger's mother said, "I hate this house."

"You love it," her father said. "You're angry because I forgot to open the cellar doors and windows this summer to air the damp out."

"I'm angry because that means *I* have to remember it."

Charlie said, "There's always something to take care of."

"Unless you live in a—in one of those *old* places," Ginger's mother said.

"No," Charlie said. "No. I wasn't saying that."

"You know how many perfectly rational, intelligent people get *dumped* into those places?" her mother said.

Ginger's father said, "Don't *worry* so much. I promise. As long as I can drawl and drool and mutter, I'll remind you that the cellar needs its airing out."

Her mother limped into the house and they sat in the memory of her tension. Ginger sighed. Then she said, "Oh, look at that *moon*!" It was full and threw a startling light, which appeared to go no distance but to burn in place. Ginger's father called for his wife to return. "The moon," he called. "Come look at the moon."

They waited, like children who had built a version of the sky, for the disgruntled elder who would come and maybe approve. She did come, with decaffeinated coffee, an offering.

Ginger's mother said, "What planets are those alongside it? Or are they stars?"

Ginger said, "Isn't one of them red? Wouldn't that be Mars?"

"It might be," her mother said. "But it might be a star."

Ginger's father said, "There are two more—I can't name them. I didn't know they clustered like that, all together."

"It's probably rare," Ginger said.

Ginger's mother said, "Probably *very* infrequent. Yes. *I* never heard of it before. I can't imagine how long it might take for them to shine together again."

Charlie said, "It probably happens once a week."

Nobody laughed. The reddish star or planet was above the moon, and they could see a larger, brighter body glowing orange-white above whatever it was that shone like rust, or terra-cotta. Something else—surely it was a planet, Charlie thought, naming it Jupiter, knowing that he would think, right or wrong, of Jupiter when he thought of tonight—seemed a great white balloon.

"Imagine," Ginger said. Charlie knew that she would say it—how would one not?—and he regretted it for her. "Sue Ellen and Aida can see this." Charlie squeezed at the bridge of his nose, hoping to shut off her speech. "And when we talk to them," she said, waving at the terra-cotta planet or star, the blue-white, brilliant maybe-Jupiter, "we can say they saw—we all saw it together. What nobody might see again for who knows *how* long."

Ginger looked up to see her mother glancing down. No one needed to say who would not be on the surface of the earth to look at the sky so many years from tonight. But no one seemed capable of saying anything diversionary. So they sat for what seemed a very long while as the darkness deepened, and as the stars and planets in their slow but fugitive formation rose in the blue-black sky.

Then Ginger's father rumbled, deep and happy, from the chaise on which her mother sat. He was still sitting on his chair, at the other side of the porch, but his voice rolled out from a bulky cassette recorder with which her mother was fiddling. He spoke of negotiating with a Taiwan national, and of how the man had outwitted him, and his voice was cheery and possessive: he clearly knew that he was being recorded, and he seemed to enjoy letting someone preserve what only he could tell.

"I've been making little tapes of some of Dad's stories," Ginger's mother said. Ginger sighed a long and shaken breath. Her mother said, "Don't worry. I won't take down anything you say, dear."

Ginger said, "I don't mind."

Her mother said, "When children grow up, they sound different. The most they can do is talk about what it was like when they were young. But they don't sound the same."

Ginger said, "No."

"That was a hell of a story," Charlie said.

"He robbed us blind," her father said, "because he was

out-and-out smarter than I was. He did his job better. I couldn't help admiring him."

Charlie nodded in the dark. Ginger's mother played more tape-recorded sounds—Baltimore orioles calling, her own voice saying, "It's a soft, wet night," a neighbor saying how she had spent her day—and then Ginger's father's voice returned, sounding nothing so much as pleased. It was as if he knew that one day his voice would speak about the Taiwanese, or about the man who had tried to sell him a slum in Bedford-Stuyvesant, and that his tones would be charming, his story engaging, and his body long gone. He was winsome for the future, Charlie thought. He was speaking from the grave. And there he sat, before his wife, who mourned him already, and before his daughter, mostly absent these days, whose daughters were now mostly absent as well. Charlie's eyes ached. Jupiter glowed below the moon, and Mars above, as Ginger's mother played the cassette.

In the darkness, Charlie could barely see any of them now. Ginger's mother said, "I want you to hear something near the beginning of the tape. It's sort of funny. Dad tells about the man from the aircraft company. The fellow who couldn't tolerate dust. Did he ever tell you about that?"

"I must have bored them with that one a dozen times."

Ginger's voice said, "Tell it, Daddy."

Her mother said, "Let the tape tell it. Wait. I have to find it. It's near the beginning. Wait a minute." She clicked buttons, reversing the tape. She pushed another button that sent it forward. She clicked and pushed, making the tape whine and jump and say fragments of sound.

Ginger said, "Daddy, go ahead."

He began to talk while they sat back, invisible to one another. The hum and snick and sudden voices of the tape recorder played like a background tune in a shop while her mother searched the tape for his story. He was saying, "You see, his work involved the manufacture of instruments for fighter planes. One airplane in particular, an interceptor. They called it an all-weather interceptor. Well, you can imagine how an airplane that was supposed to fly in fog and rain might rely on its instruments. So of course the delicacy of their manufacture had to match the delicacy of the performance expected of them. Men were going to be sealed up, alone, ten miles in the air, surrounded by tons of metal alloy and wires and high explosives and kerosene, and they were going to rely exclusively on those instruments—except for their wits, of course. And who knows better than present company how little *those* can sometimes be counted on?"

As if he had rehearsed, he paused for polite laughter. Perhaps if they had sat in daylight he would have expected a smile and a nod. In the background, on the tape, Charlie heard a sound that startled him. It confused him. Ginger's father continued, "Not to mention matters of perhaps intercepting a bomber headed for the United States, or one of our military bases in Europe. So it was crucial work. He headed— this fellow I'm speaking of—he ran the team that was in charge of the final assembling of the controls display. In their lab, they wore masks and caps and gowns to keep their hair or skin off their work. They wore gloves, of course, and the lab was immaculate. One speck of dirt, as I understand it, and some gizmo might go haywire. Boom! Millions of dollars and a human life: just ashes. So he was, not surprisingly, a very nervous man. He trembled, he said, except when he was on the job. I remember saying to him, 'You had best love your work, then.' The poor guy. We were writing a contract proposal for the company, and he was among the technicians' representatives in my office one morning. We were talking about wages. It was amicable, systematic, slow. This was quite a while ago. This was almost twenty years ago, my God. He sat there, shaking and pale, watching everything. He had enormous brown eyes, I remember. He was like a great big spaniel or a retriever. He watched and he watched.

"And, all of a sudden, he sat up. He'd been slouched, looking tired, just pressing his fingers on my desk top, watching. Then he sat *straight* up and rubbed his fingertips together. The expression on his face was one of horror. I'm sure you can guess it. They don't call them dusty lawyers' offices for nothing, after all." Ginger's father paused. Charlie nodded and smiled, as if they sat in the light. "His fingers were covered with *dust*, you see. The enemy!"

Ginger's mother said, "There!" Her father's taped voice in the background paused, as the voices alive on the porch did, and then the tape-recorded voice of Ginger's father said, "The enemy!"

"This thing takes forever to rewind," Ginger's mother complained. But Charlie was thinking that the sound he had heard a few moments ago, preserved in the muted chatter and mechanical grating of the buttons, was his own voice. It had spoken a syllable, now long past in the to-ing and fro-ing of the tape—a fragment of his daughter Aida's name—and he could not avoid imagining that his daughters might listen to this same broken voice on a porch in a future night, when Ginger was absent, and he was, too, and when a rare pattern of planets would have reappeared to goggle from the dark.

A button clicked and the tape recorder stopped. They sat in the darkness. Ginger's mother cleared her throat. Charlie thought of his daughters thinking of him, and then, like a delicate moth settling, a hand that reached from the darkness stroked the back of Charlie's hand. It was a tentative touch, and the hand was very light and very little—his mother-in-law's. She offered the softest caress. Charlie waited for more. But the small hand withdrew. Ginger yawned, and her father spoke of sleep.

Greetings from a Far-flung Place

SHE'D BEEN WORKING for an hour on her voice. The letter had begun, " 'Well, nuts,' I said. 'Get yourself another girl.' " She had read that in the dialogue of a minor character in a forgotten murder mystery. It didn't matter. She wouldn't mail the letter to her sister or call her on the phone or in any other way open the communications between them which had recently shut down like the factories she'd seen from the van as they raced against some world's land speed record through a small industrial city on the verge of death. They weren't estranged, she and her sister. It was more like distance. They had the same widowed mother, and they had distance.

There were three sheets of motel stationery. She had filled one side of one sheet, in her smallest and neatest hand, with beginnings aimed at helping her to locate a voice in which to address her sister. There was no stranger sleeping on the bed after tepid sex. There wasn't a cigarette burning in the shallow plastic ashtray. No liquor, tears, or perspiration stained the cheap letterhead. The room was neat, though overheated, and it smelled of bathroom cleanser. She didn't weep or shake. She sat, in her white terry-cloth bathrobe, and she worked at her trade: the voice.

Sister, beloved, here are greetings from a far-flung place.

That was all right. That was not bad. And Scranton had surely been flung, by history and currency and industry and plain use, about as far as it was possible for a city to be moved. The band had played a civic center's winter bash after a dance at Lehigh, in Bethlehem, Pa. Two engagements that close meant a satisfactory take, though not riches. She had gotten away with a Peggy Lee imitation in the boonies. She had nearly gotten away. She had stood absolutely still except for a tiny tick of the tummy and had sung very low—too low for her register, but they hadn't known, they'd thought her a throaty jazz singer—and the band had done the brassy *ooo-wa*, with a cymbal burnish on the end. Provincials like the horns that way. To her it sounded as cheap as their wages, as worn-out as her vocal cords, and as derivative as each of their other sets had been.

Sister, beloved. Far-flung place. All right. Mom of course always calls the places I go "far-flung" when she talks to you. *If* I'm the Good Sister when she talks. If I'm not, it's your turn, and I'm called "restless" and you're simply "darling" or "considerate." At which time the places I go are simply called "away." It reminds me of the bad books I read in these places we play. I spend most of my time on my back, as you and Danny doubtless have said to one another, but I have to disappoint you by saying that it's time spent reading. Most of these gigs—you were waiting for that word—consist of waiting for Ellis to see that the luggage and instruments get into the vans, and waiting for us to get stuffed and molded buttock to buttock into the vans, and waiting for the damned vans to get to wherever we're playing—Manny's Casa Roma, or a cement-block palace named the Poseidon Club—and then I wait to get dressed and I wait to be introduced by Ellis as "our girl singer," because, in spite of my being thirty-eight and in spite of its not being 1938, Ellis keeps trying to sound like a big band leader with slicked-down hair and brown skin. He can't forgive himself for being white and more or less untalented, and he's probably right.

So I wait. I read mystery books in paperback and I leave them in the room when I go. I have learned from them that death means as much in the mystery business as it does in mine, and that death after a hundred thousand words or so is usually meaningless, and that a favorite trick of the police is the Good Cop–Bad Cop routine. During the interrogation, one cop rages at the suspect and threatens a long prison term, immediate harm, and the prospect of jail-cell rape. The other restrains the Bad Cop and finally gets him out of the room. He offers the suspect cigarettes, which every suspect smokes, I've learned, and soft advice. Between them, the Bad Cop and the Good Cop break the suspect down. The poor bastard finally signs a confession.

Can a mother be two cops? When she's tough on one of us—when she intimates quite clearly how much the Bad

Sister has hurt her in one of a thousand awful ways—then she makes the other into a Good Sister. And what sister does not strive to be good in the eyes of the law? She does her cops, we does our rob-hers.

She had one side of the paper left. She drank from a can of sugar-free soft drink and she stood to remove the bathrobe. Though she didn't look in the wide mirror, she did suck her stomach in and pull her shoulders back, as if the mirror looked with someone's eyes. She walked toward the bathroom, away from the gaze. But there was another mirror, over the sink. She said to it, "Not bad for forty-one. I mean thirty-eight. On the other hand, not that good either." She squeezed her belly and although there wasn't a lot to get hold of, a grip was not impossible.

Gripping herself was preferable, this moment, to being gripped by Henry, their sad drummer. He called like a cat when he made love, and he often was apologizing for something. Which explained, to her satisfaction at least, why the band could never, ever, swing: nobody was there to drive it. She had tried talking to Henry about Basie's rhythm section, but he never wanted to talk about Basie or the free-fall let's-not-stop-and-anyway-we-can't pouring onward that musicians and even their girl singers experienced a few times in a career. She liked Henry, and he used marvelous cologne, and though he was fifty his body was hard, like a younger man's, and his skin was exactly the light brown of the pottery made in Bybee, Kentucky, which her sister had brought home from college as the start of her dowry. His only drawbacks were occasional whining, and a need to be comforted that equaled his need to make trouble or cause excitement. He was not a topnotch drummer and, because of him, by the end of a long set they always swam in molasses. But he worried about her. And he was a chum. And when you don't have husband, children, dogs, cats, canaries, or the real sense of having done too much to write home about, you keep hold of your chums.

It was really called the Hotel Meridian, and it truly was in Altoona, Pa. All the way from New York in the van, she'd realized when they arrived, she had been expecting the city *not* to be Altoona—because she didn't want to be the singer in the kind of band that played Altoona for the kind of money they'd make. It was a very large motel with a parking lot you could fly a jumbo jet from. *Plenty of Free Parking*, she figured their ads would say. Hail fell, and she stood and watched the little granules bounce and roll on the hood of the van. Henry came up beside her, square-shouldered and tall with a short strong neck, elegant with his scarf so white against his black coat, and he took her right hand. He brought it up to her face. "Look," he said, and she saw that her cold pale hand was a fist.

"I'm keeping my fingers warm," she said.

"You're turning into a knot," Henry told her.

He picked her fist up and kissed it. She felt about six years old for as long as the kiss lasted. Then she felt cold and stiff. And when Henry saw that she wasn't going to open her hand, he walked around to the back of the van, and she heard his deep voice take on a bantering tone with the others: men unpacking luggage at motels after driving. The girl singer went to the desk and then to her room. This was on another trip, another time. There were plenty of other times.

Her sister, Cindy, was pale and big-eyed, thirty-six years old, married to Danny, and living in a 1969 Mediterranean villa house not quite as important to her as breath or her only child, Bud. The shower was a little too hot at first but she kept it that way to open her throat. She was about to begin her voice exercises, she even had her jaws open and was projecting against her palate, when she decided instead to sit on the floor of the tub beneath the almost-scalding water, and weep. She did it with her eyes open, and she watched her legs go from their winter whiteness to red.

This, dear sister, is what they mean by seeing red. And greetings from a far-flung place. Or am I, this time, merely "away"?

She crawled into the scald and then stood up beneath it and called, in a rugged harsh voice. The water against her ears and skull rumbled and she called again. That was enough. She turned the water off and stood, dripping, trying to pant. But she hadn't run, she hated jogging, even, and she could no more tolerate her own hysterics than she could tolerate Henry's or those of anyone else. There was wisdom and cunning distilled from mistreated generations behind the words, good ones to try to live by, that were the unsurprising credo of a shabby band of serious and only so-so jazz musicians: Be cool.

She turned the cold water on. She winced when it hit her shoulders and thighs, but she stood beneath it until she really was gasping. Then she turned it off and sang, softly and pretty well, and with the self-mockery of actual blues. God bless the child, she sang.

Not bad for a woman of thirty-eight.

So, Cindy, I've been thinking about the last time we were together for forty-seven hours and change. I'd been in Michigan City, Indiana, with the band, if you remember. That's where Scranton or Bethlehem will go to get their brain death confirmed, Michigan City, Indiana. Ellis had been down so far, he'd begun to do his little red medications, and the bus we'd chartered out of Chicago was run essentially by joint power. They were passing so many up and down the aisles and around, the bus driver began to giggle—he wasn't toking, mind you—because there's apparently a sign near Chicago that directs traffic to Nashville, which, you'll remember, is not near Illinois. You'll also remember my visit, I think. I was wiped out. I hadn't wanted to come. But I'd been talking on the phone to Mom and she'd mentioned how confining your life with Danny was. And how, sometimes, you weren't "considerate," which meant I hadn't merely been "away," but had been out in the far-flung places while you were pinned at home. Which meant that you were the Bad Sister, I was the Good one, and if I wanted to stay that way I would do what our mother said. Can a sister be a stool pigeon? Can a mother be two cops?

The time of which I'm thinking is memorialized by the fact that I possessed slightly longer hair, a slightly slimmer waist, and slightly more voice. It was spring, and we were sitting in the Mediterranean villa on the edge, the good edge to be sure, of Mamaroneck, N.Y., waiting for Danny to come home from another day spent adjusting insurance claims. I always think of him using screwdrivers and hydraulic jacks and metal cutters. Bud was fourteen, I think. He was ripe. We were drinking Danny's Scotch, as you seemed to enjoy calling it, and Bud was sitting with us and watching us drink. Alicia Brooks née Bernstein, girl singer, was sitting there with her long and, let's admit it, pretty damned good legs, propped up on the coffee table. My Liberty print skirt was hanging around my thighs and I knew it. I was wearing a sheer tank top and poor Bud was getting plenty of nipple. He was also looking right along my big black boots and partway up my crotch. I sat there and I moved my legs apart. Just the slightest bit. I did. And I was doing a joint. I hadn't wanted it. I hadn't remembered I carried the damned thing. I looked into my bag for a tissue and I found a scrawny joint that a music lover had sent me. "Dear Ms. Brooks: Tonight I am going to get high and dream of washing your entire body in cognac while you sing 'Love for Sale.' I hope you will accept the enclosed. I would like to think of you getting stoned and dreaming of me as my washcloth slides down the etceteras and into your usuals." And Cindy, babe: something made me light it up while you glared and stared and were too polite to throw me the hell out. And something made me shift my legs just a little, so the kid I used to feed when he was a baby could do a visual pelvic on me. His face was so serious and red! And what it was, of course, was Mom. I was there because of her, I knew it, I despised us all, and I did the number on your baby's bones instead of Mom's or yours or my own.

We were on the phone, and I had just finished telling her about Michigan City, Indiana, and for some reason I stitched on the fact that Benny Goodman played there once.

"A Jew," Mom said. "It's so hard to think of Jews playing jazz music."

"He dated Billie Holiday."

"She was the one took the drugs?"

"She was the genius who was black, Mom. Benny Goodman dated her for a while."

"If I am not mistaken, a famous composer composed for Mr. Goodman—"

"A clarinet concerto. Goodman hired Teddy Wilson for his piano man. It was Bartók."

"Also a black?"

"Billie was black, Teddy was black, Bartók was white, Mom. Who did you have in mind?"

"Excuse me." I could hear it coming, Cindy. "Pardon me for not giving you a reason to make fun of me earlier. A mother, I forgot this in my pleasure at hearing your voice on the telephone. A mother has to take abuse no matter what age or the child's age."

"Mom. Don't fight."

"It takes two to make a fight, Allie. And with you, it only takes one."

"Don't cry."

"I cry when you talk to me that way. It's simple. Excuse me: isn't that why you do it?"

"Mom. How's Cindy? Tell me about Cindy. Don't fight. Don't cry. Talk to me about Cindy. How is she?"

She did the long shuddery sigh. Then she said, "Cindy. Oh, Allie, she is so inconsiderate sometimes. She doesn't mean to be. She's a nice child. But she has her problems. I understand this. I don't meddle and I don't pry. I wouldn't do that. But she has a lot of problems and sometimes they don't permit her to—to *see* us, you and me and the other people in her life. Well, on the edge of her life, if you know what I mean. Allie, it isn't as if she's traveling the way you are. You know, with a career that takes her so far. She isn't what you'd call *busy*. I mean, how many times can you vacuum-clean the house? She's at home, the child goes to school and then with friends, she stays home, and Danny is there at night to eat and sleep and believe me, take it as truth, not a lot more. So I can understand why she can't get in touch. It's sadness. It makes you stand still in the middle of the room sometimes, you couldn't move if you wanted to. And sometimes you just don't want to. But there *you* are, every far-flung place I have ever heard of except Alaska, and believe me, I wouldn't be surprised to hear you calling me from *there*. That's the point. You would call me from there. Cindy can't call from Westchester County. She's unhappy. She is so unhappy that she doesn't have time. I know about depression, believe me. That is a depressed girl. So, Allie—would you call her? You'll call her tonight or tomorrow? Maybe visit her one of these days? Tell her the furniture's nice. I don't know. Let her talk to the big sister a while. Darling, you remember Cloris, the maid who is colored? How's your friend in the orchestra, I forget his name, it escapes me."

You know?

Greetings, babe, from a far-flung place. Did I tell you that the folks in Bethlehem were more depressed than the folks in Scranton? The *air* in Bethlehem felt brown. Only the college boys smiled any more than they had to. Scranton's okay. Bethlehem's okay. You're okay. I am too. We're all okay and we're all ofay, except for Henry and eight other guys in the band. Did I tell you about the one who plays sax and clarinet for us? He thinks he's Gerry Mulligan because he's white and plays baritone.

She was in her white terry-cloth bathrobe and the motel stationery from the night before was next to the motel stationery from tonight. There wasn't any liquor in a glass and there wasn't a cigarette burning in the plastic ashtray and the TV set wasn't on. No man was sprawled in his shoes atop the cheap coverlet of her motel bed. She was clean from to-night's shower and her feet were in her snug furry slippers. She held the ballpoint pen against her lips and did not write.

The boys in their tuxedos were mostly handsome because very healthy and very young. The girls in their open-backed gowns were mostly ditto because ditto. You could have got-ten away with some of those numbers because you're so scrawny, Cindy. Scrawn is in. It sounds like some kind of New England chowder: scrawn. Listen, I could tell you New England stories, complete with chowder, chowder-heads, and heavy items with actual guns in their suits. I mean it. But this is a Pennsylvania number, and the items I have in mind were wearing rented midnight-blue tuxedos without guns. Ellis looked so classy in his dinner jacket. Henry was particularly gorgeous. Most of the boys looked like their shirt hurt their neck. After a while they didn't. That was because they got so drunk. It was loud. The kids were pre-tending to be classy. We played swing numbers and they tried to jitterbug and Lindy. They mostly ended up doing sloppy Charlestons and falling either prone on the floor or into break-dancing.

There I was, our girl singer, doing "I'll Never Smile

Again" and of course smiling. The baritone sax does a solo riff, a little one, just before the end. Our guy had his cheeks out like Mulligan. I thought his face would explode. Ellis was laughing so hard, his hairpiece shifted. Then we broke, the guys drifted out to smoke on the front lawn and the kids got loaded some more.

I went outside the fraternity house onto the back lawn. That was where they'd put a lot of their furniture to make room for the dance. It was cold, but I was hot, and I sat on one of those big old leather easy chairs with my feet on an ottoman. I was sitting there with my eyes closed and my feet up, cooling off and worrying because in the middle of "A Fine Romance" I'd forgotten the name of the town we were in. I was also worrying because I was a lot older than these boys and girls, and in the middle of "A Fine Romance" it had struck me that I couldn't remember a good deal of how I'd got that way.

Nobody was out there. Then some boys showed up, four of them, and one of them had his tie off and his studs out and he had a neck on him you'd need a road map to drive around. He had that blond-red hair that Bud had when he was a baby. Except this guy was about six foot two and he weighed a lot more than two of me. Well, two of you. He was red down to his collar, and sweaty. The steam was coming off him. He looked so much like a big white horse. He was smiling at me with teeth and skin and eyes, except he was steaming like an animal and he was going to jump all over me. I could tell. He had watched my little Peggy Lee number and he and the other ones, big, all of them, were going to take a few turns with me. I rose up above myself as if I'd died. I became my own ghost. I looked down. I saw myself in the white satin-lookalike floor-length gown with the cleavage above it. I saw my legs, up on the ottoman, fully extended and a little apart. All propped up for rape, and no place to go, and they were going to split me open and pass me around. I saw myself in my Liberty print and my black boots and my legs apart and your little boy Bud in front of me, staring.

It was big boys now. They were very drunk. They were *all* giving off a kind of smoke in the cold air. The one with the neck was unzipping and then zipping his fly, up and down, up and down. They were looking at me and waiting for the one with the neck to move. The way they were looking at me and looking forward to me reminded me of how Bud hadn't.

Henry said, "Go away."

The one with the neck said, "You work for me, or what?"

Henry said to me, "Come inside now. It's cold. All right? Come in."

I did not cry. I thought about higher education. I said, "Good of you to join me, Henry."

"Good of you to join *me*," he said. He turned back to the boys and said, "Go away now. Go to bed. Go home."

"You're *in* my home, man," Neck told him. Then he said to his friends, "I'm just like calling a spade a spade. You know?"

I turned around and I was going to announce to them what they were and who they were and why they were. Henry put the gentlest pressure on my elbow. He cupped it and guided me around and up the back stairs and in. I was angriest, just then, because on their faces I had read their

119

utterly faithful reliance on the fact that sooner, or perhaps regrettably later, I was going to be willing to do, or have done, what they'd have forced me to—although it was just beyond their comprehension, those wide healthy faces had told me, that a girl singer in a second-class band would not want to shudder underneath a truckful of them. I thought about Bud, looking along my legs. I thought about you and I thought about Mom. I mostly thought about me. Henry lit a cigarette and put it in my lips. I dragged on it. He called a cab and sent me back to the motel in it. I bathed.

She moved the pen against her lips and looked at the pages she had written two days before. God bless the child. She tore the letterhead up and she put the pen on the dressing table. She swiveled in her chair and leaned back to put her crossed ankles on the edge of the bed. Her bathrobe fell open and she looked at her legs. She closed the bathrobe and put her legs together. Her hand lay on her lap. It was in a fist. She looked at it and waited for the fist to open.

This is to remind you about Bud and how he sat and looked at me because of what I did. This is to remind you about how you didn't do anything about it.

This is also a reminder to Mom that I will not sign the confession.

This will serve as a reminder to me that I already have.

And now, here in the Members' Room of the Hotel Imperial in Red Bank, New Jersey, and on behalf of the fellas in the band, ladies and gentlemen, I'd like to invite you to join us in giving a big welcome to our girl singer, Alicia Brooks, who tells us "I've Got the World on a String."

Sister, babe.

Far out.

 Naked

RUDY MADE ME PROMISES, and they came true. He was our doctor and had always been. In his high, bright voice—a loud and happy shout no matter its announcement—he would cry, "You have the *measles*, hon!" Or: "We're gonna take your *tonsils* out, you can eat all the ice cream you *want*!" Or: "Your head will feel better when it's *exactly* twenty minutes past dinnertime!" When I was eight, I heard my mother describe him as a rascal. When I was ten or so, I knew that, according to my father, he was a presumptuous bastard. To me he was Uncle Rudy, and in the forties and fifties, he was at my bed when I was ill. If I were home from school with a flu or one of the many childhood diseases no one then was vaccinated against, I lay in my room and listened to the wood-cased radio with its golden crosshatched speaker: "Helen Trent" and "Our Gal Sunday" and, later in the afternoon, "Sky King" and "The Green Hornet."

On lucky days, I heard the Dodgers play—Jackie Robinson throwing to Gil Hodges—and, despite the music about me, and the radio voices, I always heard Rudy, or always thought I did. He drove the newest, sleekest cars, Packards, I remember, and Lincolns. Their windows rose and fell when Rudy pushed buttons. He parked with impunity in front of the fire hydrant at our curb. And, although they were tuned and silent cars, I always thought, when I heard Rudy climbing the steps, that I had heard his motor cough, or his brakes mildly squeak. I liked pretending that his process up the stairs was no surprise. And so it wasn't one, for years and years.

He was light on his feet, and his step was a sort of spring. His shoes had leather heels and soles, so he clacked as he climbed, and our wooden steps made groaning noises under him. I always thought it unfair that a man who could bound like that, and click as sharply as he did, still had to walk on stairs that made him sound fat. He wasn't thin. He couldn't have been taller than five feet seven or eight, and he surely weighed over two hundred pounds. He frequently dieted, choosing faddish and unproven methods, and once, I remember, exciting my mother to complain for his safety. Once in a while he bought new suits to flatter a slenderer shape that he would own for a couple of months. But usually Rudy seemed round: his bald head was round, and it sat atop his big chest and belly, and his thick round legs, his little feet. I heard the feet, when he came to care for me with his magic, and then I saw his round, gold-rimmed glasses on his happy pale face.

He beamed when he saw me, and he stood above my bed

and looked at me, then examined me with eyes and hands. He probed, he listened, he squeezed, and always he smiled the happiest smile. His breath smelled of chewing gum, and his voice carried total conviction. He might say, "This fever will break at—wait a minute. What time is it, Michael?"

I'd consult the same clock that he was looking at and, with a grand sense of drama, tell him, in my weakest voice, "Two o'clock, Uncle Rudy."

"This fever will break at seven o'clock tomorrow morning at the *latest*. Do you understand? You'll feel better by seven tonight, and by seven tomorrow morning, you'll have a normal temperature. Which is?"

"Ninety-eight point six," I would recite, as if such knowledge were wisdom.

Rudy would smile as if it were. He would nod. "Perfect!" he'd shout. "You get yourself into college, and I'll take care of med school for you. How old are you now, Michael?"

"Seven," I would say, as if reaching past six had been a feat of art.

"Well, we've got some time," Rudy would say.

And only then would he admit my mother, home from work to care for me. He always kept her outside my door because, as he often told her, he had his time alone with me, and then he had his time with her. While Rudy talked with me, my mother paced the hall. I'd hear her high-heeled shoes. And, at seven that night, I would ask for food. At seven in the morning I would register ninety-eight point six. And Rudy would have had his time alone with my mother, after his time alone with me.

Rudy's wife, Dorothy, had always been kind to me, and

though she often came with him to our house for social evenings, I didn't think of her in any special way. At dinner,
when I was thirteen, my mother announced to us that Rudy
had left Dorothy. "It's the way all these Jewish doctors do
it," my Jewish mother said with disgust. "They marry wom-
en with money who help them pay off their debts from
medical school. They buy the office equipment and pay for
the nurses—and you *know* about the nurses, yes?—and then
the doctor leaves them when they're ugly and old."

My father said, "I would consider calling Dorothy ugly a
massive favor to her."

"She can't help what she looks like," my mother said.

"Maybe she can't help it," my father said, "but she makes
Spike Jones look like Dorothy Lamour."

"That's stupid," my mother said. "All the people in the
world to think about, and you pick Spike Jones? Dorothy
Lamour? This is what you talk about all day in the office?"

"All day in the office," my father said, "we talk about
numbers. We say 'six' and 'eleven.' We say 'Ninety thousand.' But we never say Lamour or Jones, unless it's a client's
name. And we don't have a client named Lamour. These are
names I learned after extensive reading of the *World-
Telegram & Sun*. I hope they aren't too far beneath us for
me to be saying them at the table. How was school, Mike?"

"Excuse me?"

"Without question," my father said, pulling his bow tie
off and setting it beside his napkin on the table. "Absolutely.
You're excused. Do you think Spike Jones would divorce his
wife just because her chin, where she needs to shave it a little,
was falling down onto her neck?"

"Huh?"

My mother's fork clanged on her plate.

My father, who was usually mild if not silent, and whose square face rarely carried much expression unless he grew teary while listening to Perry Como sing songs about parting, put his lips together, puffed his smooth cheeks, and widened his eyes. He looked like a fish, and I started to laugh, although I was puzzled—frightened, really—by these meat loaf and baked potato antics. My father saw my expression and he must have understood. He said, "Just wait, Michael. Wait." And I still don't know if he meant me to wait for seconds or for years.

My mother hardly waited seconds. She pushed the yellow Fiesta Ware pitcher so hard that water spilled from it onto a yellow, chunky Fiesta Ware plate. I thought again of our door. "You know how old he is? Rudy?"

My father answered her by smiling and nodding his head. He didn't make the fish face, and I was grateful. I told my mother, "No."

"This doesn't concern you," she said, her pretty face white, her thick lip reddening under her teeth while she waited an instant, and then said, "Forty-four."

My father smiled broadly, then *he* reddened. Then he leaned back in his chair and smiled at something on the ceiling. I looked up, saw nothing, then looked down at my brown, grainy meat loaf. I waited for more. There was silence, and then my father's voice: "I know it."

"You know his age. Yes. But hers? Do you know *hers*?"

"Oh," my father said, as if he mugged for an audience. "You mean there's another *woman*? Well. I must say, I don't know how old *she* is. I'll bet, though, whatever her age is, it wouldn't take too many numbers to write it or say it. And I bet you're crazy with it."

"I'm not crazy with it!"

"Michael, is she crazy with it, or what?"

"Don't you do that to him."

"*You* do it to him and it's all right. He sits here and you get crazy and it's right. I *ask* him about it and I'm wrong? What is this conversation *about*?"

Now, I was old enough to know that something more than minor was going on. I was also young enough to be tempted, for an instant, to cry out loud—for Rudy, or for everything my parents seemed to threaten to leave behind, or for what I couldn't discern in the murky innuendo of their talk. But I was old enough to succumb to none of those temptations. I took a breath, I bent to my plate, and I ate the meat loaf, pulpy as usual (my mother never thought we'd have enough) with too much torn-up bread.

My mother said, "The woman is twenty-four. Rudy is forty-four. She is twenty years younger than he is. She—"

"No," my father said. "No. You deprived me of the pleasure of announcing the *fullness* of this catastrophe. You really owe it to me to allow me to finish the cliché. Now, if I remember it—wait. Yes. Okay. I think I have it now. *She is old enough to be his daughter*. Right?"

"No. *Young* enough," I said.

My father's breath hissed. My mother said, "*Michael*."

So I said, "Excuse me," with what I thought of as dignity.

In my room, among my books and flung-about clothing and the drawings of spaceships and space suits and other apparatus of a future I saw as free of gravity and full of colorful wars, I lay on my bed and looked over the lights of our neighborhood in Brooklyn, and tried to make sense of my parents' life together, and mine with them, and ours with Rudy. It was spring, the limbs of giant high trees were whipped by winds that came up, then died, with no pre-amble. At one moment, the skies were quiet; at another, they softly roared. The dark blue air looked grainy, and moving branches with their new leaves sliced the light from houses on the block behind us and made the brightening moon seem to dance in its place, low above the neighborhood. After a while, I did some homework and didn't think of Rudy or my parents until I heard their footsteps as they climbed the stairs.

"There are dishes to be dried," my mother said at my closed door. "Most children your age have to wash them too."

"You all right?" my father called.

"It's all right to come in," I said.

I waited, but I heard their bedroom door close, and I knew that the fight—about *what?*—was moving to private quarters. When they'd come up the stairs together, the house had seemed to shake. I had looked from my window as they climbed, to see whether the moon seemed to vibrate more than before. The winds had slackened, the moon had looked still, and I remember that I'd smiled with gratitude. My con-tentment stayed with me that night, and it came down to breakfast with me in the morning; I was prepared to let their mystery be theirs. Rudy was coming to dinner that weekend with his fiancée, as my mother called her, and I would wait until then for further clues.

My father seemed apprehensive on Saturday, though as usual he worked in the garden, wearing his World War II fatigues. He'd begun to talk about how few men his age could still get into their army-issue clothes. Pausing often to catch his breath, he clipped what rarely needed cutting back, he painted a portion of the high fence that screened us from our neighbors, he mulched and raked and swept; he made time away in a place that was away, and he thought to himself about matters of which he never spoke to me. Or so I concluded. His face, when he worked, was someone else's, and I often watched him with curiosity. I never worked beside him, though: I was the usual thirteen. He was showered and dressed quite early, and he was early at his inventory of liquors and mixers and pickled onions and candied fruits and ice. I wore clean corduroys and a shirt with a starched collar that irritated my neck. I was watching wrestling on television while my father made the living room ready for peanuts and drinks, and while my mother slowly dressed.

I saw my father look at the ceiling only once—I was reminded of his upward glance during their argument—and I don't know if he was thinking of my mother upstairs. But I was. For I was listening, over the cries of the fans of Bruno Sammartino, to her feet. She was already in her high-heeled shoes, and I listened to their slow, lassitudinous rhythm as she drifted from her bureau to her closet mirror, then back to her bureau drawers again. Her footsteps at first seemed almost random. She surely didn't dance on her bedroom's parquet floor. But something under the percussion of her heels did suggest to me a kind of dance—she moved from *here* to *here*, from *here*, then, to *there*, and purpose changed her position, though nothing like a plan. Bruno, fighting clean while his lighter- longer-haired opponent used illegal blows and outlawed holds, persevered, then triumphed. He used his famous flying dropkick, and he won. I watched the referee count the opponent out. As the canvas slammed with the final count, and as Bruno sprang to his bare feet, I understood: I had heard my mother *thinking*. The sharp and aimless-seeming sounds of her staccato shoes had been, in fact, an accompaniment kept by her body for the thoughts—and hadn't they been stabbing thoughts—that were sounding inside as she picked out earrings or brushed at her glossy brown hair. All at once, my mother's footsteps upstairs grew purposeful. She marched across the floor. On our groaning stairs, she came down.

My father, as if signaled, went to the hall closet for his sportcoat. He turned to my mother and said, "You look nice."

"I look fantastic," my mother said.

I stayed with a tag-team wrestling match and didn't look up for a while. But they'd both looked pretty good to me, and awfully nervous, and I hoped, suddenly, that I wouldn't hear Rudy's car at the curb, and that he wouldn't come. It was the first time I had not wanted to see him. It was the first time I'd considered *whether* to want to see him or not. I was enough of a child to think of grown-ups—and surely of Uncle Rudy—as climate, neighborhood, a feature of my life, and not what I *voted* on. My own will made me itch.

And I did hear the faintest protest of brakes, I thought. And I surely heard feet that shuffled against the broad brick steps outside, and that thumped on the wooden floor of the porch, and that shushed on the mat before our door as the doorbell rang. My father answered the door, and his voice was full of bonhomie. My mother joined him—the sound of her feet across the foyer reminded me of black men who tap-danced on Ed Sullivan's show—and she was cordial, though grave. I turned the set off and went to be a cute nearly-nephew to Uncle Rudy and the woman my mother had known in advance she would hate.

I hugged Rudy; I usually did. He looked at me and, as usual, he beamed. "You look like a million bucks, fella!" he said, so clearly glad to see me that I almost hugged him again. I did put my hands on his shoulders and squeeze, and he said, "By Jesus, I love ya!" I noticed three things as he spoke—the heat of my reddening face as my field of vision included the woman with Rudy; my mother's teeth on her lip; the new woman's height and stunning beauty. "Meet Genevieve! Michael, this is Genevieve. I *completely* love her. I wanted you to meet her because I wanted the two of you to love each other. Isn't this great?"

Genevieve was taller than Rudy, taller than my mother and me. She and my mother shook hands gingerly, I noticed. My father actually took Genevieve's hand and raised it to his lips. My mother bit hers. Rudy smiled and smiled, and he pounded my father's shoulder and rubbed the back of my head and told us all how grand things were. Genevieve stood without moving, as if she were a mannequin. Her hair was the blackest I have ever seen. Her skin was so pale, it looked like the waxy yellow-white of an antique doll's. Her eyes were very large and dark in an oval face that was slightly rounded at the cheekbones, but slender nevertheless. Her figure, slim according to the standards of Hollywood in the fifties, still required my attention, and her suit, made of something white and fine, struck me as unusual. When we sat in the living room, I stared at her legs, which were very long and slender and on which she wore smoke-colored stockings. I had never seen hose like that except in magazines purchased by the fathers of my friends. I looked at her every time I thought I could study her without getting caught. She sat on our yellow sofa next to Rudy, and she said little. He touched her often, and I watched his beefy hands. When she spoke, Genevieve talked about European cities, and music I hadn't heard of. Rudy often spoke of her as though she weren't there. Looking at my mother, his old friend, he would reach out and tap my mother's knee, then say, "Isn't she a dreamboat? She's *my* dreamboat. I treated her for a sore throat! Imagine! I looked down her throat, and I wanted to climb in after the tongue depressor!"

"Rudy, you're disgusting," my mother said.

"But you're honest, Rudy, aren't you," my father said as he mixed more drinks. "You're an honest man."

I remember Rudy as a brilliant man. He seemed that way that night, in spite of his playing what I would later think of as the middle-aged fool. Light came off his glasses as he sat up higher on the sofa. His eyes grew wider, and I watched as he saw what was invisible to me. My mother was saying something patronizing to Genevieve, who nodded but didn't reply. Rudy said to my father, "You have the sound of a man with something to say."

"Oh, no," my father said, opening a bottle of club soda. "No, I'm a CPA. I just work with numbers. You know. My work involves nothing more than what adds up."

Rudy said, "As in two plus two equals four, and no latitude for interpretation?"

My father passed a tall iced drink. "Twos are twos," he

said. "Fours are fours. That's it. Yes. And I've worked with those numbers."

Rudy said, "And for some time?"

"Yes, for some time."

Rudy said, "I wonder if I know what you mean."

"Oh, sure," my father said. "Yes. You do."

Rudy raised his glass and looked at my father with a smile of, I think, admiration. "Here's to your guts," Rudy said. He drank, then raised his glass again. "*Salud*. And here's to your perspicacity." He drank again, then turned to Genevieve. "Hon? You know what that means? Perspicacity?"

My father sipped his drink, then quietly left the room. My mother watched him. She said, in a voice that imitated the sounds we make when we jest, "Are you two fighting again?"

"We never fight," Rudy said, smiling. "Sometimes we disagree, but then we only argue, and just for fun. The way that old friends do." He paused, then picked up his glass. "Sweetheart," he said to my mother, "here's to old friends."

My mother raised her glass, but didn't drink. She looked at Rudy, and kept on looking. Genevieve raised her eyebrows in her otherwise immobile face. My father, returning, said, "Sorry."

Rudy drank some more and said, "Let's not be sorry."

My mother put her glass down and said, "I have to cook. Michael, tell them about school. What happened yesterday. You remember. I have to go cook." She still looked at Rudy, but he had turned toward me, so she stood and left the room with loud, quick steps.

I had always performed at my parents' evenings, and with Rudy I never had minded. But it was Genevieve, leg and thigh, breast and throat, arched thin eyebrows, long white hands, at whom I looked as I told how a fellow named Green, several years older and a foot taller and a lifetime more dangerous than the other boys in our junior high school, had been plucked from Industrial Arts by two policemen. "He shot a kid," I said. "He shot a kid in the eye with a zip gun he made. A pipe thing, lead pipe, with a bullet in it. You use a really heavy rubber band with a nail, that's the firing pin—it explodes the bullet," I explained to Genevieve. "You put a wooden handle on it with tape. He shot this kid and they had to take out his eye. The kid didn't die, though."

Genevieve asked, "What kind of school do you go to?"

"Public school," I said, assuming that creatures such as she went only to private schools in major European capitals. "Andries Hudde Junior High School," I said, hating its provincialism. "It's on Nostrand Avenue." I was searching for ways to make myself die, which seemed the only appropriate response to having sat before this exotic person to speak to her of Ralphie Green and his zip gun, and a school named Hudde.

"I never heard of that school," she said.

"Oh," I answered, "that's all right." And, blushing sweatily, smiling goofily at Genevieve, at whom Rudy goofily smiled, I finally said, "Will you excuse me please? I have to go help? I'll be *right* back." I fled.

And in the kitchen, which was around a corner and down a short corridor from the living room, in a litter of black pans and wet potholders and a smoking leg of lamb, I found my parents in a sad and knotted embrace. My father was saying, "No, no. It's all right. It's all right. No."

"I don't have any right to be comforted," my mother said.

"Sure," my father said. "Everyone does." But he moved back from her a little.

"By you?"

"By me," he said. "Why not? Who else?"

"I don't really hate her. She's so young, though! I don't mean that. I don't know if it has anything to *do* with her. Does it?"

"I'm a CPA," my father said. "I know about numbers. Look how long I didn't know about you. Don't ask me that kind of a question."

"What do you know about me now?"

"Not a lot."

"When?"

He said, "What?"

"You know. When did you know?"

"I'm not talking about it," my father said, drawing farther away. "Not when or where, not how many times. None of it. I didn't talk about it before, and I'm not talking about it now. Let him get married to his dream girl and that's that. No more. And pay attention to tonight. The man is moving on. He doesn't want the old parts of his life anymore. He wants a divorce."

"*I* don't. I mean, from you."

"You should have," my father said, stepping farther back. "A long time ago. It isn't shameful. Everyone wants a divorce."

"*You?*"

"Everyone," he said. Then he said, "But what in hell do *I* know?"

I went upstairs, waving at Rudy and Genevieve as I passed the living room, smiling some sort of smile. I shut my door and walked about my room, touching objects. I heard my name in living room murmurs, and then I heard feet on the stairs. They cracked and creaked, groaning their old-wood noises. It was Rudy. He didn't knock, as my parents would have. They were enlightened parents who read the columns by psychologists in the old New York *Post*. Rudy just walked in, because he was welcome, he assumed, and because he loved me. As far as Rudy's reasoning went, I think, love gave you permission to do anything to anyone. What he did was save my life and keep my health. And make love to my mother. First he had his time with me, and then he had his time with her. I cannot remember him leaving a lot. But I remember him entering—through the front door, up the steps, or into the kitchen or living room, or swinging open the door to my room. He was always on his way in. So no wonder, then, that my mother could not imagine his departure. And his tall, pale Genevieve, so different in size, coloring, ripeness from my mother—she was Rudy's signal good-bye. Although he did love us all, I think, and even my father; and he surely wanted to share his happy news.

But he was leaving as he entered. I could tell. I started to cry. Rudy, with his sweet breath and giant chest, leaned against me and hugged me with his short, strong arms. He pulled and pulled.

"Did you ever think you were adopted, hon?"

I remember feeling my body grow cold. I couldn't bear any more news, I thought. I was always very careful about how much stress I accepted. I shook my head.

"Well, you aren't. But I always thought you were more like me than him. That's not fair to say, is it? But I thought so. I wished. I totally love ya! Remember that. Remember me. I knew your parents when we were all skinny intellectuals in the Communist Party. Did you know that? We ate lousy food and drank lousy wine and told each other lousy lies about lousy goddamned liars in Moscow. Did you know that?"

I stayed against his chest. I shook my head.

"And we were so goddamned happy! And your father and I loved your mother, and then your father won. He's— sneaky. Because he's so tough. So watch your ass with him. He's *tough*! When you see those lousy movies where the movie's always on the side of the guy who's taking the pretty girl away from the boring accountant—well, whatever. Don't believe it! The accountants always win! And I *love* ya! I'm happy as hell you could meet Genevieve. Don't you love her? Don't you *love* her?"

He pushed me back, but held on to my shoulders. I didn't look at his round white face, which I knew would be grinning while his dark little eyes studied me intently. I stared at his light brown sharkskin suit, the vest across which he always wore a gold chain that rose and fell according to his progress through dangerous diets. His tie, I remember, was maroon wool with small tan figures on it. I wonder if he was studying me the way I studied his tie. I couldn't look at his face. I only remember it from other days, because I didn't see it again.

He said, "You want to forgive them."

"Who?"

"Don't play stupid. You're the brightest boy I ever knew.
You know who I mean."

"Why should I forgive them? What for?"

"For not being happy."

I pulled away, and he let my shoulders go. I was surprised,
and nearly fell, but I stood my ground. I looked, still, at his
turned-up cuffs, his narrow short shoes, polished to a gloss.
I couldn't look farther up, but I stayed where I was and said,
"No."

"No, you won't forgive them? Or no, they're not unhappy?"

"No!"

"Sweetheart," he said. He sighed. "Who am I to tell you?
But I know something. Listen, when you're naked you are
naked. Understand? All you are is—naked." He grunted as
he moved his arms. I had closed my eyes by then. He said,
"It's eight fifteen. Lie down, listen to the radio, get yourself
some sleep. By the morning, by half-past seven, you're gonna
feel *wonderful* about the world. I swear it!" His arms pulled
me in toward him, but I resisted. I didn't know why. I don't.
"You'll feel great," he said. He squeezed as much as his little
arms allowed, and he went out. It is a law of brain development that you will, when grown, remember every departure
by every person to whom you should have called good-
bye, and whom you ought to have embraced, and on whose
cheeks you could have dispensed a couple of the dammed-up
tears you persist in hoarding. I heard him on the steps.

Fed and sheltered, surrounded by what I had picked for
my pleasure, and sullen because the people downstairs were
getting along as best they could in their sad, short lives, I

decided always to live alone when I grew up. And then I turned the radio on and listened to Henry Morgan's show and laughed. At 7:30 in the morning, true to Rudy's word, I woke. I looked through glowing green leaves at a Sunday sky under which a boy played stickball or he *died*. He didn't. And he did grow up to learn how everyone, no matter who has loved him for good or for ill, no matter whom he loves, is faithful to that cruel and careless, easy childhood vow.

In Foreign Tongues

L ET ME MAKE IT CLEAR: I have my work. The
group is more of a *social* outlet for me. I am far from
discontent. We were at the Beatrice Inn on 12th Street in
New York, and we were making believe. Solly was pretending not to think about food, even though he studied his Fat
Book. Ouida spoke of her mother-in-law in a manner suggesting that life on the same planet was feasible for them.
Boris, whose son had quit a fine arts major at Skidmore to
join the submarine service of the navy, spoke about his boy
as if he liked to. Maybe he did; I hated to hear him. I swore
that his son was fascinating, though, and that Ouida's life was
free of influence from the rise or fall of her mother-in-law's
blood pressure, and that Solly—he looked a pound or two
larger than when he'd begun his diet—struck me as fairly
trim.

In other words, we were doing what we'd done for the hour just past: sitting in a group and, for the sake of mental health, confessing as truth what might be lies. We were the core of Peter—Petey, we called him—Pasternak's Wednesday night group therapy session. We were in our early middle age, and often sad. We sat on Petey's beanbag chairs, all of them fire-engine red and filled with treacherous granules that gradually, as the hour passed, let us down and down and down, until we lay nearly flat, looking up at the pressed tin plates of Petey's ceiling more than over at each other, and talking about what we wanted to hide and maybe still were hiding, and goading each other to come out, come out, come out. And every Wednesday, after Petey praised us, as if we had accomplished more than talk, we went to the Beatrice and we sat some more, and once more talked. We were afraid to stop, I think. I think we were all so lonely that we might have talked all night, each day, all *week*, if there had been anyone unselfish enough to listen to so much Solly, Ouida, Boris, and me besides myself and Solly, Ouida, and Boris.

The Beatrice was a short flight down from street level, and was always noisy and bright, never pretentious, and never unhappy. We went there for inspiration, I think, and for the shrimp—low in calories, Solly said, dipping his bread in the olive oil which they oozed—and the sense of its being a *family* restaurant, a place to which we belonged and a place which was ours.

So we were sitting after dinner, drinking coffee and sambuca, smoking cigarettes—Boris was once more swearing to quit—and in an instant of silence, the sort that always made me afraid that someone might begin to weep, Ouida said, "I had a remarkable student for the first time this morning."

Boris, predictably enough, asked, "Did you have him on the piano bench, or were you patient?"

Tall and slender Ouida, with her hair as ever in a honey-colored bun on the back of her head, said, "Don't worry. He was nowhere near as thrilling as you once were."

Solly blushed. I laughed the laugh I hate—a kind of horse's snicker—and said, "Could I be thrilling, once, Ouida?"

She looked at me and frowned. Her large ears seemed red with heat and drink, and her brown eyes grew hooded. "I think so. Yes."

I snickered again, then laughed like a human being, and Solly said, still blushing, "He tries, but he just can't talk about sex. It's what Petey said, you know?"

"You don't have to *talk* about sex," I snarled at all of them. "You can just *do* it."

"Oh, goodie," Ouida said. "When?"

"We're engaging in the most hostile damned repartee I've heard since maybe our first session," Boris said. "You realize that, people?"

Ouida said, "I was only trying to talk about a student. A *girl*. She's going to be a decent player, I think. I mean, she's serious. There's money, of course. Upper West Side—Central Park West someplace. High eighties. Her father's in—entertainment. Uhm, television, actually. She's in the sixth grade, and she can think about music. And other things. That's what I wanted to tell you, so will you *listen*?"

As she spoke, Ouida was lining up anything she touched—clean silverware, uneaten crumbs of risotto in chicken liver fragments, little packets of artificial coffee sweetener. Solly was entering "scampi" in his Fat Book, a spiral notebook in which he wrote each morsel of intake, and its caloric value, for the perusal of his nutritionist, who weighed him every two weeks, and then scolded him, and took a hundred bucks. He said, "What?"

"*Listen!*"

"Yes," Boris said. He sought agreement in much, and especially with Ouida; he found very little, or none.

"This girl, Elizabeth Church, is doing the Czerny she's so proud of—actually, she ought to be—and she stops, she looks at me from out of all her pale skin and a storm of freckles, and she says, 'I always think that outward signs *can* tell inner tales. Do you?'

"I reply, I *stammer*, that I hadn't thought of it.

"She looks at me and says, 'Hmm. No. Well, it's not the sort of thing people talk about, I suppose. It's just that Daddy was talking about a script he had to read for homework.' She giggles, thank God, and sounds like a girl for a change, and she tells me her father brings home television scripts, things that people propose to make films of. He has to approve them. 'He had one that didn't have a lot of words in it,' she says. 'Mommy wondered how the people could tell what it was about. She said it sounded confusing. But Daddy said that outward signs *can* tell inner tales.' "

"Inward tales," I said to Ouida.

"You know the man?" she asked.

"No. Of course not. I would have said—just *inward*. That's all. It sounds better."

"Wait a minute," Solly said. "Ouida"—he pointed across the table at me—"was it one of *his*?"

"It had occurred to me," Ouida said.

"Not a chance. You *know* my scripts don't get produced," I said untruthfully. They hooted and booed and threw imprecations about self-pity. I told them, "You're painting me rich and successful so I pick up the check." I felt glad.

"But it's a wonderful question she asked," Boris said. "Outward signs and inner tales."

"In*ward*," Ouida said, mocking me.

"Well, either one," Solly said. "Of course."

"It's true?" Ouida asked him.

"*I* think so," Solly said. "Look at good movies. Good TV, even. *Books.* Or all those short stories where people just sort of talk very tersely and not a lot happens, but you know *some*thing's supposedly been said, something important, you know? And then the story's over and nobody knows what happened except self-control was exercised?"

"I should think of that as an argument *against*," Boris said.

Ouida said, "Yes. What about body heat? Doesn't an outward sign of something within—inward, darling—have to give off some human *warmth*?"

I said, "This is boring. Let's talk about ice hockey. Or even the New York Rangers."

Ouida said, "Why not talk about soft-boiled *eggs*, for God's sakes?"

Solly said, "I want to talk about what Ouida said."

"I'll bet you do," Boris said.

"No, Boris. I want to on account of she's right. She's talking about me. Well, you know. Not the piano lesson part, you goof. You know what I mean. I mean—*look*." Solly held his Fat Book up. It was yellow-tan and, once hardbound, now a flabby envelope of green-ruled pages. "I take this everywhere. You know it. It's on my bedside table. My cats take turns crowding their bodies onto it for warmth on cold mornings. I take it into the bathroom in case I inadvertently swallow *mouthwash*. When I'm making breakfast for me and the cats, I'm entering what I'm going to eat. I take it to work, of course. It sits on my desk. My supervisor sits on it when she needs to talk to me, the cat. She does it because all I can look at, I find, when she does that, is her skinny little ass, pressing down on it. She knows it too. And I'm always looking up the calories in my calorie counter, and writing them down, planning my intake, *confessing* my intake—you know, all of you. You know what I do."

"You just did," Ouida said, patting his pudgy hand and making him blush.

He nodded. "I do it every day. All weekend, I eat and I write down what I eat. I write and I eat. On Monday, and every day of the business week, I sit at my machine and work with other people's numbers and accounts, but I'm also writing my own. I wonder which are true? Because I write down what I'm going to have for lunch, for example. One slice diet bread, forty calories. One stalk undercooked broccoli, ninety-four calories—that's a *big* stalk, by the way. Half a three-and-a-half-inch water bagel, seventy-seven calories. You get the idea."

"Yech," Ouida said. She dipped her finger into the congealing oil on Solly's plate and slowly sucked it off her finger. Solly blushed once more.

As if to fight her finger with his own, Solly lifted his thick index finger into the air and made his point: "But I don't *eat* what I *write*. I go down to the Brazilian Coffee Shop and I have black beans and rice in their sauce, five hundred calories. I have the duck at Quatorze: seven hundred, maybe a *thousand* calories. I mean, green peppercorn sauce? And then I go to see the nutritionist, and I stand there on his scales. I get *covered* with perspiration, and it isn't just the heat or being fat. It's shame." He looked at us as if he hadn't been saying something similar for months. His eyes were enormous and wet. His pause was so significant to him, dear man. And he said, lower, "Shame. So you go tell me inner signs and outward tales."

Ouida picked Solly's hand up and kissed it. I thought he would suffer a stroke. She held his hand and caressed its soft, hairy back as if it were one of his cats.

"Jesus, Solly," Boris said, "that's not so bad. We've all *told* you so."

"No," I said, "his point is the inner-outer thing, not badness."

"Both," Solly said. His voice came gently, as if he were afraid to move lest Ouida set him down.

"Well, it's understandable, Solly," Boris said. "What the hell. You think one way, you do something else, that's everybody in the world you're talking about, pretty much."

"But could you tell from his Fat Book," I asked Boris, "what's inside his gut?"

"I could tell what's on his *mind*," Boris said.

"Or maybe just what's on the page? Solly's more than just a Fat Book."

Solly's eyes were nearly closed. I expected to hear him purr.

"Well, that's *life*, dammit," Boris said. "That's all. You can't know everything about people by reading from the outside in."

"Elizabeth Church's father says you can," Ouida said.

"And Solly just proved that you can't," Boris answered.

"No," I said, "maybe Solly commented on the nature of the relationship between the inward and the outward. Instead of saying there isn't a relationship, maybe he helped to define one."

"Too complicated," Boris said. "Too abstract. Too hard."

Ouida said, "This, from the man whose son—"

"Don't start," Boris said.

"—comes home on leave from an atomic submarine—"

"I'm asking you not to," Boris said.

"—where he's in charge of listening to the whatchama-callit."

"Sonar," Solly crooned.

"Sonar," she continued. "He comes home, after listening for all those weeks to blips and bloops, not talking to anyone, just listening. He hears whales and scampi, for all we know, and masses of cold water. Am I right? Cold water gives an echo? And he *hears* all this. And then he comes home to Boris and Barbara's apartment—"

"We don't pay rent anymore. We bought it. You could at least call it a condo while you make me nauseous after dinner. After-dinner betrayal, anyone? Or will you stick with booze?"

"—and he spends his leave, when he's there with them, not talking. *He never, ever talks.*"

"He's tired," Solly said.

"It's possible he just isn't used to saying a lot because of his job, Boris. I did suggest this. You dismissed it," Ouida said.

"Well, I should have. I mean, I supply prosthetics to hospitals. I'm a *leading* supplier. You think I should go around limping? In a wheelchair? *What?*"

Ouida said to us, "He hasn't a leg to stand on." Solly laughed, silently, until his face was crimson and his chest was heaving. But Ouida still let go of his hand. He kept it on the table before her, as if it were part of her dessert, forgotten for now, but there for nibbling.

Boris didn't laugh. He wiped and wiped at his unstained mouth with a corner of his napkin. He finally said, "Not funny."

"We know it's a problem," I told him.

"From Mr. Warmth, no less," he said. "Tell Barbara. She's the one starts crying as soon as he comes in."

Solly said, "Maybe that's why he doesn't talk."

Boris nodded. "I barely talk to her myself," he said from the corner of his very clean mouth. Then he said, "Joke."

We all nodded, and soon were silent and serious, tired, worried, I think, about the silence seeping in.

Boris said, "Not that much of a joke. He looks so—peaceful. He doesn't complain, he doesn't sulk. You talk to him, he smiles and answers happily. Gently. And then he crosses his legs and puts more chewing gum in his mouth and very sweetly sits there and looks at the wall across the living room. Barbara put a chair there, where we used to have a planter. So she could sit and watch his eyes and know when he was seeing her and wait for him to respond. But then she got hysterical when he didn't. 'You're turning me invisible!'

she'd shriek. And he'd say, 'Huh? Excuse me, Ma?' and she'd go absolutely nuts. So I made her stop sitting there. Now nobody sits there. He comes home and he stares, and he smiles, he eats dinner with us and looks at TV, and he doesn't talk. I forget the name of his boat. I forget where the hell he sails in it. Whatever they do in submarines—do they call it sailing? Who knows? *I* don't. He doesn't tell us. Barbara's been bleaching her hair a very bright—really, a ghastly shade of blond."

Boris looked up. He'd been studying a line of matches laid down by Ouida. He wiped the corner of his mouth and folded his napkin on the littered tablecloth. "You think that's like your Fat Book, Solly?"

I asked, "How many calories in hair coloring?"

Ouida giggled and Solly, when he saw her reaction, smiled.

Boris said, "Beep. Beep. Beep. That's what he hears. Beep. Maybe it's all that he needs."

I said, "He interprets his world through the noises, Boris. He reads the world. Those are the signs the kid was talking about, her father, really, was talking about—the piano player?"

Boris said, "We did not raise our only child ever, in the history of our lives, to learn the world through earphones. Please *don't* tell me it's all right."

Ouida said, "I didn't mean to be cruel, really."

Boris said, "Oh, no."

"But maybe it's more satisfying to him. The electronic noise, the filtering out of everything else."

Boris said, "More satisfying than we are, you think."

"Well," Ouida said.

Boris said, "Yes."

"I mean, I *understand*," she said. "Don't forget—"

"We remember about you," Solly said.

"Dear man," Ouida said, but she didn't, to his patent disappointment, stroke his hand. "Don't forget that I am the only young—nearly young—widow I know whose mother-in-law is still offended by a marriage she hated. Even though it ended when Richie died, she insists on fealty from me—I mean, I have to feel sorry for her. And she does remember. No. She *knows*. She can tell me things about him I never suspected. I receive some of him that way. I always swear I won't, you know. I promise myself that I won't. That I will never see her again, or ask her to talk to me about him, or sit there to be insulted, demeaned. While she sneers at me because she cannot *bear* that I was me, not her, when we were married. It's like the Fat Book, Solly. I keep writing down that I won't ever eat that again, but I go out and I *dine*. I feel so horrible afterward."

Solly nodded and nodded, like something on an antique German clock.

"I'm so dutiful, I make myself sick," Ouida said. "I ride out there on the train to Harrison. I take a cab to her house. That maid admits me, the one who never talks. And I wait. I mean, I've *telephoned*. She's said, 'You'll have to come for tea.' It's like a horrible medicine one of us has to swallow. Both of us. And then I sit there, in a dark anteroom that always, always, always, always smells like wet raincoats. Even when the sun shines. And I try to read but I can't, because it's unlighted and I'm scared. As if I were waiting to play a recital!

"She has a room out there that the maid always shows me into. It's filled with uncomfortable chairs and all kinds of hairy plants—you can't see anything, some kind of fern or bush or little tree in a little pot or tall spindly chair with no cushions is always in the way. She sits there. She frowns at me. She pours me tea. She puts it on the table in front of her, and I have to come over from whatever slab of hard wood I'm sitting on to fetch it. We sit. She sips without making a sound. I, of course, always slurp. I can't help it—the tea's too hot. And then she talks. Only then. 'Well, how are *you*,' she always says. She's reminding me that I haven't asked about her, I suppose."

"No," Boris said. "That's the tone Barbara takes when he comes home. It's fear of disappointment."

"I will not be made guilty about this, Boris."

"It's only a suggestion," he said.

I asked, "Are we talking about the same outward signs that mean *different* inward things?"

"Inner," Solly said.

Ouida nodded. "Wouldn't that make life complicated? Not to mention stories like this one about it."

"Tell yours," I said. "And don't be guilty."

"I wasn't suggesting that anyone feel guilty," Boris said.

"I apologize for growling at you," Ouida said. "I have to protect myself."

"Not if you tell the story," I said.

"Clever," Ouida said.

Boris said, "I don't get it."

Ouida said, "So we sit and I slurp and then she beats me with good manners about the head and neck for a while. We talk a *teensy* while. And then—I can't help this—my head turns on my neck while my brains fall into my stomach. They keep shouting up, 'Don't turn! Don't *turn!*' And I look over at her little table. It's near a window box. She keeps—junk, I guess. Memorabilia, would you say? I don't know. It's like her horrible *mind*. She has all this stuff on it. Little Russian babushka dolls, one inside the other? A big set of them. Sometimes everything's inside the biggest one, sometimes they're all out. Sometimes one or two are out. And I keep trying to figure out what she *means!* There are nineteenth-century page cutters to be used on old books that she never uses them on, as far as I know. And paperweights from Italy that don't hold any paper down, and inside of the glass it looks like little *squids*, not anything lovely. And a very beautiful small ceramic watering jug with a crack, it looks like, running down the side. I suppose she pours water onto her jungle from it, if it doesn't leak all over. I've never seen her do it. And the Pennsylvania Dutch figurines."

"Oh," Solly said.

"I'm sorry. I can't help it. I can't even *believe* it."

"No, I wasn't complaining," Solly said. "I don't remember you ever talking about them before."

"Sure, she did," Boris said.

I shook my head. "Never."

Boris said, "Oh."

Solly nodded.

Ouida said to him, "So why did you say 'Oh'?"

"It sounded mysterious," he said.

"Oh, that's *sweet*," she told him. She patted his hand. He went nearly incandescent. "But I never talked about them?"

We all shook our heads.

"Well. Well, all right. I mean, we *are* talking about outer signs here. All right. So I look over, every time, and she sees me. She's watching. She sees me, and she starts in talking about Richie. How he didn't wear his snowsuit in the Blizzard of 1947 or something. And I really want to know that. I do. It's something to have. There *was* one in 1947 where they lived. Everybody stayed home, all the parents and the children, New York City closed *down*. Richie built a snow tunnel that went all the way across the street. They lived in Forest Hills, then. And he refused to wear his snowsuit. It was an adventure, he told her, and no adventurers *ever* wore anything *like* a snowsuit in any of the books that he'd been reading. He was always a terrific reader. So he went out in corduroys and black rubber galoshes—with those metal fasteners? He got sick. She thinks he got scarlet fever because of that. *I* think he got it from living with her. People *can* really get you sick, I believe. Oh, I'm—yes. Yes. I'm storing it up to keep for when I'm alone, but I'm also looking at her table. She has these figurines. They're made of cast iron, about four inches high, three-dimensional—statues, I'd guess you'd call them. Little Pennsylvania Dutch farm people. And they're always changed! She moves them around, depending on her mood. They have these painted-on dungarees and gingham shirts, and there's a daddy and a mommy and a little boy and a little girl. Their smiles are huge and empty. It's frightening. When Richie and I went to visit, the little children would be standing close to the parents, and we'd know it'd be all right for a few hours or a day. Or they'd be a couple of inches apart from the parents. Then we'd know she was hating me again for taking her son, whatever it was I did. Do. I don't know. And we'd make jokes about it when we were alone. But never with her. Because, one time, Richie asked her why she kept moving the figurines around that way—Richie wasn't ever frightened of anyone—and you want to know what she said? Not 'I don't.' And not 'I have my reasons.' Not 'I do?' or 'Do I?' or 'Huh?' She looked her son right in the eye, pausing only an instant so she could frown up through my eyeballs and into my brain, and she said, '*Which figurines do you mean?*' "

"Perfect," I said. "Excuse me."

"No, you're right. It *was* perfect, it was so insane. Almost as crazy as my going to see her."

Solly said, "You don't want to *lose* him, Ouida."

She held his left hand with both of hers. He patted the knot of hands with his free hand, then kept it there.

"So I go there," she said, "and I do the tea, the slurp, the look, all of it. And I end up caring where she's put the silly cast-iron damned *statues*. Last time, the girl was lying down. Lying on her stomach on the table!"

"Voodoo," Boris said.

"Jewish voodoo," Ouida agreed.

I asked her, "Did you fall?"

"I worked so hard at making sure I didn't, you know, trip on the doorsill going out or something, I ended up falling into the cab and banging my shin. I cried all the way to the station. I hated myself. I *blamed* myself. *That's* Jewish voodoo. Solly, dear, my hands are hot."

"Oh!" he cried. "Geez! I'm *sorry*."

"No," she said, "not at all. I probably worry too much about my hands."

"Solly'll read a lot into that," Boris gloated.

But Solly, emboldened, looked up at Boris and said, in a very high-pitched voice, "Beep."

"So," I said, "how do we feel about Ouida's new pupil?"

"It *was* your script," Boris said.

I asked Ouida, "Was it about a father who pushed his son to play high school football? Did the boy wreck his knee in a nasty accident on the playing field? Do we see the father, a month later, looking down at the leg of his sleeping son? Looking at the scars as if they're routes on a frightful map?"

"You did write it," Solly said. He smiled broadly. "Say, this is exciting."

Ouida said, "*I* don't know. She only talked to me about her daddy and a script and what he said. I never read it."

"But you did write it. I can sense it. Right?" Boris asked.

"I don't have sons," I said. "I don't have daughters. Or wives. I don't write scripts about sons. I never wrote a script about a knee. Can you think of anything worse than a movie about knees? Or sons? Or wives?"

"A movie about cast-iron figurines," Ouida said.

"A movie about the sonar operator on leave who never talks," Boris said.

"A movie about a Fat Book," Solly said.

It was ending. It was over. I nodded, accepting the return of my credit card from our waiter, and adding a handsome tip. We were ushered from our table with much courtesy, and we all uttered tourists' broken Italian as we left. *Buona sera*, we called, as if we lived where such a phrase was spoken. *Buona sera.*

And outside, adjusting clothes and hefting parcels and bags, we clung a moment more to our company, breathing dark Manhattan air, absorbing the sounds of cars and sirens, readying ourselves to cross Eighth Avenue or climb down into the subway or walk crosstown.

Ouida kissed us each on the cheek. She held the lapel of Solly's jacket and smiled to him. Boris and Solly and I shook hands. "Another week," Ouida called. "Another week."

Solly looked as though he'd weep. And so, really, did stern Boris. I wondered if I did too. Ouida looked happy and brave.

Boris moved hesitantly toward the corner where he crossed each week.

I said, "Don't wait. Good night, good night. See you at the session, Boris. Good night."

He nodded, and soon he stood at the curb.

Solly didn't know which way to walk. I told him. I said, "Solly, go home."

"Right," he said, turning toward Greenwich Avenue. "Right. I ought to feed the cats."

"Been a long day for them," I said.

"Solly, take care," Ouida said.

Solly uncertainly said, "Yes."

In her long, broad-shouldered melton coat, her cheeks flushed with drink and conversation, Ouida looked to me like the spirit of New York City in the winter. I belted my double-breasted trench coat, and I pulled the buckle tight. "I think I'm gaining weight," I said. "All these dinners at the Beatrice."

Ouida put her hands above the belt, as if to feel my ribs. "Oh, I don't think so," she said. "But if you're worried, you can read a few pages in dear Solly's Fat Book. All of his pages are dietetic, you know." She kept her hands on my ribs. I put mine on her shoulders. "Do you ever feel lonely?" I asked her. "Besides missing Richie?"

Her smile moved my hands to my pockets. She moved hers too, but to gesture happily at the milky glow of Manhattan's evening sky, the bright and growling confusion of its traffic. Across at Greenwich, Solly waved, a boy on the landing of the stairs at bedtime. I waved back.

Ouida said, "Well, this is the *city*. This is where people *always* feel lonely. Aren't we supposed to, sometimes?" Now she waved good night to Solly too, and he went out of sight toward his cats. "Am I misunderstanding something?" she asked.

Good night, Solly.

Good night, Boris.

Ouida. Good night. Good night. *Buona sera.*

I said, "Nah."

 Gravity

BUDDY AND HIS WIFE are big. They're big on sports and big on work and big on marriage, big in fact. Because LuAnne works for the state, spreading news as the governor's aides understand it or wish it understood, she gets tickets to the basketball games, very few of which are lost, since the university spends as much on a player in a year, she points out (though never in print), as the governor's office will spend on her annual pay. Together they sit, bulking large on the narrow wooden bleachers, and they make great noise.

Not *fat*, Buddy points out. He stands almost six feet four, he weighs about 235, and his ribs still show when he strips to shower after racquetball, if he sucks the gut in just slightly. "Where the ribs *used* to be," Buddy will say, pounding his belly, which is hardened by the deep breath he takes against his own assault.

LuAnne wears a size sixteen and looks like a fourteen because she's nearly six feet tall. Her shoulders are wide, her back is broad, her arms are long and muscular. Her hands, wider than the average man's, can wrap a softball firmly enough to make it curve at high, unhittable speeds on staff picnics. She has a girl's face and soft heavy hair that she wears long, the way she wore it when, across the street, in the state's university she sees every day from her office window, she wore a size fourteen and felt slim, looked glamorous, and was pursued by Buddy Wolfe. Buddy dropped out of premed, got twenty-eight of his credits toward the Ph.D. in what he calls pure science, changed his mind again and earned the master of arts in teaching, became an instructor of high school earth science, telling louts and drug merchants, the usual earnest students, and one or two of the Midwest's rampaging killers-to-be that oxbow rivers are formed by the centrifugal force of the stream that spins tiny fragments of earth toward its outer edge, where they chew at the bank and make the straight water crooked. "This is a function of gravity," Buddy tells them in the ninth grade every year. "Gravity, ladies and gentlemen: what makes you fall down each and every time. From the top of Old Capitol, from the top of the Pizza Hut, and from the edge of the Sauquoit River. And you will fall if you're a feather or a sack of cats. Gravity. It turns a piddling little baby river into a sharp-toothed *saw*. Hello? Do my words fall on deaf ears? *Fall*, I said. Is anyone home? That's what the Lord asked in Eden. Just after the Fall. Hello?"

They aren't more than thirty-five, but they'll never have children and they don't tell anyone why. LuAnne's office mates talk about her time in the hospital seven years ago. Buddy's friends remember the tests he kept taking at the university's clinics. And Buddy and LuAnne go to games, as now, in the midwestern winter, with vicious winds blowing mounds across the roads and stranded drivers asleep in their trucks, with hot air fogging Buddy's glasses when they enter the gym and LuAnne grinning like a great big girl on a date fifteen years ago, as the cheerleaders toss one another around and assure that privacy, for a couple of hours, becomes an offense against the common good. "Come on," they cry in unison, for unison. "Come *on*, make a little *noise*, they don't have the *guts*, they don't have the *poise*—two, two, two, two, two, two, *two!*" The crowd raises its common voice and its individual fingers, calling *two*, huffing it like an engine, and Buddy and LuAnne do it and keep on doing it as the home team runs out, one at a time, for introductions.

This was the morning in their lives that LuAnne feared, and she could never have told him why she had feared it so long. Buddy was talking, over Friday morning coffee, about the Building Council meeting of the afternoon before. The malfeasances of a middling-efficient principal, the ambitions of a very short guidance counselor—"the goddamned troll," Buddy always called him—and the advances made on the high school librarian by an English teacher who thought that teaching *The Good Earth* by Pearl Buck would raise his students' awareness of "a culture other than one's own," as he always called it: Buddy was reciting the little moments of friction he had slept on. LuAnne wasn't listening. She said to herself: I can hear it, but it's going over me. I'm a hot rock in a cold river, and it's going directly over me.

LuAnne was remembering Skip Milgren, who raised her after her parents died in the usual middle-western wreck: sixty cars accordioned, folded, pleated, and torn, then scattered for a mile on the I-80, with twelve people dead and most of the rest sliced by glass and crushed by the momentum of heavy engines and big cars, all the frozen slush and heaped ice and slippery concrete red with blood and glittering like jewels because of the shattered windshields. Skip had served in the marines with her father, had coveted her mother—she'd been sure: until his death he had spoken of her father with tears in his eyes, but had not been able to say her mother's name—and he had raised her with the clumsiest bachelor's delicacy. No one had been alive to contest his custody of LuAnne, but no one, after a month or two, would have dared, she was thinking. And while she was thinking it, Buddy spoke of the Xerox machine's malfunction, and the fellow who, caught smoking marijuana in the boys' room, had locked himself in a stall, refusing to come out until granted amnesty. "You ever hear of a kid taking a toilet hostage?" Buddy asked.

Skip, or Skipper, as her father had called him, had been taller than Buddy by several inches, and heavier by thirty pounds. "But I wear the best damned looking shoes," Skip used to say, smiling at his vanity and at his bulk. "I've got very graceful arches on my feet. And I wear nifty socks."

Behind his house—it then became *their* house—Skip had installed a concrete pool in the ground. It was narrow but long, and in the worst days of August and September, Lu-Anne had swum after dinner with special boyfriends, and she and Skip, during the still, moist, sulphurous afternoons, had sought refuge in the water. Skip's hair was always crew cut, even when, in his forties, he went through his reformation. His doctor had warned him to lose a good deal of weight, and to stop using salt, and to drink less, and to exercise. He had warned him of the stroke that, even in the early September of her sophomore year, was on its way. LuAnne thought of it, always, as an arrow, shot high into the air from far away, from beyond a hill perhaps, but surely aimed, and barbed at the heavy point, and on a perfect arc toward Skip. She thought of the arrow striking that balding but brush-cut head; sun exposing the skin among his few short hairs had always made him look vulnerable.

Crew cut, then, even while priding himself on buying his clothes a size smaller, tan because of his time at the pool, and less short of breath because of his exercising, enormous nevertheless and still embarrassed when seeing her in her swim suit—two pieces of yellow terry cloth she was too shy to wear with anyone but Skip—he was coming from the house when she saw him as the world, and not the girl whose parents had left her alone in it, must surely have seen him. He was a brownish-olive giant. His arms and legs were very long. While the fat lay in pads on his arms, she could still see the long, thick muscles. His legs, in the old-fashioned woolen briefs, were round and a little blubbery, though firmer than one might expect. His legs were covered with heavy black hair, while his arms and chest seemed hairless. His tattoos—a palm tree over his left nipple, the snouty face of some kind of beast on the biceps of his left arm—seemed darker underneath his tan than they seemed in the winter. Of course, he rarely let her see him without a shirt except in the summer, at the pool. His belly, though a little smaller, bulged nevertheless, a long graceful slope that began at his chest and went on beneath his bathing suit. She remembered thinking of the flesh beneath his bathing suit for what struck her as the first time, on that steamed September morning of her nineteenth year. She was certain that she'd blushed.

"Because I wouldn't want some kind of policy that re-warded kids for *not* learning," Buddy argued, pouring them more coffee. "Hell. The only thing they're denied, as it is, is combat pay for knife fights in the courtyard."

And the girls with chunky thighs and high socks, the ones who had better legs and showed them with greater verve, the boys who smiled sneakily and bounced on their rubber-soled shoes, all were swinging their hips and leading the crowd to cry two, two, two, two, two, two, *two!*

Skip had walked from the sliding glass-and-aluminum door at the back of his house. He had spread some suntan lotion on his somehow sleek strong body, and he'd lit another Camel, which, in his long, thick fingers, looked more like a match than a cigarette. He'd always pulled the smoke in hard and sighed it out as if in loss. He did it again, left it in his mouth awhile, and walked along the pool's side to stop half-way and call her. "LuAnne," he'd said. "Baby."

"Hi!" she'd answered. "I'm wilting out here. Do I look like a big dead cornflower to you? Feature the heat, Skip. It's murder. What I won't do for a tan."

"LuAnne," he'd said. "I didn't have the honor of seeing you off to school at the start of your freshman year."

"Didn't you have dinner with Mommy and Daddy about half a dozen times that summer?"

"I don't mean that," he'd called from his pausing point, halfway around, on the opposite side of the pool. "I mean, I wasn't responsible for you at the time."

"No."

"I am now."

"Oh, Skip."

"I have to, dear heart. I'm responsible now." His voice had been surprisingly high, LuAnne remembered, watching with actual interest as their point guard raced the ball across the half-court line and then pulled up to wait for his slower forwards. She remembered remembering Skip's high voice that morning while Buddy made the raisin toast and put a napkin over the knot of his necktie to keep the melted margarine from staining his blue oxford button-down shirt. The shirt had annoyed her, she recalled; she didn't know why. As the cheerleaders squatted out of bounds, behind the basket, pom-poms at the ready, white smiles never far away, LuAnne remembered remembering what had happened in her body when Skip Milgren had called her "dear heart."

Her stomach had tightened as if at the first sudden drop of a Ferris wheel. And she had felt poised at the top of something, she remembered thinking as she drank her coffee. Something is happening to me, she remembered feeling. And there she had sat, legs gleaming with cocoanut oil and pink rubber noseclips wound by the pink elastic band around the fingers of her right hand, left hand holding hard to the plastic armrest of the aluminum chaise. And she had felt the lift and then interior swoop before the drop, and the sounds of *dear heart* had rattled inside her like frightened riders in the Ferris wheel's box. She had waited for the wheel to turn further and let the box fall.

Skip had said—he nearly had cried it—"LuAnne, I need to take care of you now."

"Oh, Skip." She had almost wept, she'd remembered over

coffee and toast with her large, handsome husband, his eyes dark and wet with the passions of small politics. "Skip," she had called, as if he were miles below, on the ground, and not across the narrow swimming pool, "Skip, you *do*. You always do."

"You're beautiful," Skip had said. She had wondered if it was possible that he was not lying. She had wondered why she felt almost ratified because he had said it, truth or lie. He had said, "You're a handsome young woman and boys chase you." Then he'd stooped to seize his lighter and cigarettes, then had pulled and pulled at the smoke.

She'd hoped to rescue him by saying, "Skip, it's fine. It's all right. They—in school, they taught us everything about that in school."

"They never teach you everything in school."

"And Mommy and Daddy told me. Really."

"*I* have to tell you." He pulled at the cigarette and, reinventing her as his daughter just as surely as Buddy Wolfe had reinvented her as his wife, Skip looked at the sky, his head swiveling as if he first had to see all of it—as if a foe or a danger were upon it—and then Skip had said: "LuAnne. I love you. I respect you because of the love and respect I had for your folks. Still do have. And because you're a fine person. If I had a daughter. Well, of course, you *are* my daughter. That's to say—you're my daughter, period, finished. Understand me?"

She had nodded because her voice wouldn't work.

"LuAnne: you're too precious to be taken for cheap. That's to say—don't be easy on no man, and don't be easy *for* no man. This isn't an insult, you understand. LuAnne: it's

164

the facts of life. And always remember: you can't get ketchup out of a bottle if you keep the cap on tight."

And, poised at the top, hanging there, she had begun to laugh and cry at the same time. She had done it silently, she'd remembered that morning, stacking the breakfast dishes in the dishwasher. She had reached for a towel and had rubbed at her face and underneath it she had giggled and wept. From beneath the towel she had said, "I know what you mean, Skip. Thank you very much."

"And I love you," he'd told her.

"Oh, Skipper darling, I love *you*."

Peeking from the towel, she had seen him: enormous and almost naked, a great baby of a middle-aged man with a small boy's haircut and a soldier's cruel tattoos. He had stubbed the Camel out. He had walked back to the house. There, turning around to face her, across the small patio, across the small pool, he had looked at her and had nodded, not knowing himself to be seen. Instead of walking with his usual ponderous dignity, Skip, then, thinking himself hidden by LuAnne's towel at her face, had run. Great belly bouncing and round thighs loose, tall and wide and with his face made tough by his crew cut, Skip had run and then had leaped into the air in something of a dive. With an explosive splash he had come down, outstretched hands making his body look pointed, like the arrow that was on its way to kill him by stroke in fifteen years, and he had sunk beneath the water. Surfacing with a vast gasp, he had shaken his head and rolled onto his back. There he had lain, supported by the water, his arms and legs outstretched, relaxed, his chest and belly heaving, but his head back, loose and still.

Weightless at last, LuAnne had thought.

And while their strong forward was merciless in his re-
bounding, landing with the ball and flailing with his elbows
to clear a lane for the break upcourt, Buddy was shouting
for two, two, two, two, two, two, *two* with everyone else,
and LuAnne was remembering how, this morning, she had
remembered Skip Milgren.

The bounce pass was too far in front of the guard who'd
run parallel to the fast-breaking forward. But the guard
dived, swatted the ball up and back, and the long skinny
forward in turn flipped the ball up and over his head, so that
it hung in front of the basket as their trailing center, flying
through the air, seized it, pumped, and then stuffed it down
through the hoop. The building roared like a furnace.

The blue oxford-cloth shirt that Buddy had worn this
morning, was wearing now, with its frayed button-down
collar and its double white buttons at each cuff, had been
Skip's. They had, when LuAnne could bear it, gone through
the small house, making piles to dispose of, piles to give away,
piles to keep because LuAnne remembered their weight in
her life, and because it had seemed proper that Skip's clothing go on a while in his lieu. Buddy had agreed at once to
take some of Skip's clothing—she hadn't known whether because he thought it her wish, or because Buddy needed new
shirts.

And this morning Buddy had worn Skip's shirt. He probably hadn't noticed that she was wearing a sleeveless blue
pullover that Skip had often worn. It was lamb's wool and,
while it was large on her, it was baggy in a way that now was
in fashion. She wore it because she liked the look of small

women in large men's clothes. She knew that dressing the way she did was either prayer or despair. As the clock over the court told two minutes to go in the second period, LuAnne looked expectantly down at Buddy's ankles. He wore the loose aquamarine socks that Skip had bought in the K mart. Skip had always called the store Special K, and he had always bought what he considered bold but tasteful colors—cinnamon, banana, aqua, sky-blue. The opponents, unable to penetrate the zone defense, began to shoot from too far out. The ball wobbled high and slow against the game clock with its four faces, suspended from the ceiling. And here we are, LuAnne thought. What's left of Skip we're unpeeling in little pieces of clothing. Mummy-bandages, she thought. You take the socks and I'll take the sweater. You wear the shirt and I'll wear the pajama tops. One of these days, she thought, we'll pull away something else, an undershirt, a tie, and there won't be anything left. There won't be anyone there. That poor big man diving into his pool, there had to be somebody there if all that water splashed up. And if Skipper disappeared, she knew, so would she.

That was when LuAnne saw herself as poised, and almost-falling, and on the edge, and as surely in danger as she had remembered, this morning, that she'd felt at the poolside fifteen years before. As the ball, again thrown up in frustration, hung high in the air before them, Buddy leaned over and he kissed her, as a baby might, on the cheek.

She turned to him and smelled the fruity perfume of his chewing gum. He had been that close beside her throughout the game, she realized. He had been watching her as the legs of the cheerleaders shone and their pom-poms shook and they flashed their teeth, calling two, two, two, two, two, two, *two*.

The ball came down as the buzzer sounded to close the period. Thrown by the opponents in desperation, it fell through the hoop and barely shook the net. The cheerleaders stared. The crowd only hummed, then went silent. But Lu-Anne, to her surprise, had stood. She had suddenly stood, and she was looking down to her husband, Buddy, the boy she had known for a very long time. Buddy's face looked young and lean and sad in its bewilderment.

"Where are you going?" he said.

But he really had to know something, LuAnne thought. You don't kiss your wife like that unless you are smart and probably frightened, and you suspect her of being about to disappear into her history, or someone else's—unless you know the world is a dangerous place, and people disappear. He looked up at her, and LuAnne, in the stillness and disappointment of the great hall, wearing Skip's sweater, hanging in her life above the man in Skip's shirt and Skip's socks, called down to him as if he were a youngster, and she the heavy veteran of wars: "Dear heart." With a ladylike smoothing of the hem of her skirt, and with her legs side by side as she seated herself, LuAnne floated down.

Dog Song

I

HE ALWAYS THOUGHT of the dogs as the worst. The vet's belly heaved above his jeans, and he cursed in words of one syllable every time a deputy tugged a dog to the hypodermic, or trotted to keep up as a different one strained on its chain for its fate, or when a dog stopped moving and went stiff, splayed, and then became a loose furry bag with bones inside. The deputies and the vet and the judge, who also did his part—he watched without moving— did it twenty-six times, in the yard behind the sheriff's offices. The air stank of dirty fur and feces as though they were all locked in. The yelping and whining went on. When they were through, one deputy was weeping, and the vet's red flannel shirt was wet with sweat from his breastbone to his belt. The deputies threw the dogs into the back of a van.

They might be dangerous, Snuyder had decided. They might have been somehow perverted, trained to break some basic rules of how to live with men. So they had died. And Snuyder, doing his part, had watched them until the last lean mutt, shivering and funny-eyed, was dead. He thought, when he thought of the dogs, that their lips and tails and even their postures had signaled their devotion to the vet or to one of the deputies; they'd been waiting for a chance to give their love. And as the deputies flung them, the dogs' tongues protruded and sometimes flopped. When their bodies flew, they looked ardent.

The dogs in the yellow trailer had drawn the attention of the people in the white trailer across the unpaved rural road: their howling, their yapping, the whining that sometimes went on and on and on. Lloyd and Pris, the man and wife in the trailer with the dogs, came and went at curious hours, and that too attracted the attention of the neighbors, who had their own problems, but somehow found time—being good country Christians, they *made* time—to study the erratic behavior and possible social pathology of the couple in the bright yellow trailer edged in white, propped on cinder blocks, bolstered against upstate winters by haybales pushed between the plastic floor and the icy mud. The neighbors, one working as a janitress, the other as a part-time van driver for the county's geriatric ferrying service, finally called the sheriff when there was a February thaw, and the mud all of a sudden looked awfully like manure, and an odor came up from the yellow trailer that, according to the janitress (a woman named Ivy), was too much like things long dead to be ignored by a citizen of conscience.

But only one of the dogs was dead, and it died after the deputies had kicked the door in, and after it had attacked and had been shot. It died defending a mobile home that was alive with excrement and garbage. Turds lay on the beds and on the higher surfaces, counter and sink. Madness crawled the walls. Lloyd, the husband, had written with dung his imprecations of a county and state and nation that established laws involving human intercourse with beasts. Twenty-six dogs were impounded, and the couple was heavily fined by the judge.

The awful part, of course, had been the dogs' dull eyes and duller coats, their stink, their eagerness to please, and then their fear, and then the way they had died. Later he decided that the nurse with her hair that was thinning and her arms puffed out around the short, tight sleeves of her hissing uniform was the worst part so far. The first sight Richard Snuyder had seen, when he fell awake like a baby rolling from its crib, had been a man on crutches at his door, peering. The man had sucked on an unlit filter cigarette, adjusted his armpits on the crutches, and said, "I heard you did one *jam*-jar of a job. Just thought I'd say so. I was raised to express my appreciation of the passing joys."

Snuyder, hours later, had thought that the man on crutches, apparently a connoisseur of catastrophe, was the worst. He wasn't. The worst became the orderly who brought in a plate of mashed potatoes and open hot roast-beef sandwich in glutinous gravy, who was chased by the nurse who brought the doctor, whose odor of dark, aged sweat and stale clothing did little to dispel that of the roast beef, which lingered in the room as if the pale orderly had hurled it on the walls to punish Snuyder for being on a liquid diet.

The doctor, who had mumbled and left, Snuyder thought for a while, was really the worst part of it: his dandruff, his caustic smell, his dirty knuckles that gave the lie to the large scraped moons of fingernail above the tortured cuticles. This is the worst, Snuyder had thought, though not for long.

Because then the candy striper with her twitchy walk and bored pout had stood at his door, a clipboard in her hand and an idle finger at her ear, though carefully never in it, and had looked at him as though he weren't open-eyed, blinking, panting with pain, clearly stunned and afraid and as lost while being still as dogs are that stand at the side of the road, about to be killed because they don't know what else they should do.

After the candy striper had left, the balding nurse with great arms, and no need for such forms of address as language spoken or mimed, came in to adjust something at his head and something at his leg. His neck didn't roll, so he couldn't follow her movements except with his eyes, which began to ache and then stream. Looking at his legs, she wiped his eyes and took the tissue away. He was about to ask her questions but couldn't think of anything that didn't embarrassingly begin with *Where* or *How*.

He tried to move his legs. That was next, as soon as the nurse left. He worked at wiggling his toes and each foot and each leg. They moved, though they were restrained by something, and he called aloud—it was a relief, during the cry, to hear his own voice and to know that he knew it—because the right leg was pure pain, undifferentiated, and the left, though more flexible, hurt only a little less. His legs, and the stiffness at the neck, his aching eyes and head, a burning on the skin of his face, the waking to no memory of how he had come there, or why, or when, or in what state: *he* was the worst so far. He suspected that little would happen to challenge this triumph. He'd been born someplace, of an unknown event, and every aspect of his arrival on this naked day could be measured against the uncomforting hypothesis that, among the local discomforts he knew, he himself was the worst.

His legs could not be moved, he could not be persuaded to move them again, and he lay with all his attention on his torso, thinking *I will be just chest and balls, I will not be legs or ankles or toes.* He panicked and felt for his legs, then moved an ankle—he yelped—in response to his fear: he did have his legs, and they would move at his command, he wasn't only a chest. *And balls?* He groaned his fear, and groaned for the pain in his legs, and then he groaned with deep contentment: he had found them under his hospital gown, both of them, and everything else, including the dreadful catheter. So all he needed to know now was when he would stop hurting over most of his body, and why and how he was here. *All right. First things first. You have legs, your balls are where you left them, and a little panic is worth a handful of testes during times of trial.*

I have not gone berserk with worry for my wife, he thought.

Do I have a wife?

How do I know my name, if I don't know whether I'm married? How did I know about balls? Are you born with a full knowledge of the scrotum? So that even during amnesia, you still—

I don't want *amnesia.*

I don't want *to be a pendulum in a ward, swinging on crutches and sucking on cold cigarettes and laughing at people forever and never* remembering.

What about my kids, if I do have kids?

The same nurse, with thin dark hair and wide white arms, was at the head of his bed, looking into his eyes this time as she wiped them. She had the voice of a twelve-year-old girl, and the teeth of someone long dead. She said, "Mr. Snuyder? Do you remember you're Mr. Snuyder?"

He tried to nod. The pain made him hiss.

"We'll give you something for pain after we X-ray your head again. But could you tell me if you know your name?"

"Thank you," he said.

"Yes. And your name?"

"Woke up knowing it was Snuyder."

"Good *boy*!"

"Woke up. Found out I had my scrotum, and I never knew if I had any children or a *wife*." He was crying. He hated it.

"You'll remember," she said. "You'll probably remember. You did take out a telephone pole and a good I say at least half of a Great American Markets rig. Worcestershire sauce and mustard and beerwurst smeared over two lanes for a quarter of a mile. If you don't mind glass, you could make a hell of a sandwich out there, they said."

"Kill anybody? Did I kill anybody?"

"Not unless *you* die on us. The truck was parked. Trucker was—how do you want to put it?—banging the lady of the house? You must of pulled a stupendous skid. The troopers'll be by to talk about it."

174

"Did you look in my wallet?"

"Doctor'll be by too. I'm off-duty now."

"You don't want to tell me about my family? There wasn't anybody with me, was there?"

"You're supposed to remember on your own. There wasn't anybody killed. You take care now."

"Won't dance with anyone else."

"Good boy."

"Wait," he said. "Wait a minute." He winced. He lay back. He heard himself breathe.

She said, "That's right. You lie down and be good. Good boy."

He woke again, with a thump, waiting for the nurse to speak. He saw that she was gone, the room dark, the door closed. He couldn't remember waking, ever before in his life, so abruptly, and with so much pain. And that wasn't all he couldn't remember. He thought *baby, baby, baby* to himself, as if in a rapture, and he tried to think of a lover or wife. Was he divorced? What about kids? He thought a gentler *baby* and looked within his closed eyes for children. He thought of maps—blank. He thought of cars and couldn't see the one he'd driven. He remembered that the nurse had evaded the question of who had been with him. But at least she wasn't dead.

And how had he known that his passenger was a woman? And how could he know he was right?

He was tired of questions and tired of hurting. He remembered, then, how they had rolled him through the halls for a CAT-scan and how, when he'd been rolled back, they had looked at him like magic people who could make him fall asleep, and he had fallen. He wanted more magic. He wanted to sleep some more and wake again and know one thing more. A woman in the car with him. Should she have been with him in the car? Should she have come with him to this room?

And he woke again, one more question not answered, to see a light that sliced at his eyeballs and to hear a general commotion that suggested daytime and what he had doubtless once referred to as everyday life. The door opened in, and Hilary was inside with him, and through dry lips he said, "I *remember* you!"

She said, "Can you see how little I'm cheered by that?"

No: she started to; he finished her statement in his mind, fed by memory, and he smiled so triumphantly, his face hurt. In fact, Hilary said, "Can you see—"

And he said, "Hilary. Hil."

She shook her head as if winged insects were at her, and then she wept into her wide, strong hands, walking slowly toward him, a child at a hiding game. But she was not a child and there were no children—not here, anyway, because the boys were at school, of course, and he and Hilary, Richard and Hilary Snuyder, were alone, they were each forty-seven years old, and they were working at being alone together while Warren and Hank went to school in other states. The states were *other* because this one was New York. Hilary was tall, and she wore her pea jacket, so it must be autumn, and her upper lip came down on the lower one as if she wanted to make love. Richard did, then, and his hand went down to grip himself in celebration where it had earlier prodded for loss. "Hilary," he said. The catheter guarded his loins, and his hand retreated.

She wiped at her eyes and sat on the chair beside the bed.

"Come sit on the bed," he said.

She sat back. She crossed her legs and he looked with a sideways glance to see her jeans and Wallabees. His eyes stung, so he looked up. He sniffed, expecting to smell perfume or soap. He smelled only gravy and the finger-chewing doctor. And Hilary said, "How could you decide on—going away like that?" She said, "How could you *do* that? No matter what?"

"Hil, I'm having a hell of a time remembering things. I didn't remember *you* until you came in, the boys and you and—would you tell me stuff? You know, to kind of wake me up some more? I don't remember going anyplace. They said I smacked the car up."

Hilary stood, and something on her sweet, pale face made him move. The motion made him whimper, and she smiled with genuine pleasure. Her long hand, suspended above him, was trembling. He felt her anger. His penis burned. He closed his eyes but opened them at once. He was afraid of her hand descending to seize him as if in love or recollected lust, but then to squeeze, to crush the catheter and leave him coughing up his pain and bleeding up into the blanket. He saw her playing the piano with strong bloody hands, leaving a trail of blood on the keys.

She said, "I have to go outside until I calm down. I'll go outside and then I'll be back. Because unlike you I do *not* run out on the people I love. Loved. But I'll leave you a clue.

You want to remember things? You want a little trail of bread crumbs you can follow back into your life? How about this, Richard: you drove our fucking car as hard as you could into a telephone pole so you could die. Is that a little crust of some usefulness? So you could leave me forever on purpose. Have I helped?"

The awful doctor came back again, adding the insult of his breath to the injury of his armpits. He was thick, with a drooping heavy chest and shoulders that came down at a very sharp angle, so that his thick neck looked long. His fingers were large, and the knuckles looked dirtier now—this morning, tonight, whenever it was that the doctor stood at the bed, telling Richard where the orthopedic surgeon was going to insert pins of assorted sizes and alloys into the hip and femur, which the instrument panel had cracked in an interesting way. The neck was all right. The back was all right. The head seemed all right, though you never can tell with the brain. A little rancid laugh, a flicker of motion across the big jowls and their five o'clock shadow. And the ribs, of course, although CAT pictures showed no danger to the lungs. "You'll be bound."

"I'm a judge," Snuyder said.

"Good man."

"I'm a district judge with a house in the suburbs and a wife and two kids and two cars. Three cars. We have an old Volvo my son Hank fixed up. A '67 Volvo. It runs pretty well, but it's rusted out. Bound over—you say that when—"

"Yes, you're a judge. Good man. I was talking about a restraint for the ribs, is all. Two ribs. You're lucky."

178

"Of course, I'm lucky. And I didn't aim to hit some telephone pole."

"You remember what happened?"

"No. But I wouldn't have. People with a—people like me don't *do* that."

The doctor looked bitter and weary. "No," he said. "I can call the rescue squad, if you like, and ask them to take you back and drop you off at your car. I'd have to call the garage and tell them that it isn't telescoped. Totaled. All but small enough to use for a Matchbox toy if the grandchildren come over. Of course, you'll probably benefit by using less gas in it from now on."

Richard blushed. He couldn't shut up, though. He said, "I meant suicide."

"I know."

"I meant people like me don't *do* that."

"You want anything for pain?"

"No."

"Don't be stubborn, Your Honor. A petulant patient is still a patient in pain. Can be. Call the nurse if you hurt. I'll leave orders in case you do. I'll see you before they sedate you. It might be soon, but I think they'll wait until tomorrow, or late this afternoon. We're crowded. Sick people, you know."

"Unlike me."

The doctor let his face say that he was ignoring Richard's childishness. And Richard felt an overwhelming need to cry.

"So if you're so crowded, how come you put me in a private room. Why don't you keep a suicide watch on me? Who *says* it's suicide?"

"First of all, we didn't. Second of all: Two kids in a car,

one pedestrian walking her dogs, the cop who was chasing you for DWI and reckless endangerment and all the other violations you probably pronounce on people at your place of work. I'm going. We aren't having much of a doctor-patient relationship right now."

And when he left, Richard lay back, breathless with rage. He panted with hatred for his wife and his doctor, the nurse, the orderly, the hospital, the cops behind him during the chase, and the fact that he had not slowed down when they came into his mirror, no siren on but a band of white and red light that made him blink before—he suddenly could see himself—he crouched over the wheel and then leaned back, pushing his arms straight, locked at the elbows, jamming the accelerator down until the bellow of the engine and wind and, then, the siren of the following police, were almost as loud as the howl that he howled and that he kept on howling until the impact shut him, and everything else, up.

He heard his breath shudder now, in the salmon-colored room, mostly shadows and walnut veneers. Then he heard a man say, "You wanna nurse?"

"Who?"

"It's me. You can't turn, huh? Listen, Your Honor, it's such a pain in the ass as well as the armpit, the crutches, I'm gonna stay flat for a while. I'll visit you later on, you can look at me and remember. I'm the guy said hello the other time."

"You're in here with me?"

"Yeah. Ain't it an insult? You a judge and everything. Like the doctor said, it's real crowded."

"This is *too* crowded."

"Well, listen, don't go extending any special treatment to

me, Your Honor. Just pretend I'm a piece of dog shit. You'll feel better if you don't strain for the little courtesies and all. Your wife's a very attractive woman, if I may say so. Hell of a temper, though."

Richard rang for the nurse.

His roommate said, "All that pain. Dear, dear. Listen, remember this when you wake up. My name's Manwarren. Emanuel Manwarren. Manny Manwarren. It's an honor to be with a Your Honor kind of deal." Then, to the entering nurse: "His Honor is in discomfort."

Richard lay with his eyes closed until the nurse returned with water and a large capsule. He looked at her. She was young and intelligent-looking, and very tired. He said, "How shall I take this medicine without drowning? I can't sit up."

She said, "He ordered it by spansule." Her voice was flat. She was expecting a fight.

"He would," Richard said. "What if I die taking medicine?" He heard himself: he sounded worried about dying.

"Don't fret," she said. "I'll telephone for an order change, and I'll bring you a shot."

"You're a charmer, Your Honor," Manwarren said.

"Are we going to engage in class warfare, or whatever this is, for all the time we're in here? Mr. Manwarren?"

"Call me Manny. Nah. I'm a prickly personality. I hate the cops, authority figures like that, judges—you know what I mean?"

"Manny, why don't you think of me as a miscreant and not a judge."

"Can I call you Dick?"

Richard closed his eyes and listened to his breathing and the rustle of Manwarren's sheets. The pain was in Richard's bones and in his breath. He said, "There *was* someone with me, wasn't there?"

"Dick, in cases like this, there usually is."

11

They lived in a renovated carriage house at the edge of a small country road outside Utica. Simple country living at a condominium price, Hilary liked to say. They couldn't quite afford the mortgage, college tuitions, cars, the McIntosh stereo rig—Snuyder felt like a pilot when he turned the power on—or the carpets from Iran or Iraq or India, he forgot which, that Hilary had lately come to buy as investments. He thought of them as insulation.

Looking at his lighted house at 1:25 in the morning, observing a close, clear disk of moon, a sky bluer than black, and veined with cloud—it was a dark marble mural more than sky—Richard said, "We get by."

Hilary was in the living room, at the piano. She was playing little clear crystal sounds with occasional speeded-up patterns of dissonance. He watched the tall, pale woman at the piano, her body rigid, neck tense, all pleasure residing below her moving wrists.

"Hello," Snuyder said softly, removing his jacket and then his tie, dumping them on the sofa. "I was working with the clerks on a case. It's a terrible case. Then we went out for some drinks."

The repetitions in the music came in miniature parts and were very simple. There was a name for that. He was unbuttoning his shirt and he had it off by the time she sensed him and stopped and turned on the piano bench to see him wiping the sweat on his chest with the wadded shirt.

"Ugh," she said, covering her eyes with her big hands.

"How."

"Richard, stop. It's ugly."

"It's a sweaty night," he said. He went for his welcoming kiss. She hugged his waist and kissed his belly.

"Yummy," he said.

"Salty," she said. "Phoo." But she held him, and he stayed there. "Vhere vas you so late?"

"I told you—clerks? case? Just now?"

Richard carried his guilt and his dirty shirt toward the shower and Hilary followed. She stood in the doorway as he slid the cloudy shower door closed and made a screen of water that sealed him away. He groaned and blubbered and shook his head and shoulders and, loosening at last, dopey with comfort, shed of the sweat and oils and inner fluids of somebody else, he heard only part of what Hilary had said.

He called, "What?"

He turned the water off, and her words came over the stall. "I said you sounded especially like a whale tonight."

"Thank you. You did not. The Satie was beautiful."

"Thank *you*. It was Villa-Lobos, a *Chôros*. I don't think it's possible to confuse the two unless you've got me at the piano, the Snuyder Variations, eh?"

"Hilary."

"Sorry. Sorry."

"A number of other performers also dislike playing to a live audience. Glenn Gould, I remind you, for the one-millionth time, stopped playing concerts altogether. He was not, I think you'll agree, a shabby tickler of the ivories."

"Can you see how *little* I'm cheered by that? I'm sorry Gould is dead. I wish he'd been comfortable at concerts. But he made *recordings*, Richard. He made wonderful recordings."

"And you will too. It'll happen." He made his voice sound matter-of-fact, sincerely casual, casually sincere. But he knew how impatient he must sound to her.

He had intended to leap from the shower, dangle his body before her, and roll her into bed—and pray for performance this third time tonight. But when he came out, tail wagging and his smile between his teeth like a fetched stick, she was gone, his stomach was fluttering with premonitions, and he was very, very tired. He decided to settle for a glass of beer and some sleep. Hilary was in the kitchen when, wearing his towel, he walked in. She was peeling plastic wrap from a sandwich, and she had already poured him a beer. "You always want beer after a day like this. At least I can make the meals."

Richard drank some beer and said, "Thank you. You're very kind, though sullen and self-pitying."

"But I make a fine Genoa salami sandwich. And I look nice in shorts."

She was crying at the sink, turning the instant boiling-water tap on and off, on and off. The mascara ran black down her face. She looked like a clown. He realized that she'd made herself up for him—when? midnight? afterward?—and had worn the face she had made for him to see. He visualized himself, proud as a strapping big boy, stepping from the shower to greet her.

He finished chewing salami and dark bread. He said, "I hate to see you so damned unhappy."

She turned the boiling water on and off, and steam fogged the kitchen window. "So you make me cry to express your dismay with my sorrow?"

"Actually, I wasn't aware that I was making you cry."

"You're such a slob, Richard."

"But well-spoken, and attractive in a towel."

"You aren't unattractive," she said. "But you're so tired, you could never make love. Could you?"

Richard sighed with fear and satisfaction as he drank his beer. "We can do some middle-class perversions if you like. Many were developed for the tired husband after work, I understand. We can—" He had by now stood and moved to her, was moving against her as they leaned at the sink. "We can do a number of exotic tricks they practice in the movies that the D.A. confiscates."

Hilary's eyes were closed. She was unfastening his towel. Her upper lip was clamped over the lower one; and he watched it when it moved. "Movie perversions?" she said. "Where would you pick up movie perversions?"

"You know those evidentiary sessions I sometimes hold? We all sit around and watch dirty flicks."

She said, "Pig."

His skin had been cool and hers hot. His body, had it been a creature with a mouth, no more, would have sung. But it was very tired, and it was crowded with his mind. He thought, now, here, in his hospital room, not about—*damn* it—whoever he had been with in a motel room in Westmoreland, New York, before he wrecked his car. He could remember that—the room, the bedspread's color, the light lavender cotton skirt on the floor, and not her face. He couldn't see her *face*.

Richard, in their house, in his memory now, had taken off his wife's clothing and had wooed her away from what was sorrowful and true. He'd loved her in their kitchen to the exclusion of everything, for a very little while. And now, in the hospital room, he couldn't see or say the name of the woman he had loved more than Hilary and whom he had washed from his body to preserve her to himself. Naked of clothes and towel and her, they had lain in a nest of Hilary's underwear and blouse and dark Bermuda shorts—skins so easily shed. And Hilary had been watching him. He'd seen her eyes rimmed with black and filling with darkness. She had figured him out, he knew. He had wondered when she would tell him. In his hospital room, he remembered hoping that she would find a way to make it hurt.

III

It took Lloyd and Pris nearly a month to arm themselves and gather their courage and rage. Then they came, through the main doors of the county office building, and past the glass information booth—"Can I help you?" the woman in beige had said to the profiles of their passing shotguns—and down one flight to the basement offices. They thought the dogs would be in the basement, Lloyd later said. "I couldn't figure on anybody keeping animals upstairs where the fancy offices was bound to be." They took eleven people hostage, including a woman who cried so long and loudly that Lloyd—"She sounded like one of the goddamned *dogs*"— hit her with the pump-gun barrel. She breathed quietly and shallowly for the rest of their visit and was hospitalized for a week. The police at first remained outside and were content to bellow over battery-powered hailers. "*I* couldn't understand 'em," Lloyd said. "It sounded like some goddamned cheerleaders on a Friday night over to the high school game. Except Pris and me wouldn't play ball."

They passed out a note that said, "26 PRIVAT STOCK CRETURS PLUS FREEDOME OF CHOICE PLUS $10,000." The money was for Pris's sex-change operation, Lloyd said in his deposition. They wanted to be legally married and live as man and wife. Pris was tired of costumes and wanted *outfits*. The police got bored and flushed them out with tear gas, then beat them badly before the arraignment. Lloyd later said, "I don't think the operation would of made that much difference, to tell you the truth. Pris, he didn't—she—whatever the hell he is. *It.* I don't think he loved me the way you want somebody to love you." Lloyd was starving himself in the county jail. Pris was defended from rape by a captured counterfeiter out of Fairfax, Virginia, and their affair was two weeks old and going strong.

And Hilary had not come back. Manwarren had paid for a television set while Snuyder had slept the sleep of the sedated, and Snuyder now lay looking at the dimpled ceiling panels, clenching his fists against the pain, and listening without wishing to. Game-show hosts with voices as sweet and insistent as the taste of grape soda cried out with delight and mortification as army sergeants and homemakers and stockbrokers selected numbers and boxes and squares marked off on walls and were awarded either bounty or a consolation prize consisting of a lifetime supply of scuff-resistant, polymer-bound linoleum clean-'n'-polisher for the busy woman who has more to do than wax, for sweet goodness' sake, her floors. Manwarren also watched soap operas that had to do with misplaced babies and frantic adulterers, always on the verge of discovery as incestuous. There were snippets of old movie, fragments of cartoon, crashingly educational disquisitions on the use of C— "C, you *see*, is also in *ka*-ristmas ta*ree!*"—and Gilligan, eternally trapped on his island with Tina Louise and constitutionally incapable of hurling himself upon her, continued to invent ways of extending his imprisonment.

Manwarren, a real critic, commented with alert smugness and an eye for the obvious. "You believe she couldn't remember who invented *noodles*?" he sang. He crowed, "Numbers are from the friggin' Arabs, dummy! No wonder he's a garbageman." Snuyder kept waiting to hear the suck-and-pour of passing traffic on the arterial highway leading into downtown Utica, but all he heard was Manwarren and the objects of his derision. "Hey," he said, "hey, Judge. You handle yourself like this 'Family Court' guy? He takes *no* crap offa nobody, you know? He's got a courtroom fulla morons, by the way. No wonder they ended up in court. They wouldn't know how to cross the *street*." A "M*A*S*H" rerun drove Manwarren into silent sniffles, but he covered well by saying, in a gravelly voice, "I don't think that's a very realistic way to talk about the Korean conflict." Of "Robin Hood," he said, for the first time approving in tone, "I never knew Glynis Johns had knockers like that, Judge."

Snuyder listened. The pain made him blink in disbelief. He looked at the ceiling panels and waited for Hilary to return. She didn't. The balding nurse, this time in a long-sleeved dress, came in with a sedative shot. He was so grateful, he felt embarrassed. His orthopedic surgeon, a tall and slender man who not only didn't smile, but who made clear both his disapproval of the patient and of having to explain to him, explained to him what he would do inside of Snuyder's hip and leg. Pins. Something about pins that would staple him together again, he remembered, after the surgeon was gone and the ceiling had dropped a few feet, and then the orderlies came to roll him away to be pinned into shape.

There was something about dogs, and their terrible odor, and somebody riding one around a muddy country lot. He said *No!* And, knowing that he dreamed while he dreamed, he awaited the dream that would tell him who had sat in the front with him while the police car chased him and he drove—by accident, he insisted to the unseen audience his dream included—into the slow breaking up of his bones. The dogs whined and whined, as if steadily, increasingly, wounded by someone patient and cruel.

The intensive care unit was dark and silent and Snuyder was in very deep pain. His hip burned, and his stomach, and the groin he ached too much to reach for. He kept seeing the skin slide open as the angry surgeon sliced. He yelped for assistance and then shuddered to show the nurse that it was he who needed her promptest sympathies. He was hooked to a drip and a monitor, she explained. Soon he would be taken back to his room. He was fine. The procedure had seemed to be effective, and now his job was to sleep. He slept, but the burning followed him, and he dreamed again of dogs whose fur was stiff with filth, whose eyes dripped mucus, and whose droppings were alive with long white worms. He heard the dogs' howling and he hated Lloyd and Pris. The television set was low, and a curtain divided him from Manwarren, but he knew, waking later, that he was back in his room, and still burning, and all right, alive, not dreaming anymore. The world was in color on the other side of the curtain where a voice electric with triumph told someone named Cecelia that the car she'd won had bucket seats. She screamed.

The woman in the car with him had screamed.

Tony Arizona, his senior clerk, was there in the morning to discuss adjustments of his trial calendar. He brought a cheap glass vase filled with blue flowers that Snuyder couldn't name, and a fifth of Powers' Irish Whiskey. He showed Snuyder how his cases had been distributed among the other sitting judges and that certain others—very few of them—had been postponed. Snuyder said, "No. You gave the boys with the dogs to Levinson."

"He wanted it. He hates queers."

"He *is* queer. I want that one, Tony. Hold it over as long as you can before you give it up. And try not to give it to Levinson. He'll be corn-holing them in chambers by the end of the first hour. Oh, boy."

"They cut you up some, I understand."

"Not to mention *I* cut me up."

"Judge. Dick. I have to give the dog people to Levinson. State wants your calendar cleared. You understand? I'm sorry."

"The suicide thing?"

"They think they might want to look into it."

"Tony. *You* think I tried to kill myself?"

"I think you bent your car around a telephone pole. For what it's worth, I don't care—I mean, I *care*, but only about you. You did it, you didn't do it, you'll work it out and the accident's over, that's that. It's not the suicide thing. It's the woman."

Snuyder heard himself sigh. He could see the letters coming out of his mouth and into a comic-strip bubble: Ahhhh. He waited for Arizona to tell him who she was, and whether he was in love as much as he thought he remembered he once had been.

Arizona said, "They have to do it. *I* don't know anything. And nobody else is gonna say word one. I expect a superficial investigation, announced vindication, and a prompt resumption of jurisprudence as usual."

"And then there's the matter of the law," Richard said.

Arizona, handsome and intelligent, with great brown eyes and a fondness for dark striped shirts such as the maroon one he wore, smiled a broad smile. "Absolutely," he said. "There is always the law, and the public trust, Your Honor."

Manwarren called over the curtain, "You guys believe this? They want me to believe this bimbo just won a trip around the world for two, all expenses paid, by telling greaseball over there with the microphone that Columbus didn't discover America?" The muted shrieks of the victor poured around Manwarren's voice.

The woman in the car had screamed. Arizona poured Powers' into Snuyder's glass with its plastic straw, then he held the straw low, near Snuyder's pillow, so the judge could suck it up. He emptied the glass. Arizona might know her, he thought. But he couldn't be asked. Snuyder was ashamed to remember his wife and his children, his work even down to the specifics of the cases he had tried months and years ago, when he could barely remember the presence, much less identity or necessary intimate facts, of a woman he had carried with him toward jail for certain, and possibly (if Hilary was right) toward death. But she wasn't dead. The nurse had told him that no one was dead. He thought of someone with no face who sat in a wheelchair, paralyzed. He saw her—she was like a burglar in a stocking mask, terrifying because faceless, unnatural—lying in an iron lung, crushed in a fetal sleep forever, staring through a window and drooling, staggering like a monster with hands like claws at her waist, serving the judge's sentence and locked away from his mind.

Arizona slid the Powers' into the drawer of the bedside table when he left. The pain pills and the Powers' combined, and Snuyder flinched. The doctors would have to cut and cut before they found out what was wrong with such a man as he, he told himself. He closed his eyes against the undeniable blade, as if they were cutting, as if they were at the flaccid organs and slimy bone, searching for what was the matter. For him.

It was Hilary who woke him when she sat in the visitor's chair with some effort, swearing as she fell back into the deep seat. After a silence—she breathed as if she had a cold—she said, "How's your catheter, Judge?"

"Hil. Do you know who she is?"

Manwarren turned the volume down.

Snuyder whispered: "The woman in the car?" He took a breath and then shouted, "Manwarren! Turn the sound up! Mind your own business!" He felt as though he'd been running. "Bastard," he said. He shouted it: "Bastard!"

The sound came up slightly, but Snuyder knew that Manwarren was unchastened.

Hilary said, "Why, who would that be, Your Honor? How *is* your catheter, by the way?"

"I hurt all over. Okay? I'm in a lot of pain. I'm humiliated. I'm under investigation, Hilary. They're looking into my comportment on and off the bench."

"I didn't know you'd done it on the bench. And you can't really blame them. A suicide is not always the most stable interpreter of the law, never mind his other little quirks and foibles."

"It's apparently because of the woman. That was all I could get from Arizona."

Hilary said, "I wish *I* could get more from Tony. He's really a piece."

"Please don't talk like that."

"Do I really need to tell you about the hypocrisy of this discussion?"

"No."

"You know I'm disgusted with you. That's an easy one.

Disgust is easy and seeing it's easy. But what *kills* me—"

"Hil, I can't remember a lot. I remember *us*, overall, you know. And a lot of times and things. But I can't remember a lot."

"And that includes the slut in the car? *That's* what kills me. It's so *sad* for you that you can't. I feel *sorry* for you. You son of a bitch."

"Hil, she's literally a slut?"

"Oh. You boy. You infant. You expect me to keep track of your infidelities and log your bedroom transactions, don't you. You'd ask me for help. You know, knowing me, I'd probably give it. You—*boy*." She wept mascara lines down her face.

Snuyder said, "I'm promiscuous? I thought I remembered that I really loved her." Their silence widened, and a woman on the television set said, "I wouldn't dare tell them that!"

Hilary sighed. She said, "I think I'll go home. I understand they'll bring you back for therapy, and you'll use a walker. You'll be able to walk someday. I feel sorry it's so bad. Also, Richard, I'm moving. During the latter part of the week. I'll telephone you."

"Where?" he said. "Did we decide to do this?"

Hilary shook her head. "It started when you told me *you* were moving out."

"Yes," he said. He remembered at once, and as if he looked through transparent overlays: long arguments, slower and longer conversations, Hilary on the phone, Hilary weeping black lines while holding a teacup to her mouth, himself standing before her and wishing aloud that he were dead. He remembered the words about remorse that he had tried to say, and the fear of how they'd tell their sons. Hilary had told him about Warren, calling from college, in tears, because he had sensed that it all had gone wrong. Snuyder said, "I'm sorry. I don't remember women. A woman. *The* woman, I guess you'd call her."

"Yes," Hilary said.

"I apologize. If it's because of her, I apologize. I don't suppose it would make any difference now, seeing that I don't know her anymore. Is she the—"

But Hilary was up and moving. She was at the door. He heard the squelch of her crepe soles on the linoleum floor.

He said, "I suppose not."

She said, "See you, Judge." Then, too brightly, she said, "Actually, I'll see you in court." She laughed too hard, and she left.

Manwarren called over at once. "You know what, Dick? I think you shoulda hit the pole a little harder, you don't mind my saying so. You're in a pickle, to say the least, big fella."

"You think I'm in a pickle, Manwarren?"

"Call me Manny."

"I'm going to make a call, Manny. While you sleep. I'm going to have a man who runs a chain of fish stores in Syracuse—I'm going to ask him to have an employee in the Manlius packing plant come over here while you're sleeping and kill you. He's going to open your chest with his bare hands, and he's going to tear out every vital organ in your body one at a time. And he won't wear gloves. His nails will be dirty. He picks his nose. Do you understand me, Manny?"

The sound increased in volume, and bright voices clung

195

to the ceiling tiles. She had been in the car with him. She had screamed when they'd hit. Hilary was leaving because of her, and he didn't know who the woman was. The set cried out and the voices rose. He was alleged to have attempted suicide. He would never walk normally, and his sons would not come to him. He knew that too. Hilary would take all their money and the men on the ethics committee might remove him from the bench. He thought they wouldn't, since none of them was terribly honest either, and each was equally impeachable. They would probably reprimand him, and he would suffer a trial-by-headline. But he would return to the bench, he thought. He would live alone in an apartment such as the ones near the Sangertown Mall. Or perhaps he might move into Clinton, where the old large houses east of town were divided into Victorian cells for bachelors and men such as he. He would drive alone to work and sit in his courtroom. He would say who was right in the eyes of the law. He never would know who the woman had been, or what they had been together, or why.

It was an empty mourning, he thought—abstracted, like a statement about how dreadful the starving African babies are. He wondered if the woman he loved and didn't know might have told him she was leaving. Perhaps he had aimed at killing *her*.

He heard himself whimpering, and made himself stop. He heard Manwarren's television set, and then the dogs in the trailer who'd whimpered, he'd been told by the deputies, before they heard the foot on the door; once rescued, they'd begun to bark and wail. He thought of Lloyd and Pris, armed and marching, in their terrible fetor and loss, to recover their starved, sick dogs. They were separated now. Poor Lloyd: he had taken the hostages, and only when his prisoners lay on the floor in the deeds-recording office had he realized that he wanted to insist on one more prize, the operation that would change Pris's sex. It was then, Snuyder remembered realizing, as he'd read Lloyd's deposition, that Lloyd had understood how permanently separate he had always been from Pris and probably always would be. "He don't love me," Lloyd had said. "How could he?"

It was a case he had wanted to try. They were accused of a dozen public-health violations and twenty or more violations of the civil and criminal codes. And they were so innocent, Snuyder thought. No one should be allowed to be so innocent. Shots rang out on a TV show, and wheels screamed. Snuyder jumped, remembering the sound of locked brakes. She had been there with him, in the same small space. And he had leaned back, locked his elbows and knees, and had driven at the pole. He had. And he would not know her. And even that was not the worst part.

She *might* return. He would have to decide about trying to heal, or waiting for her next door to death. He forced himself to breathe evenly, as if he slept. The TV set made sounds. The dogs stood on the bed and chairs, they cried their pain and hunger, their fear. Manwarren cackled. The police would come soon with questions. He was held together with pins. He was going to die, but of natural causes, and many years from today. He knew it. He smelled the dark air of the trailer, and he heard the gaunt dogs whine.

One More Wave
of Fear

I DID NOT GROW UP despising nature on Argyle Road, at the far southern edge of Prospect Park, in Brooklyn in the 1950s. But I did come to hate the upper-case initial with which my parents said the word. Our house was set back from a street on which few children but a lot of lean, straight men and women lived. As I remember them, most were white and Protestant and wealthy, and apparently convinced that their long black cars should frequently be washed but rarely driven. My parents also called it Natural History, or The Out of Doors. My father taught science in a junior high school on Nostrand Avenue, and he loved his work. It didn't seem ever to stop. Lanky, almost thin, with great swollen knuckle joints and knees, with elbows that were sharp and a chin nearly pointed, a nose that led him as he was leading us, my father, with his Ed.D., was considered a master teacher by his colleagues and his principal and many of his students and himself. While my mother cooked, he lectured on asparagus. When I rode with him in our DeSoto, he talked about the flowers that grew in vacant lots and through the sidewalk cracks. And on weekends we took wearying walks with the Audubon Society or the Brooklyn Bird Club and, when I grew older, we hiked with the Appalachian Mountain Club on trails in upstate New York. I remember those trips as a blur of similarities: the same swarms of insects at the nose and eyes; the same wet heat that was pooled about us by the same clinging brush; the same unnatural, galloping pace that suggested flight from the birds and plants and marshes we had come to pursue.

I sulked, at eleven and twelve and thirteen, when they forced me to stroll through Prospect Park while searching, say, for the pileated woodpecker: eighteen adults, in various stages (to me) of decomposition, and one slouching kid, who hunted through touch football games and horizontal lovers and the droppings of unleashed dogs for a bird. My mother hit me after the woodpecker trip. She swung her fists against my back, chasing me up the stairs and into my room, shouting that I'd ruined Nature for her. That night we made up. She explained, my small and never-placid mother, that her difficult childhood in the slums of east Manhattan had led her to marry my father, and to read many books, and to seek the consolations of The Out of Doors. In the darkness of my unkempt room, my mother sat on the chair at my desk, and I lay on my bed, and she told me how little fresh air she had breathed as a girl, and how she had longed even then for Brooklyn, and such a neighborhood as ours—"You know, the suburbs," she said—and how she felt at peace when with my father on what she called a Field Trip. Those words were another signal for me, like the phrase The Out of Doors, to long to get as far inside and close to walls as I could.

We forgave each other, sometimes almost daily, and my father lectured, my mother wrote her books about the children of the slums—aimed at children, and written in medicinal sentences (they were good for you, but unpleasant), and published at last by a vanity press, and finally piled in our basement, under heavy pack frames and canvas rucksacks and three sets of snowshoes that we'd never used. My father, the heir of wealthy parents, was a Socialist who used to be a Communist. The more his colleagues turned each other in to education vigilantes—those were the days of naming names to such as the House Un-American Activities Committee—the less Communist, the more Socialist, and the more secret about each, he became. I think he feared to lose his job because, like many compulsive teachers, he was a voice in search of ears on which he might fall. He forgave America, I forgave my mother, and she forgave the need to have to make me understand her. And we walked the hundreds of acres of Prospect Park, and my father pointed at leaves, and told me which were diseased and which could be brewed as a tea, and which would make me itch. I played at "Captain Video," my favorite television show—"Hand me the atomic hammer!" he would cry to the Video Ranger, as they waged their war against the evil Doctor Pauli—in the farthest place from Nature I could find: my mind. And they *all* made me itch.

One Sunday morning, when I should have been playing

stickball with other thirteen-year-old boys, or—better—looking at Don Winslow of the Navy on TV, I was entering Prospect Park with the rest of the bird club, walking from the assembly point in Grand Army Plaza, under the great arched monument. My mother wore her 9 x 30 binoculars, and my father his, on thin leather neck straps. I had been loaned a pair, which I kept in their case and carried, like a book, in my hand: I didn't want to be mistaken for someone who cared about birds. My expression, I am certain, was that of a recent lobotomy patient; it was crucial to me that no reflection of feeling or thought be visible on my flesh. Demonstrating nothing, and looking at nothing, I followed the Leader, as he was called, a man named Ted who pointed at birds and named them.

Ted, fat and round-faced and sweaty, as he looked through his binoculars suggested to me the attentiveness of U-boat captains in war. "Nothing," he said, lowering his glasses. "Garbage stuff."

"Well, a towhee," my mother said, noting its existence in a little spiral book she carried.

"No," my father said. "No. Sparrow. A tree sparrow."

"You mean eastern sparrow," Ted said.

"Well, they're one and the same," my father said, entering the bird in his own spiral book.

My mother said, patting my father's arm in a friendly way, while breezes blew her hair, "I think it's a towhee." She chanted it.

My father shook his head. He smiled at her, but I knew that smile. Its ferocity kept me in check on trips such as these. I stood and I waited. He said, "Sparrow."

My mother smiled and shrugged. I guess my father knew

what the shrug said. He blushed, and his voice deepened. He said, "Your towhee is too small by an inch, lacks a round black spot on its breast, and is making the strange mistake of *calling* wrong. Listen."

Ted moved closer to my parents, while the others in the group moved on, making do without Leadership. Ted and my father cocked their heads; my mother didn't, but she stared at my father, as if he were another curious bird.

"There!" my father said. "You hear? *Teelwit!* he's calling. *Teelwit! Teelwit!* Am I right?"

My mother nodded.

He asked, "And your towhee?"

"All right," my mother said.

"Your towhee?"

"*Fine,*" she said. "You're right."

"What does your towhee sing?"

My mother looked at him, and then she turned and walked to the rest of the group. Ted looked away from my father and followed her; the group moved along.

My father, his face still red, turned to me and looked, with no sign of seeing *me* in his eyes that I could find. He lifted his binoculars, then lowered them gently on their strap until they hung. They seemed to be heavy on his neck. He said, "As your mother well knows, your towhee calls *Chewink! Chewink!* You can't mistake *Chewink!* for *Teelwit!* Can you?"

In those days, there were waves of fear in Brooklyn neighborhoods—anyway, in ours. There had been a wave of fear about Germans possibly landing at night at Plum Beach, near Sheepshead Bay. There had been a wave of fear about the shabby men spotted chalking arrows in the street and on the curbs of certain blocks, one of them ours; the fear had been that Gypsies or tramps would be flooding the streets of Brooklyn, begging for food and clothing, hiring out for work they'd never perform. The men, we had finally learned, were marking routes for the delivery of new telephone directories. And of course there had been waves of fear over polio epidemics and the arrival on the block of Negro families. The wave of fear when I was six was squirrels. Brooklyn was filled with pigeons and squirrels, and the squirrels, with their thick gray pelt, their long graceful tail, their clever paws and large dark eyes, had been a part of my childhood, like curled cats and wandering dogs. But to householders they were like the rats to which they were cousins. They scrabbled in attics and ate the insulation of electrical wires, it was said. They stored nuts uninvited. They were invaders. They were part of all the movies of my childhood. James Arness and James Whitmore in *Them!* Giant ants, atomic mutation, man's meddling with nature. It invaded a small western town. Just like the squirrels in Brooklyn. Or *Invasion of the Body-Snatchers.* Or *Plan 9 from Outer Space.* Or how about all those Japanese things with one American actor and a huge *moth* running amok, everybody milling around, talking Japanese a mile a minute, which gets dubbed as "Remain calm. Tranquillity is better than dying of fear and disorder. Get your guns." It was as if the *squirrels* were pillaging and looting. In *Brooklyn.*

At breakfast, my parents discussed the attic noises they had heard at night. My mother's lips curled with loathing. My father frowned with distress, and his voice deepened.

"We can deal with this," he said. "I know how to control a situation like this. I'll be home from school late, and then we'll see."

That day, he drove off to P.S. 240 with a certain harried look that I later came to associate with serious thought; he was showing my mother that he was working. And he did come home late that night, long after we had eaten dinner without him. He carried under each arm a long rectangular machine made of what I think was tin. There were tilted doors inside each contraption, and wires that banged as he walked from the back door through to the kitchen.

"Traps," he announced, slamming them onto the kitchen counter. "*Humane* traps. We catch 'em, but we don't kill 'em."

Above us, as my father in the attic labored to bait and arm the traps, the small gray squirrels ran beneath the eaves and in the walls. They had grown confident, and at night I heard their claws unhesitatingly march on our wood. At first I had been frightened that a squirrel would chew through my walls and enter my room and bite me. And then I remembered my barefoot days in the backyard during the summer—I was never allowed to go barefoot on the sidewalks because, as my mother summed matters up, "Where I haven't looked before you walk on it is dirty. That's the rule." The squirrels had never bothered me out back, and the house, I figured, was still more ours than theirs. So I grew too confident, myself, and I listened to them racing in the woodwork at night, and I smiled for my parents' despair. Cataclysm was really all a kid had going for him until he was taller than his parents.

When I woke and heard my father going to the attic to

check on the traps, I fancied that I had heard them going off at night, and that I'd heard the shrill cries and frantic searching of trapped gentle Disney-creatures, prisoner in my house. Then my father would descend and say, "Nope. Nothing."

More and more, my mother greeted his report with a low and guttural wordless statement of woe—as if my father had struck her. He took to coming down in silence. I would listen to their soundlessness as he dressed for breakfast while she, always in her robe at breakfast time, sat with him in their unstated failure. And at night, they would work again on the bait. They went through cheese, Ritz crackers, soda biscuits, Arnold bread, then cups of Planter's peanuts, then cups of nuts that my mother cracked in the afternoon while we waited for my father to come home. Finally, because peanut butter was my father's favorite food, I suggested that he use it in his traps. I was watching him eat a peanut butter and jelly sandwich, and I was thinking that, with his thin fingers at his mouth, he seemed to nibble like a squirrel. My mother shrugged, and my father raised his brows; that night, they baited with Skippy. Smooth. I recall thinking how gummy the mouths of the squirrels would be.

It worked. There had been no strangled squirrel cry, no slam of gates into place, but in the morning, as my mother waited in her gathering tension, my father went up to the attic, scrambled about a bit, and then came down slowly, clanking, and bearing trapped beasts. "*Yes!*" he called, carrying Natural History. "*Yes!*"

When I came to breakfast, I expected to find them happy. But they were—if not outright huddled—concentrated at the far end of our kitchen table, as far away from the traps on the kitchen floor as they could be. Inside each trap was a squirrel, shivering. The slanted doors had dropped to perpendicular, and the squirrels were walled inside them. Now, my father told us, sounding as if he tried to sound buoyant, but talking in a way that made me look at him as sharply as I looked at the squirrels, *now*, all that had to happen was that someone take the squirrels to the park—far away from the house, as far as someone might feel like walking—and then set them free.

"Someone," my mother said.

"You," he told her. "I have to teach."

"I don't *know* anything about squirrels—you're the scientist."

"Yes," he said. "And I told you everything you need to know. You carry the cages by the handles on top. The squirrel can't reach you, no matter how he tries. Then you trip the door in each cage when you're a good long distance from the house. The squirrels run away. Then *you* run away."

"That part I know about," my mother said.

So I did not wait for the school bus that morning. I dressed for autumn weather in my brown corduroy jacket and peaked brown corduroy hat. My mother, who chose to wear gloves that morning, hefted each cage by its handle—her face suggested that she carried each squirrel by its tail—and we slowly made our way up Argyle, across Church Avenue into the Parade Grounds, where kids skipping school played ball, and across which we were going to walk to reach the lowest tip of Prospect Park, near the lake.

Brooklyn in those days, and especially in parts around our

neighborhood, was filled with trees and rich bushes, thick hedge, undeveloped fields that weren't even vacant lots yet—they were more like scraps of leftover forest—and everyplace in the giant trees, it seemed to me that morning in fall, squirrels swarmed, their tails floating behind them, softly flicked pennants of my mother's dismay.

We had to pause a lot, because my mother carried the traps away from her body, and her arms grew weary. I offered to carry one and was refused in the way parents decline the assistance of children—a signal that sacrifice of some considerable quantity is going on. We made our slow unhappy progress over the Parade Grounds, walking across baseball diamonds and having nothing to do with play; when I ran down the first-base line and waited for my mother to catch up, her face informed me that second base was not in my immediate future. We were on business, her frown made clear, and as far as I was concerned, from that moment on, the day was one more Field Trip.

We had a long distance to go, we were still rather far from the park itself, but the trees grew thicker, and the squirrels on them seemed to multiply. I noticed them, and I noticed that my mother noticed them. How could she not? They crawled, they scurried, they sat up and nibbled, they ran; sometimes, scrambling up a tree, one would stop, then turn, then hold there upside down, like a salamander on a stone wall in *National Geographic*. The squirrels made chattering sounds, and long loud squeaks, and some of them silently ran, in bursts, along the tree limbs. I remembered my parents talking of how squirrels hunted down birds, and I did cheer them on, though silently.

My mother said, "Enough."

"Daddy said—"

"Daddy wants to say, he can come and carry the squirrels and tell *them*. Mommy says enough. Get back where it's safe. Go back."

I retreated obediently, so that no vengeance-seeking, human-devouring squirrel, mutated by nuclear testing, or inhabited by invisible beings from another world who sought our blood or souls or air supply—or which were simply part of the enormous danger my parents always discovered— could attack. My mother, in her gloves and long, tent-shaped tan tweed coat, bent above the cages. I saw the squirrels shrink from her. I watched her shrink from them.

I heard a sharp snapping sound, and then something clicked, and a squirrel paused at the end of a trap. It moved back inside.

"Shoo," my mother said. "Go on." She waited, then kicked at the side of the trap. "Shoo!" The squirrel remained. My mother said, "Go *on*!" With the tips of her fingers, she picked up the closed end of the trap and shook it. She shook it harder, then banged on its side with a fist. "*Go!*"

The squirrel scampered down the incline of the trap and ran away, pausing to inspect; it ran again, paused, then ran farther. It went to a nearby tree and disappeared. The second squirrel went at once, and then my mother sat heavily down on an empty trap.

I watched the tree to which both squirrels had run. It was extremely broad at the base of the trunk, and its heavy thick branches were alive with squirrels. They ran, they paused, they hung upside down and right side up, they chattered and made their high-pitched sounds. As I watched them, they became the central object of vision; the tree they ran on was secondary to what inhabited it, and the tree receded, the squirrels advanced, and that was true of neighboring trees as well. The ground, too, seemed to ripple with their motion at the base of every tree.

My mother sat on her trap on the endless green-going-ocher of the Parade Grounds, looking up at the trees, the ceaseless motion of the squirrels as they worked and as the winter came in upon them. "They'll come back," she said. "You can't keep that—that"—she swung her arm in its heavy coat, she pointed with her finger in its glove, indicating trees and what swarmed in them—"there's no *way* of keeping them under control, believe you me." She diminished, staring up at them, like the pretty girl in the horror film who at last understands what has come for her.

 North

IN THE PICTURES of us you can see how willing we were from the start. We smiled so hard for the camera. We did what we were told. You go explain that to a dry-goods salesgirl in the largest independent variety store in the Mohawk Valley (except for Utica), New York.

I told her, "No. It wasn't the Starving Artists Show. It wasn't the Adirondacks. That's just a silly thing of mine. Look. Finally, it worked out to where it was, you know, time. There wasn't anything. I mean, we'd got to the point where I had a framed picture of him hanging up next to the little Drexel cherrywood desk where I sat when I paid the bills."

"Good reason," Franchot said. She was a tall blonde with a high waist and yellow teeth. She didn't mean it unkindly, and she blushed to prove it as she lit another Kool.

"It was the picture his parents had shot when he was eight years old, Franchot. With the white shirt with the big collar? And the wide, short necktie with big raspberries on the bright blue background?"

"Oh. Well, that's cute."

"Sure is. Sure was. And you know what he had in his office? Well. His cubicle. You know what?"

"*Your* picture."

"My picture. Me, six years old, in the pinafore with the white buttons and the white lace collar."

"What color pinafore?" Franchot asked.

"The picture was in black and white."

"And you don't remember the color?"

"No, I don't. That's not the point, is it?"

She shook her head. Her fine light hair spun. She waited for me to tell her what the point was—why I had left a husband after four years.

Vigary came into the back room of the store, just then. "Hi, girls," he said. Franchot smiled, but I nodded coldly. I was not about to be called a girl by a man who was wearing the bottom half of a green clown's suit, wide flat blueberry-colored feet and all. His upper half was in a light blue oxford button-down. I could tell it wasn't good cloth. It was one of those drip-dry combination fabrics with the wide pores. All those cheap shirts have a kind of weave to them, if the man wearing one doesn't have an undershirt on his belly hairs stick out the tiny little holes. So there was Gene Vigary, with his belly hairs and his blue plastic clown's feet.

He looked at my face, but I refused to smile for him. He'd have to learn. He set down a large carton and he sighed. He smiled at Franchot and she showed her yellow teeth in return.

"United Parcel just came through again," Gene said. He motioned at the opened carton. "Our costumes."

I said, "My former husband used to wear shirts like that. Every day. He had eight of them. He rotated them so the armpits didn't get, you know, stained or stale. They can turn yellow on you, from the sweat. I washed one a night. For four years. One thousand four hundred and sixty-one shirts."

Vigary nodded. He closed his eyes, the way you do when you count up in your mind. I knew from the way he had nodded that I talked too much about my former husband. Women my age do, I noticed: widows and divorcées, as my mother liked to call us. I thought she thought *divorcée*, being French, was something like *whore*. "You figured in an extra day for leap year," he said at last.

I said, "What did you mean, Gene, our costumes?"

He pointed with pride at the carton as if, in the storeroom consisting mainly of steel shelves with cartons on them, it had already earned pride of place.

"All the way from Warren, Ohio," he sang. He rubbed his hands as if they'd done some work. I looked away, because I knew the news was bad. I didn't have to watch to know his jowls shook, and his red-orange hair threatened to fly off from where its one lank hank, parted starting at his left ear, tried to ride his bald head as if it belonged up there. He said, "Beel and Steinberg, Costumes and Wigs."

I wanted to ask him if he'd bought himself a red-orange wig to wear in place of the dye-job-and-hair-shaft he was featuring. But I needed a job, and this was a job. I looked at boxes of one-size-fits-all baseball caps, and rabbit-shaped cookie cutters. On the far wall was the framed picture of young Gene Vigary standing next to a dark-skinned man named Sandy Amoros. He'd told us proudly how he'd seen him make some wonderful catch off of some famous baseball player in New York City. Nobody else who shopped in the store seemed to care either. This black man in the picture with Gene wasn't Jackie Robinson, and that was all I knew or cared to.

"I don't intend to wear a costume on Hallowe'en," I said.

"Oh, I want to," Franchot said. "I love dressing up."

"I love dressing up, too," I said. "But dressing up isn't wearing huckleberry-flavored shoes. With all due respect."

"None taken," Vigary said. "But there is a costume in there for you, and I think you're gonna love it. I do hope so, on account of tomorrow, the thirty-first of October, the employees in Vigary's Dry Goods are gonna be wearing the uniform of the day. And the uniform of the day—well, lemme see"—and he sounded like his mouth was full of honey and Hershey's Kisses—"Franchot, she'll be wearing"—like a clown sent to cheer up the orphans, he slowly pulled it out— "a Playboy Bunny costume!"

Franchot actually squealed. She actually slapped her palms together. It put me in mind of nothing so much as one of those TV contest shows, where women jump up and down in costumes and shout at each other about how much kitchen appliances cost.

Vigary held up a few pieces of black cloth and some mesh stockings with some sort of insects on the weave, cloth butterflies or moths, I thought.

He handed her outfit to Franchot, and she examined it, as if it mattered. He said, "Kelly?"

It was like getting news from the dentist.

"Yes, Gene," I said.

"Here."

I turned back to look. It seemed to be some kind of flimsy blue-black nightgown.

"What's that, Gene?"

"Your costume."

"You sure it's skimpy enough? I mean, will you have enough skin showing in the store tomorrow?"

"Couple of pretty girls like you, I thought we should show ya off."

"You sure did. Who am I?"

"You're Elvira."

"Elvira?"

"The lady with the big—you know! Witch lady shows the midnight horror movies on TV? She's kinda sarcastic. But really put together good. You remind me of her."

"I've been getting all the horror I need before midnight," I told him.

"Now, don't you be a spoilsport, Kelly."

"I'd really like to not have to wear this, Gene."

"But it's part of the job," he said. "Isn't it."

"It really is?"

He nodded. His face might just as well have been an elbow or a knee for all the expression it gave me. His little dark eyes looked out from behind his face. His bright hair flapped. I thought the clown costume would suit him well. I always thought that clowns were mean, crazy people inside of those noses and lips.

Franchot said, "I could come over early, Kel. We could make up and everything before work."

"Great," Gene said. "Great initiative. It's *business*. It's what holidays like Hallowe'en are supposed to remind us."

"I thought it was when the dead came back," I said.

He said, "Come on, Kelly. That's for kids."

Sid had told me I should keep the house. He'd have told me anything he thought I'd want to hear. Either he was convinced that I'd wake up, like the princess on her funeral bed, and forgive him while asking his forgiveness, or he figured he was so guilty of something that he owed me all he could give. The poor man was wounded, and I couldn't give him so much as a bandage when I left. I got my own apartment, not too far from the mall on Route 12. It's north of Utica, and I could hear the low gears of the trucks. It always sounded to me like they were winding up for the long haul north. Route 12 went up to the Adirondacks, and I always thought that one day I'd pack what I could into the AMC Eagle and aim myself for some lakeside fishing town up there, and in the shadow of the mountains I would sell mosquito repellent and bait from behind a counter, and live in a little cabin, and meet people who were there to find out what really mattered—or, even better, who knew. I still could do that.

The apartment wasn't bad. The walls were made of not much more than Sheetrock, of course. Everything's built that way, these days. But the moldings were nice, and the wall-to-wall carpet wasn't called champagne. You get to appreciate that, apartment hunting. It was a nice dark color called toast, and the paint on the walls was closer to an ivory, or parchment, than just plain white that they all tried to give you. I had the old bedroom suite from Sid and me, and some old furniture from my parents' garage. Every once in a while, I bought a painting of a mountain or a lake that I thought might be in the Adirondacks. It was only a two-hour drive to get there, but I had never gone. So I guessed about the high pointy mountains I had heard of, and all the lakes. Every now and again there would be a Starving Artist Sale at the Holiday Inn in Rome, New York. All these painters couldn't sell their work, so they painted mountains and lakes and cute animals, and all the pictures, all framed already, were stacked up in the convention center at the Holiday Inn, arranged by sofa size and chair size, according to where you needed a painting. I never saw the artists there. I'd have liked to talk to one. You need to meet people who guess at what's what and who believe in it enough to starve. I only saw Franchot and Vigary, and the ladies who dragged their children in while they shopped for incense candles and potholders and trivets with blue pictures on a white background of Dutch windmills. I didn't date. I didn't want to have to describe myself or explain myself or listen to anyone's lies describing them to me.

I fried up some onions and peppers with yesterday's rice, and I made a hamburger. I always bought ground round because I figured you owed yourself something. I listened to the news report on the radio, and I drank a whopping belt of Cutty Sark. I learned that one thing from Sid: "Hey, Kelly," he used to say, when I had a bottle of something cheap in my hand. He'd point at the Inver House and he'd say, "Kelly. You're gonna put that stuff in your *stomach*." That was a good true thing to remember.

I took my dinner into the living room, and I finished my drink. The local news was on the TV, but they didn't really know anything I didn't. They knew the *details*, but I could have told them, walking in the door and not even bothering to turn the set on. Two-car collision at some street corner. Baby burned or beaten or neglected out in the countryside someplace. A factory closing down. A politician hoping for something out loud, or wondering if we really needed it anymore. And weather coming, a little warm, and then cooler, and some jokes about trick-or-treat, and don't let your children eat razor blades or glass. And then the sports.

The thing about Cutty Sark is it tastes like the ground it comes out of. Especially if you drink it warm, which I did, because I didn't want to have to go for ice cubes when I splashed in the little extra bit more. There I was, I thought, drinking the peat (whatever that was) and the water out of Scotland. That was a place I should go to, I thought.

Then they showed Elvira. They said she'd be showing movies at midnight, on Halloween. She came out in her skin-tight black dress with all the skin between her tits showing down to her belly, and they were so big. Plastic, I thought, or—what was it they used?—silicon. I wondered if silicon was the same as plastic. Sid had always talked about silicon in the computer he sold, and I thought about giant tits that stood straight out in a slinky dress, ticking away inside with little computer chips. Breasts that can think, I thought. I heard myself laugh, and I hated the sound.

I made myself clean up right away. I turned the TV off and changed my clothes in the bedroom with its big bed. I was standing in there alone, pulling jeans up and sliding down my Champion Mills hooded sweatshirt that said Green Bay Packers, on sale at the factory outlet, and I stopped. I stood in there next to a pretty painting of a lake and a maple tree dropping its leaves onto the still surface of the lake. My pants were undone, and my sweatshirt was up around my neck, and I just stopped still. I put my hand on my stomach, and I jumped because my palm was so cold.

I was remembering how Sid had cried. I think he'd been as impressed as I was, because he kept saying, "Look at me. I never cry, Kelly, ever, and I'm crying! For *you*!"

That had made me cry. We'd stood there, in the kitchen of our big house out near the Clinton reservoir, and we'd just cried at each other. It seemed to me, later on, that we were trying to see who could show the most sadness.

"Sid," I remembered telling him, "you win."

"Oh," he had said, like a little kid. "Kelly. We're not going to do this?"

I said, "I meant you're sadder than I am."

And then he'd really started in to cry.

And that night, Halloween eve, in my new apartment off Route 12, I felt worse about his crying than when he had cried. It was like I suddenly understood what had happened. No. I understood how much damage I had done. You'd have thought that my belly would warm up my hand, or that my skin would get used to my fingers. But nothing got used to anything. I stood half-dressed, with my fingers feeling cold to my belly and my belly feeling hot to my hand. We'd wanted some freedom at the start, we decided, so we didn't try to have kids. I thought about Sid and me, hanging each other's childhood photos on the wall.

I was thirty-five years old, and I hadn't touched a man for almost a year. I wondered if I was going to be a new kind of nun, one of the Sisters of Annulment. My mother told me she had changed her church because she couldn't face Father Boris. I had offered to change my name, if that would help things, and she'd cried. There wasn't anybody I had not made cry who loved me.

The bodice was held together with a dark mesh. But it still didn't plunge right, the way Elvira's dress dived down between those unmoving melons. The mesh looked wrinkled, and so did I. The dress hugged me tight on the hips, and the slit seemed too far front, instead of to the side. And the bodice drooped. "I'm an underdeveloped nation," I told myself in the mirror that morning.

Franchot came over for tea, and she looked wonderful. I was jealous of her black mesh stockings and her long round legs, and the way her breasts threatened to jump out and sing. Her little rabbit's ears flapped in her hair the way her bosom wobbled when she walked. I figured that Vigary would either throw her down on the floor in the stockroom, or offer to leave his wife that afternoon.

Franchot smoked Kools and drank herbal tea, and when I came out of the bedroom wearing a plain blue corduroy skirt with a blue and gray striped shirt, she hissed out her smoke and drank off some tea and said, "I thought you might."

"I can't wear a costume," I said.

"You're so stubborn, Kelly."

"Franchot, people wear costumes, they *hide* from each other."

"So? Don't you *want* to hide from Vigary? Or do you like getting felt up near the bath mats?"

"He doesn't feel—he doesn't touch me!"

Franchot lit another Kool. "I wish I could say the same."

"Tell him not to."

"Getting felt up is the uniform of the day, Kelly."

"Wait a minute."

"I really don't want to go looking for another job again."

"Wait a minute."

"I want to make my wage, and go to school at night, and get a degree and—"

"Franchot! Wait a minute."

"What, Kelly?"

"He molests you?"

"I don't know if that's the word."

"How about he violates you."

"Kelly. He arranges his whole entire *day* so at one point or another in it he can get the back of his hand, or the edge of his arm, on my chest. That's all. I mean, it's enough. But it's also all."

"And because you want to be a dental hygienist, and because he pays you a wage, you let him do that."

"I try not to let him. But he works awfully hard at it."

"Oh, I bet you he does."

"Yes," Franchot said.

I thought of myself in the bedroom, with my cold hand on my stomach.

"So he gets to dress you up like his dream."

"Oh, it's a costume, is all, Kelly."

"You tell me what you told me, and you can say it's just a costume?"

She nodded, and the smoke bounced out of her mouth in jagged little bursts.

"There's no such a thing as just a costume," I said. "You're either in disguise, or you're—sincere."

"I'm sincere, Kelly!"

"I know. I know. Franchot, I'm asking you for the sake of my *life*. Don't cry. All right? Please?"

She nodded. Her eyes were wet, but she sniffed and smiled and looked at a Starving Artist painting of a snowstorm in some hills. She looked back, and she said, "So you're going to wear the Elvira suit?"

"Only if I die and you and my mother lay me out in it."

"You don't mean that," Franchot said.

I carried it to work in my big leather handbag, along with my apple and my herbal tea. It was Vigary's, and he could have it back. The stores had pumpkins in their windows, and the merchants wore costumes. They all must have decided at the last Rotary meeting, I thought, when they ate steak or roast beef, and drank too much beer, and then finished the evening off with sweet liqueurs that made them drunk. Sid had gone to a few. He always came home randy. I figured they spent the end of the evening talking about the waitress's body, trading dirty jokes. One night, he'd come in and he'd barely waited to get his overcoat and sports jacket off before he began to grope and pinch and feel. He'd been clumsy, all right, and he'd smelled stale. But that wasn't why I'd pushed him away like a girl on a date. I'd felt my face go red with my rage. I remember I'd shouted, "Oh, no you don't, buster."

"Kelly," he had whispered. His entire existence, I figured, was slightly south of his reversible brown and black belt. His face looked young and sweet, like the face in the picture on the wall above my desk.

"Yeah. Kelly. Where was my name the last two weeks? When somebody around here was too tired, and then too busy, and then had to watch the CBS late double feature? It takes getting drunk with your rowdy toads at the Clinton Inn, does it?"

"This isn't really *that* serious, is it, Kel? We're not fighting, are we?"

"Oh, no, Sid. Why should we fight? You keep on getting drunk once a month at the Rotary, and then come in here and—what is it? Get your ashes shoveled?"

He'd giggled. "Hauled."

"That's disgusting."

"Yes. It's not what I'm—"

"Sid. Listen. It isn't a matter of *what*. It's a matter of *who*. Who you are with me. Who I am to you. *Who*. And what you're after here isn't me. If it was, you'd have been around before this. Not drunk. And not all worked up by whatever dirty talk you and the other merchant princes have been talking. You're supposed to want *me*. Actual, true, me. Not just—skin."

And he had said, "I never knew—you know, that you—"

And I had said, "Well, learn."

I said, "What?"

I was in the stockroom. I had stowed my purse and my coat, and I was making a cup of tea. The clown with the fat middle and bright green nose to match his suit and the blue wig that matched his feet said, "You're not in your costume yet."

I put my tea mug down. "I'm not going to wear one, Gene."

"Franchot's wearing hers."

"She looks adorable."

He made his green eyebrows go up and down. "You'd look adorable too," he said.

I shook my head.

"Uniform of the day," he said, like it was still a joke between us.

He held his arms out. He was pleading, the position of his arms seemed to say. His face didn't look like anyone's pleading face. It was green and red and blue, and it was a huge, happy face. That face could never plead. It laughed at whoever it looked at.

"I don't wear a uniform," I said. "Otherwise, I could have been a waitress at the Inn. I'd have made good tips."

"If you didn't give the diners an argument about taking orders from them," he said. His voice made it seem like a joke. His eyes didn't.

"But you're not ordering me to wear that dress," I said.

The clown face looked at me.

"That isn't who I *am*, Gene."

The clown face said, "And whoever told you it mattered one small jot or tittle who in hell you think you are or what you think you want? Whoever lied about that, Kelly?"

Out front, a customer whistled a wolf call at Franchot. In the stockroom, I looked at the thick painted lips that had spoken. Above the round bright nose, the eyes were dark. They were like the dark jelly you figure you would see if somebody's eyes were torn out. They were looking straight at me. Who's that, I thought.

I finally said, "If you'll give me a little privacy, I'll get myself dressed."

He came up closer, and his green gloved fingers held my arms.

"Good girl," he said. "Good girl."

His arms were at my sides. Each thumb was around each upper arm and was pressed against a breast.

He stood like that. The face smiled. The jellies watched me. The long thumbs pressed.

"I'm not crying," I said to him, or both of us.

He said, "Of course you're not. You got nothing to cry about. Now, you give me a great big smile."

Reruns

WHEN THE State Department officer telephoned to ask if I was the Dr. Leland Dugan whose wife, Belinda, was traveling as a journalist in Europe and the Middle East, I answered in a manner even I, at the time, found cagey and evasive. "Yes," I said. "I'm Dugan. But she isn't really a journalist. Of course, she *does* journalism. But she's a sociologist. On her tax return she calls herself a teacher."

One of our recent fights had been about income tax returns. Belinda had wanted to be a married woman filing separately. I'd tried to show her that such a category cost us money. She'd been resolute: "I will not sign on some line tagged *spouse*. Underneath your name. I won't *be* underneath you anymore."

"So I've noticed," I'd told her.

"In the Lebanon," the State Department officer said. His

way of saying it—*the* Lebanon, as if this were the thirties and we were in Whitehall discussing Middle East chappies—made me pay attention. I am paid to pay attention to the stories people tell. I should have done better, but it had been a difficult morning, and one of my patients, seeking to test and protest at once, had sat before my desk for twenty minutes without speaking, daring me to intervene. I hadn't, and for the thirty subsequent minutes, he'd bellowed and ranted, sweating and heaving and, finally, leaping from his chair. "I don't feel better," he'd said, like a huge, sore child. "I don't feel better at all. So *now* what am I supposed to do?"

I said to the State Department officer, "Would you tell me again, please?"

That's how I learned that my wife, Belinda, anthropology-sociology professor on leave and part-time free-lance journalist, had gone to Beirut and was now a prisoner of some group on whom the Department of State sought further information. That was when I began to think of distances—the width of oceans, the length of borders, the prairies inside lives—as personal facts, and not just my patients' reports, or my wife's.

I said, "She's alive?"

"When they keep them there, they're alive, Dr. Dugan. Dead, they come straight home."

"She wouldn't want to come straight home, either way," I said. I chuckled, but he didn't laugh back politely. He said that someone had been sent, early that morning. I was not alone, he said.

I telephoned Kate, and then I canceled patients for the day.

I thought of the man the State Department had sent. He'd have to come a winding, hesitant route. He would, as so many strangers to our cold, bleak countryside do, drift and get lost, then recover, wandering on, doubting his direction, feeling compelled to continue. He would take a route along the ground like those my patients take in time and language when they try to tell their story to me. He'd already have flown from Washington to Syracuse, or Washington to one of the New York airports, and then to Hancock in Syracuse. He'd drive the seventy-five miles in his rental car—on Route 81, then 690, then some of Route 5, then lots of 92 to 20, 20 to 12B, 12B to 12, in slow traffic through small towns, and in the wide barren spaces in between. We are so far from every-place.

I collected Linda at the central school, and I told her. She was flushed, at first, because she'd been stared at by other adolescents as she left class early. She grew pale, then, and in the stairwell, at the main doors, she said, with dry lips clacking, "But who *wants* her?"

"Nice try," I said. We went for Melissa, who was in the elementary building. As she walked into the office, Lissa, seeing us, began to cry. "It's okay, baby," I said. I kept saying it. "Baby, it is fine."

Linda said to her, "She isn't dead."

Melissa cried harder.

"We'll talk about it," I said. "She isn't sick, and she isn't hurt."

"And she isn't coming home," Linda said.

I told her, "Thank you."

In the car, after a few blocks, after listening hard and riding silently, Melissa asked, "But who kidnaps *mothers*?"

And Linda had a question, too: "You think they'll rape her?"

I asked Melissa, "Do you know what Linda's talking about?"

"Do I like know what rape is?"

"Yes."

"Mostly," Lissa said.

I had to park across the street because the cars and trucks of the news people were in our drive and on our lawn. A sheriff's deputy led us through the onlookers and rural anchor-folk. Linda was grinning, I noticed, and she slowed against my arm as they questioned us; I pushed her home. Melissa said nothing. Her face was very pale, and her large eyes looked dark. In that way, she might have been Kate's daughter. She wasn't.

Kate arrived from her pediatrics clinic, and I nodded at the deputy who called for permission to bring her along. When Linda saw her she said, "God!" Kate dodged the same fat little man I'd pushed past; he'd told me he was a reporter from a fundamentalist Christian radio station. She stood before a fellow from our local Progressive Country and Western Sounds station as he shouted into her eyes and nose, "Dr. Karagoulis! What do you think of Mrs. Dugan being kidnaped?" She shook her head. "What are you doing here, Dr. Karagoulis, if we may inquire?"

Kate said something so low, I couldn't hear it. The deputy brought her, and we went in. Kate put her hands on my shoulders and kissed me.

"Jesus," Linda said.

Melissa said, "Hi, Kate!" Kate stooped to kiss her, and then she walked to Linda, whom she hugged, then kissed on the cheek. "I'm sorry," Kate told her.

"Tell my mother," Linda said.

"All right," Kate said.

"Sure. While she's in Lebanon."

Kate said, "Wasn't that cunning of me."

"What'd you tell the reporter?" I asked her.

"I said I was making a house call." She wore white twill slacks and a soft white man-tailored shirt, white socks, and shiny brown penny loafers. "I am," she said, opening her large medical bag and presenting a smelly brown paper sack streaked with oil. She handed it to Lissa, who unpacked long submarine sandwiches and Hostess Twinkies.

Linda, who ate nearly as much as Kate, turned away, as if sickened by food. Then she turned back. Kate took cans of cream soda from her bag. "I thought we might force ourselves," she said. We went into the back room, which was big and sloppy and filled with soft furniture. Kate took the ringing phone and unhooked it from its terminal. "I'll hook it up when I call my service," she said. "You guys go disconnect the other phones, please."

Linda said, "I might be expecting a call."

The telephone rang, and Kate stared down at Linda, who was at least six inches shorter than she. Melissa said, "I'll show you how to do it, Lin."

"I better not miss any calls," Linda said.

Kate only nodded. And when they had left, and as the other three telephones one by one stopped ringing, Kate and I stood, trying to squeeze some private talk into what would be a public day. Finally, she asked, "Do you think it has to do with us?"

"*She* has to do with us," I said. "We have to do with her. We're her symptoms. Whether or not we—"

Kate said, "Whether or not we're responsible for her situation."

"Her situation's an extension of her mind. No. I don't accept this blame."

"Well, I don't *want* to," Kate said. "But—"

"Yeah."

"Yeah, what?"

"Yeah, but."

"But what?"

"What, Daddy?" Melissa asked, behind us.

"But I don't think I'm gonna get my sandwich," I said. "If that's the man from Washington." Bernie, our 130-pound Newfoundland, was roaring in the foyer.

It was the deputy, and with him, shielded by him from the newspeople, was Mr. Pontrier from Washington, with his courteous introduction, and his letter from our senior Senator, and from the Secretary of State, and his verbal greetings from—he pronounced it as a single word—the-President-himself. Kate and the girls were gone when we went through to the kitchen. He laid his coat over a chair, and I ground coffee beans and set out mugs and milk and sugar and spoons, paper napkins. I threw away the greasy bag they'd left. It reminded me of the brown bag into which I'd put Belinda's hair two weeks before she left. I had driven with it to the hospital, where I'd found Kate on pediatrics rounds. She'd been palpating the abdomen of a struggling infant, and I'd watched her close her eyes, as if to will her senses to her fingertips. In the corridor, I showed her the bag. Looking inside, she'd recoiled. "She cut it off," I'd told her. "She left it strewn through my underwear drawer." Kate had stared and stared, and tears had run from her enormous eyes. She'd wept, I remembered thinking, because perhaps she'd thought I didn't know how to. It didn't occur to me until Belinda was kidnaped that Kate might have wept for Belinda.

When I turned around in the kitchen, Pontrier had opened his attaché case and had put on the kitchen table his pad and pen, a tape recorder, and two sets of glasses in soft leather sleeves. "Will *not* wear bifocals," he said, whinnying, showing his large teeth and pink gums. "Won't admit my age. Shouldn't say that to a shrink."

Bernie walked past Pontrier to lie beneath the table.

"Hell, we listen to anything," I said. "I once had a family—"

"You do whole families?"

"Oh, yeah. Being crazy's a family project most of the time. I had this family, and I made them bring in their dog."

Hearing "dog," Bernie banged his tail against the floor.

"How'd that work out, Doc?"

"Well, I was able to help the dog. The family stayed sick."

He whinnied again, then played back "stayed sick" on his machine. He nodded. "We're ready," he said. "Tell you what I know. Ask you for information we might want later on. We need the—" He waved his long hands.

"Overall picture," I said. "Or would you say, 'big picture'?"

"Right," he said. "Right. You know Q & A."

"Q & A?"

"Questions and answers. Part of your profession, right?"

"I have a Q," I said. "How come you're here? How come the State Department phones me up, and an official"—I gestured at him, he nodded—"leaves to fight his way through the upstate wilds? How come this attention? Were you people having her followed?"

"No," he said, "it's just your wife's the second New York State citizen they've taken. Your senator got in on this. He wants *service*."

"Politics," I said, as if that explained something.

The coffee had dripped, and I set the pot on the table atop the terra-cotta tile Belinda had bought in Peru. Kate had told me once that Belinda's affection for objects made of clay was a sign in her favor. He switched his recorder on and said, in a normal voice, "Briefing of Leland Dugan, four thirty pee em, January sixteen, Nineteen eighty-seven. Eight! Eight. Still not up to date." I was afraid he was going to whinny again, but he was content with showing his gums.

"Now, Dr. Dugan." He took off one set of glasses and put on another. "Our people liaised with representatives of the International Red Cross and certain representatives of the Druse upon notification that a Mrs. Belinda Dugan of Sherwood, New York, a member of the faculty of the State University of, ah, New York et cetera, had been taken hostage. We assume she was taken hostage. No demands have been made. Really isn't kidnapping or hostage taking, is it, if they don't want something in return." He looked up. I nodded.

He looked displeased, then held up his little Japanese recorder. I said, "Yes. No."

"Thank you, Doctor," he told the machine, setting it down. "We have received confirmation—"

"They didn't cut any fingers off," I said. "Or ears? Anything like that?"

"Movies, Doctor. Movies. In our experience, this doesn't happen."

"It happened to Aristotle Onassis. Or Getty. One of those people. They sent him an ear."

"Guess you're not in the right tax bracket, Doctor," he said. And he did draw back his gums and whinny. I set my coffee cup down somewhat harder than I'd planned to. "But not a time for levity, so let's—" He looked at his yellow legal pad, with its green lines and red-ruled margin. I saw my name at the top of the pad, and a series of numbers arranged vertically. Beside each number were matters he'd apparently decided to set before me. As I watched, he crossed out what was next to number two. He looked up, saw me trying to read his pad, and drew it closer to him, as if we were being examined and he'd caught me trying to cheat. "No fingers or ears. Sorry you were so worried."

"Thank you. Does it matter who has her?"

"Does matter. A lot of these people don't negotiate. A lot of them, they're nuts, to put it in a, well, nutshell." Lips, then gums and teeth, then silent laughter.

"So's Belinda," I said.

"Clinically? Certifiably?"

"No. Although one definition of adjustment might be your ability to stay away from hostage situations in Lebanon. Or Lebanon itself. Belinda is a very, very intelligent woman of significant achievement and reputation. Right now, she hates who she is—her whole situation. She—"

"That include you, Doctor? Mind my asking? The big—"

"Yes. Big picture. No, I don't mind. Yes, I do. What the hell. Sure, it includes me. Remember what I said before? Being crazy's a family project. Being so sad. Disoriented. All of that. Any of that. Yes. Yes, it includes me. Yes."

"Tough one."

I said, "Are you married, Mr. Pontrier?"

"Twenty-nine years in two months."

"You work at it."

"Never had a fight."

I cocked my head as Bernie cocks his. Pontrier replied, "Work really hard at doing everything she says!" Lips again, then gums, then teeth and the long laughed whinny.

"Will they let her go?"

"From one of the West Bank settlements, this bunch, we think. They may not be trained to negotiate. Just take people. Do whatever harm they can. Full of hate. Socialism. Radical religion. You know."

"So what happens to my wife, Mr. Pontrier?"

"State is doing everything it can."

"I'm very grateful."

He crossed out two items. "Lines of communication are wide open. People out there listen hard, tell us what they hear. Friends of friends—you know what I mean?—keep asking about her. Just like the others."

"The others."

"You remember. Anglican. French guys. The other Americans. West German guys. Nobody's forgetting them. Maybe you forget them. State doesn't."

I couldn't have named one hostage. That was when I realized how politics, history, and extreme distances had taken Belinda from our three traffic lights, the hour's commute to her campus, the stores that stocked Sara Lee poundcake and vitamin supplements, and the house where, upstairs, Kate embraced my daughters and waited for word. Soon, I thought, people in so many lives will forget that woman's name—the one who got snatched overseas. Remember?

He looked at his list, and then he looked at me, as if he had discovered my worst malfeasances. His eyes narrowed, his leathery wide mouth frowned. He seemed to reflect on what he was going to say. Then he looked at his legal pad and said, "Nobody usually takes a woman in the Middle East."

"No?"

"You're a shrink."

"They don't value women highly. Right. But they did take my wife."

"If they don't like women, except for, you know, the obvious stuff—"

"Cooking," I said. "Child rearing."

"Screwing," he said. His eyes widened, as his nostrils did: he was daring me to rebuke him.

"All right," I said. "We'll use the State Department nomenclature."

He snorted, but didn't whinny. His cold eyes remained on me. "Have to wonder, Dr. Dugan, why they snatched her. If she's just a— Don't mean to us, of course, you or me. Woman."

I shook my head.

"Who does she work for, Doctor?"

"SUNY. Sociology."

"No, I mean over there. In Greece, or Beirut, wherever the cell was. Who was she *working* for?"

"Cell? Spies? Is that what you mean? Is that what the State Department *thinks*? Belinda Hosford Dugan, middle-aged spy?"

I saw Melissa walk in slowly and quietly. Her hands hung straight at her sides. She was nine, the age of perfection in childhood. She wanted nothing more than to give her love to much of what breathed. Her hair was drawn over to one side in a crooked, rearing wave. She wore the most innocent of miniskirts over dark tights, and her dark cotton sweater hung baggily to almost the hem of her skirt. Her legs were thin and strong. She came toward us, awaiting our discovery of her. I held my arm out, and she came to it, rolled inside it as she curled it with both hands around her waist until she stood against me.

"Lissa," I said, "this is Mr. Pontrier. He's from the government. He's trying to help Mommy."

"Will they kill her? Are these the kidnappers who kill people?"

"Heavy-duty current-events awareness," Pontrier said. "You know your civics," he told her.

"No," I said. "I don't think so." I said it as reasonably as if I were telling her that a plant was not poison oak. "Where did you hear about that, sweetie?"

"On TV," she said. "Kate and Linda and me saw Mommy on Channel Two."

"Mommy?"

Pontrier bent over to his case, and when his face reappeared, he was chewing on his lip and looking at the black plastic video cassette he held. "It must have leaked," he said. "Everything does. Knew they made a couple of copies, of course. Didn't think they would leak this fast."

I held Melissa and furrowed her pompadour with my free hand. I kept my voice reasonable, pretending that I talked to an angry dog. Bernie, sleeping, was disturbed by my fake tranquillity, and he grunted. "You're saying that a video-tape—the kind of thing—" It was what other families saw when terrorists took one of them. We were other families now, and there was no point in saying that, or almost anything else, to Pontrier, I realized. Now, at last, after the cruel arguments and breathless dark silences, after the shattered nights, finally there was nothing to say that might matter. I spoke nonetheless. I always did. I said, "There's a tape? You people let it happen that my girls saw this tape, and I wasn't there with them?"

Lissa said, "Kate was with us, Daddy. It was mostly like surprising. Except Mommy was crying at the end."

"Yes," I said. "And you're all right?"

She nodded. She wasn't. Kate was at the kitchen door, then. She said nothing, but held her hands out to Lissa. I kissed the top of her head and propelled her toward Kate.

I said, "Dr. Karagoulis, this is Mr. Pontrier from the State Department. Mr. Pontrier, Dr. Karagoulis."

"House full of doctors," he said, taking off his glasses and standing barefaced to shake Kate's hand.

She drew Lissa to her. "Is there news?"

He shrugged. She nodded.

"She's a doctor, too," Kate said. "Mrs. Dugan. She has the doctorate from Chicago."

237

"Isn't that fine!" Pontrier said.

"Excuse us," Kate said.

Pontrier looked at her as she walked away, then returned to the table, where he put on a pair of glasses, removed them, put the other pair on, and said, "My own suspicion, Doctor. They'll kick her free. On account of she's a woman. Messy things, women. You know. To the Arabs. Understand?"

I shook my head.

Pontrier shrugged, then looked at his list. "So what was it?" he asked. "Greenpeace? Socialist Workers? News Alliance for Jewish-Arab Amity? Lyndon Larouche? There's so many butthead groups. Who'd she work for?"

"Work for? When she traveled? She worked for herself."

"She free-lanced?"

"Are we talking spy novels or journalism, Mr. Pontrier?"

"Isn't always a difference," he said. Whinny, tooth and gum. "It make any difference to you?"

I clasped my hands on the edge of the table. I sat up straight and looked him in the eye. I didn't like the intimacy any more than he did, and I wound up looking at the door of our refrigerator, studded with fruit-shaped magnets holding shopping lists and Lissa's drawings and Linda's reminders (all of them ending with exclamation marks); it was our accidental map. I said, "My wife—Belinda is not entirely well."

"She need medication? We can try and work something out with the Red Cross."

"Psychic well-being," I said. "Her soul isn't well."

"You a religious guy, Doctor? Is this about religion?"

"Worse than that," I said. "I'm a Freudian. He never meant to talk about the mind. Not only. He was always saying *soul*. That's what analysis is about."

"Sounds a little ripe."

"Doesn't it. Look. Belinda's unhappy. I would call her clinically depressed. She's been doing—she's looking for something else."

He was making notes. "For what?"

"She'd love to know. So would I."

"Doctor, did she walk out on you?"

"She got as many commissions from as many magazines as she could. We're not talking whacky politics, you understand. She's a pretty typical left-wing, feminist, institution-distrusting intellectual. She wanted to find a lot of serious action and write about it. She's been giving papers on women in cultures where the politics are basically life-and-death."

"Washington, D.C.," he exploded, whinnying, showing all his teeth, every wet gum, the membranes of the linings of his lips.

"Belfast," I said. "She went there first. She did a piece for *The New Republic*. Then she went to Turkey. The next thing I heard, she was going to Lebanon."

"The next thing you heard," he said. He was a better listener than I'd thought. "So she took off on you."

"We hadn't lived comfortably together for several months."

"She did move out?"

"Can I ask you: is this relevant?"

He shrugged. "Hard to know what matters," he said. "Can't know what'll make a difference sometime down the road. We can drop it."

He made a note. His pen was thin and silver, and he had turned it to make the point emerge. Now he retracted the point. "Kind of hard not to pry," he said.

"Belinda was probably asking the same kind of question when they took her. Probably some out-of-work guy with an old gun and an older rage got tired of hearing some American woman asking *his* woman about her influence on his daily political life."

"We fix it at two months she's been gone?"

"That's about right. You checked at Kennedy?"

"We got her going into London, then out and into Ireland. She was recorded entering Athens."

"She went to Greece?"

He nodded. "Good place to hook up with radical elements."

"Look, she isn't a *spy*."

"That's what Julius said about Ethel."

"What?"

"Rosenberg. The atom spies."

"For Christ's sake, Pontrier, my wife is a burnt-out, sad, searching, decompensating person who used to think she struck a blow for freedom if she didn't shave her god-damned *legs*!"

"She won't be shaving her legs in Beirut," he said, showing some quick lip lining. "Maybe it'll bring some peace to town."

"Are you going to tell me what you're doing for her? What can I do? Can I see somebody?"

"Me," he said. "Unless the President or the Secretary needs a photo opportunity with bravely smiling families of hostages, and the main man trying hard not to cry while he says we're doing everything we can. If that doesn't happen, I'll be your contact for our saying that."

"No one's life should come to that," I said. "A *case*. That people forget."

"Never mind going there," he said. "Get ignored for a month and come home broke. Or get yourself kicked raw, die in a collapsed house with busted legs, skull fracture. Stay here. Wait. Write letters. Listen to people tell you they're doing what they can. They *will*. We spring one, especially a woman, it's political fat city. Gold." His long hand patted my fist on the table. I recoiled from the intimacy, and he seemed surprised at what he'd done. "Doctor," he said, putting his other glasses on, "let's go to the movies."

In the living room, when I turned on a reading lamp, I saw Linda at the end of the sofa, smoking. She didn't tap nervously into an ashtray. She drew it in until the ash glowed, and she held it deep, then let it out slowly, in a long luxurious soft plume. That's when I was sure that she'd smoked dope. I wondered if she and Belinda had smoked it together in the name of the mother-daughter bond.

"That's bad for you, baby," I said.

She nodded.

"I could give you statistics about strokes. We could talk about cancer. I hope to God she didn't put you on the pill."

She stood. "Hello," she said. "I'm Linda Dugan. I don't *think* my father will be doing a Pap smear right now. If there is any personal information you don't know about me yet, he'll be happy to fill you in."

Pontrier whinnied. So did I. So did *I*. "How are you?" I asked her.

"Linda's fifteen," I said to Pontrier, as if something were explained. I seized her before she could flee. She let me hold her into me, and she hugged back. With her hot cigarette behind my neck, I thought of Joan Crawford. Linda had always reminded me of her; she had my broken-looking nose and the wide mouth that on Belinda was often cruel, but that on Linda was mean and sexy at once. She was smart, tough, and damaged by life with me and Belinda. And because she was fifteen, she lived secretly. I always missed her. It was as though she too had fled to another country. She smelled a little sour, like the sweat you sweat in nightmare-heated sleep. Into her cheek and stale hair I whispered, "Baby."

She gave in and leaned on me for an instant. Her arms tightened and then let go. She stepped back and put the cigarette in her lips. "I'll go sit with Kate and Lissa." She said to Pontrier, "Are you going to leave a copy of that videotape with us?"

"Could do," he said, nodding. "Could do."

She laughed. "Could do," she said. Over her shoulder she let "Bye, Daddy" drift with her smoke.

"A little theatrical," I told him, betraying her.

"Time of great strain," he said. "Lot of stress. Pretty girl."

"Yes."

"Little like her mother. Little like you."

"Then that worked out for us." I took the cassette from him and slid it into the VCR. When the set was on, I punched PLAY.

Apparently the camera was mounted on a tripod. It remained still throughout. People walked on- and off-camera, but Belinda stayed where she was: seated in a wooden chair with a copy of the *International Herald Tribune* on her lap. She held the paper up, and I could see the date. Then she put the paper on her lap, and sat, with her arms hanging down.

I thought of Lissa's arms as she'd entered the kitchen. Belinda wore running shoes and gray, baggy, rumpled cotton pants, a dark and dirty-looking T-shirt. Her hair was chopped short, and it looked grayer. She'd lost weight, she looked exhausted. The cords in her neck were prominent when she moved or talked. Horizontal ridges on her throat were new to me. Her arms were a little puffy, and very tan. She didn't seem drugged, but she was subdued.

A small, dark man in a kind of faded khaki uniform, wearing very large and very dark sunglasses, came to stand beside her. He put his little hand on the back of her neck and squeezed. But he didn't seem to be hurting her. She straightened.

"My name is Belinda Hosford Dugan," she said. "I am an American citizen who has been interrupting—" She peered at something near the camera, and I realized that she was reading. She wore contact lenses, and I should have known from her squint that she was reading signs.

"Cue cards," I said.

"Just like Johnny Carson," Pontrier said.

"Interfering in the orderly processes of the life of the people. As a lesson to such as myself, I have been seized and am a prisoner. I am safe and well. I am not being mistreated. It's true," she said, and I knew she'd deviated from the lines they'd written. No one stopped her, though. "I'm all right. Please tell my girls—tell Lissa and Linda—" She began to cry. She stopped herself. "Hello. Darlings, hello. I'm all right. I can't come home yet. And this thing, really—" Then there was static, then silence, then the small man in dark glasses said, "Enough. For now, enough."

She hadn't spoken of me. She hadn't sent a message to me.

For several months we'd hardly spoken, except when we traded information about the house or children. Even then, our exchanges could have been by postcard. "For now, enough." I thought of Lissa and Linda, seeing her, hearing her say, "It's true," and then the little man.

"I'm too young to be as old as you make me," she'd said one morning. She was leaving for work, and I was going to drive the girls to school. She had come up behind me to put her hand on my shoulder. She'd hissed it, so the girls wouldn't hear: "You make me so tired."

And I had leaned my head back to reply, "We know it's not from sexual exertion."

And she, almost laughing, had whispered back, "We know it's not from sex with *you*."

That was the morning of the night she chopped her hair short. It was still short, and she looked pretty on the tape—hollow-eyed, exhausted, but still pretty Belinda, my childhood bride. We had taken sixteen years to fail. In the television tape, she showed those years. I wondered if anyone else could see them.

Pontrier turned the VCR off. The TV set roared the *hush* of static, and I turned it down but not off. I don't know why. It was like sheltering under something to hear that neutral noise about me. He took the tape from the machine and handed it to me. He gave me a business card, which I didn't read. I said, "That's all?"

"You don't need medical assistance, on account of you give it. And you got that tall doctor there. You understand the situation pretty good, and you can call me. You will. They always do. Eight, ten times a week, some of them. A *day*, even. Doesn't help. Doesn't hurt anything. Built the time right into my schedule. *Families*, I call it. Write it on my calendar for the week. Liaison. You can't liaise without talking to 'em. Call if you want to. Any news, you'll hear. From us. Me. Right away. Promise. Do think they're gonna turn her loose. Woman. You know." He sounded like a machine winding down.

"You have a long drive back," I said.

"Traveling's part of it. See the country. Rather see some other part of it, no insult intended."

"It's an acquired taste."

"Like okra," he said. Whinny, gum and tooth. He took his glasses off.

He went into the kitchen and soon he was back with his case and his coat, and soon he was gone from the house. At the narrow window beside the door, I watched the journalists surround him. There were two more trucks now, large white ones with lights and antennas on top. As he stopped to speak, the air and lawn in front of the house leaped into bright intensity as television lights came on. It was like a lightning strike.

In the living room, again, I put the tape on and I bent before the set. There was Belinda, her hair, her eyes, her breasts. A prurient boy, I looked behind me, then reversed the tape and looked again—she wore no brassiere. I could see her nipples at the soft fabric of her shirt. Belinda on TV, without a bra, I told myself. I rewound and looked again: my wife on reruns, available as starkly as this, and to strangers.

I looked again, and then once more. I was her audience, now. I turned off the set and the VCR and went toward the stairs to fetch Kate and Melissa and Linda. They were descending as I reached the staircase. Linda walked past me, heading for the living room. Kate, holding Melissa's hand, stood where she was.

Then a roar came from the living room, the static of the VCR. The tape began to play, and the *hush* gave way to Belinda, speaking. The stranger on TV was talking to us, and her daughter Linda sat on the sofa before her, smoking, clicking the switch to REVIEW and then PLAY. She sought the instant when her mother stopped reading her script. We stood at the stairs and we watched her watch her mother, over and over, lost and found, the *hush* and then Belinda's voice, Belinda's breasts, Belinda's hair, and Linda sighing out smoke and making her mother say to her, "It's true," "It's true," "It's true."

Name the Name

My wife isn't local. She finds it alarming that so much of where we live is named for someplace else: Pompey, Fabius, Marathon, Mycenae, Euclid, Cicero, Tripoli. Here—Syracuse and Lebanon, Rome—in the center of the state of New York, where it often snows in May and always in April, three hundred miles from Manhattan, the children are entitled. Whether they are kissed for their beauty or scalded in punishment, whipped with a belt or beaten by fists or sung to at dawn, and in a mobile home or a three-floor Colonial with central chimney and hand-adzed joists, they are the young and we allow for them in the hamlets and the trailer parks, in the yellow-brick Victorian synagogue, in the farmhouse turned by candles and chrome-plated cross into a church.

I am the man in the unwashed dark blue truck who comes

up the snow-sealed rural road or into the street behind the boarded-over tannery. If your child can't come to school, the law demands that someone bring the school to him, and I am the carrier of entitlements, with my briefcase scuffed like cheap shoes, and my long thick overcoat and clumsy gloves, with a white metal toolbox in the back of the truck that I fill each day with textbooks and ruled coarse paper, and the forms I turn in to the board every night. I am the education they must send. In Smyrna and Coventry, Lower Cincinnatus and New Berlin, I'm the chance.

At eleven in the morning, while thick wet snow fell without sticking onto crocuses and daffodils, I drank reheated coffee sweetened with condensed milk and light brown sugar by a woman too embarrassed to look at my face. She wore polyester pants with a black and white check, a man's gray sweatshirt over a heavy flannel shirt, and big slippers lined with synthetic fur; on top of each slipper was the face of a dog with a long pink tongue. She wore no socks, and the chapped rough redness of her ankles was an intimacy between us. She was feeding soft wood—scraps of lumber, chunks of pine—to a big, hot wood stove. I could smell the almost-kerosene of the creosote in her stovepipe.

Her face was wedge-shaped, and soft. Inside her fat, and under her thinning light hair, within the smell of smoke and cheap deodorant, a shy, myopic thirty-five-year-old woman was waiting for my verdict on her twelve-year-old girl. I said, "Thank you for the coffee," and while she looked at her painted-over Hoosier cabinet, I said, "Myrna's a bright girl. I'm not sure about her social studies, but I think that's only because she didn't finish the chapter. She could do it."

"I'll mind her."

"I spoke to her about it."

"I was the same age as her when I—" She pointed at her soft belly. Her fair skin was red. I saw tears behind her thick glasses.

"Not with Myrna."

She shook her head. "That would of been too young to be her. No. It was a baby bore itself early and dead. A, you know, miscarriage. I remember my grandmother—I lived with them. My mother didn't have the strength for any more kids, so she give me to them. My grandmother told me to thank Jesus it was dead. I didn't think of nothing like that, though. I cried and cried. I wanted that baby. I was like her. Twelve."

"So she'll have the baby?"

"I believe she will," she said. "Lord willing and her strength all right. She's a strong girl."

"Well," I said. "I thank you for the coffee. I'm very pleased with how Myrna's doing with her studies. Will she go back to school?"

"Oh, yes," her mother said. "I'll be helping with the baby. She has to go on and live out her life. We can afford another mouth."

"Fine," I said. "Good. And the father?"

"Myrna's?"

"Her baby's."

"No, they're too young," she said. "He'll have to live with his own mommy and daddy."

I remember how I looked at the crazy lenses of her thick glasses and then nodded. I remember being angry with myself for being surprised. I smiled my good-byes.

In the truck, I scribbled my report. I saw Myrna at the

window over the long front porch. She waved like a little
girl. She was a little girl. So I waved back. For the principal
and the board of education, for all whose rules—and weren't
they right?—required that a pregnant schoolgirl in her seventh month stay home, I waved. She would come to school
with her baby anyway, and her friends would surround her,
and certain teachers, even, would smile their applause. She
would be heroic to them, and her trophy would be eleven
years and eleven months away from a pregnancy leave and a
visiting teacher like me. I wondered if one day I would
teach Myrna's child and sit in my truck and wave to her
like this.

When I arrived at the hospital, they were removing lunch
dishes in the corridor. Outside Intensive Care, in the small
lounge, people sat to wait, and they all looked as though they
wanted to smoke. I hadn't smoked in a dozen years, and the
NO SMOKING sign always made me wish for a cigarette. I
buzzed and they asked who I was. I told them, and that I
was there for Leslie DuBois—say "Du-Boyce"—and they admitted me. I always found myself wishing they wouldn't. In
her room, one of eight in a large squared doughnut of such
rooms surrounding the ICU nurses' station, Leslie lay. I
called, above the hiss and click of her ventilator, "How's the
spider?" I had told her that she looked arachnoid, nested in
the IV feed lines and ventilator hose. Her tired eyes blinked
several times, and the urgent O of her mouth, which was
taped about the thick tube that went down her throat and
breathed for her, twitched.

She wrote to me. On the Invisible Pad, with its gray pud-
ding of undersheet, and its clear plastic topsheet that lifted
to erase what she wrote with a mute pen, a pointed red

wooden stick, Leslie wrote, in crooked block lines, NOT SPIDER FLY. Leslie DuBois had taken most of the pills in her parents' house. She had telephoned her doctor. So she'd lived. No one was certain when her brain would tell her lungs to breathe out carbon dioxide, or remind her legs to bear her weight, so Leslie, who had lived, lived here. And she was required to be entitled to me: they forced me at her, and she wrote to me on her Invisible Pad, and I called back above her ventilator, and then, for twenty minutes or so, we played school.

I said, "The Jersey Devils are the Cinderella team in the playoffs this year!"

She wrote, GRETZKY IS GOD.

"Wrong team," I called. She sweated long rivulets. She shuddered under the workings of the ventilator as if she were a ragged-running car. "Your metabolism needs tuning," I yelled.

Gray-blue pale, dank of hair, smelling sour and showing in her eyes how embarrassed she was when I bent close, she tore the cover up, then wrote HATE HOCKEY.

"Why didn't you tell me? I do too."

She tore and printed. LOVE U.

"I love you, Leslie," I said. "But you didn't do your homework, did you?"

HATE POEMS.

"Gotta read 'em. Gotta graduate on time."

WHY?

"Because when you get better you'll want to go to college. Stay up all night doing homework about poems. That's why."

BOLOGNA.

"Nothing wrong with your spelling," I called. I found on her crowded night table the Xeroxed sheet I had given her. We were doing Keats's sonnet "When I Have Fears That I May Cease to Be," which after that first line goes on to worry "Before my pen has glean'd my teeming brain." I said, "Leslie. *You* had fears that you might cease to be."

Her intensely dark eyes—the pupils looked all-black to me—swung up to lock with mine. LIFE NOT POEMS, she wrote.

"Poems are life. They can be. They can be *about* life. Very respectably. Very persuasively."

MY LIFE NO POEM.

She lay back as if she had declaimed. I was exhausting her. I said, "Let me. You're telling me, he, he does things like that 'glean'd' and that kind of phony-sounding 'do sink,' and you're probably saying to yourself, 'He stuck that in for the rhythm of the line. Nobody says "*do sink*."' Right?" She flapped a wrist. "Right," I said. "Well, I can't argue. The 'do sink' isn't his greatest work. It doesn't sound natural. Of course, you could argue that while poetry comes from a natural impulse—to talk!—it either sounds natural, like us, or it doesn't. He was writing in 1818. You have to be fair about that. Maybe they talked like that in 1818. I frankly don't think so. I think he gimmicked it up to make the rhythm work for him. But how about 'And when I feel, fair creature of an hour!/That I shall never look upon thee more'? Is he talking about his imagination? I mean, that's what the poem's about, right? A guy who doesn't want to die because he wants to get his writing done? Or is this part, the *thee* part, about, well, love?"

She was sleeping. While she slept, her chest shuddered and sweat poured up from her skin. And she wept. I swore—I swear—I could tell the difference between the perspiration and the tears. *Psychoanalysis of suicides induced through poetry by Doctor Farce! Romantic poetry a specialty!* I sat back, and in the low aqua-colored plastic chair beside her bed, in the rhythm of her ventilator's vacuum-and-compression, in the high-pitched *beep* her IV monitors cried as the clear solution in the sacs ran down through her, I closed my eyes and in the heat of her room I slept.

The tearing sound of her eraser sheet woke me. I leaned forward so quickly, my back hurt. "What?" I said. "What?"

Leslie looked across at me—our heads were almost on a level—and her eyes looked pleased. I reached, automatically, for her Invisible Pad. It said WHAT COLLEGE?

"Oh," I said—surely shouted—"Wellesley! Vassar! Radcliffe! Let's think *big*!"

Her fingers moved, and I replaced her pad in them. It made the tearing sound, and then she wrote.

SHAMPOO NEXT.

"You want me to wash your hair? Sure. How?"

She moved her hand, I gave her the pad, and she added, without tearing, TIME.

"I will. You have them get the stuff, and I will. I'll talk to you about colleges. I'll ask some questions, and I'll tell you. And I'll—you want me to bring in hair magazines? You know: magazines with pictures of hairdos? I'll give you a perm."

She took the pad back and pulled up the sheet. KISS.

So I leaned down into the clicking and hissing and tape and perspiration and her tears, and I kissed her on the cheek and on the eye. *Till love and fame to nothingness do sink.* I said, "You're right about the poem. You're wrong, but you're

253

also right. Look on the Xerox sheet, and read what I wrote for you about sonnets. About the form. The fourteen lines, the rhyme scheme, you remember. Read the poem again, and we'll talk about it. All right?"

She waved good-bye with just the fingers of her left hand. Her eyes were closed.

"All right," I said.

In the corridor, a big clumsiness of briefcase and coat and gloves and forms and pens, I said to a couple of the ICU nurses, "When is she going to be okay?" They watched as I tried to put everything where it should go. I looked up from the floor where I kneeled, my back still aching, and stuffed my briefcase full.

One of them, whose name was May, a slender woman with short legs, said, "Are we talking miracles or medicine here? And would you like the fact or the fiction?"

I stood up slowly and fought my way into my coat.

"How about you?" May said. "How're you guys, you know, handling it?"

"I'm on my way to the jail right now."

"You want some leftover lunch? You look lousy."

"You never said that when we were drinking in the Solsville Hotel," I said.

She pushed her rimless glasses back up onto her nose and stepped a step closer. She smelled like chewing gum and soap. She put her fingers over the top of my trousers and her thumb around my belt buckle. "Say hello to your wife," she said, smiling, pulling once, then twice, at the top of my pants. "Take care."

I stepped back. "I'm shampooing Leslie next week, all right?"

254

May nodded, and the other one nodded. May let go of my pants. "You're putting on weight," she said.

I shrugged.

"Misery must agree with you." She turned, and then the other one did, and they went along the corridor. I buttoned my coat and went out through the smokeless visitors' lounge, wishing as I went.

I always kept the jail for last. It was a county jail, where prisoners waited for trials or indictment for minor offenses, or were held if they were being transported from, say, Auburn to the psychiatric hospital in Rome. The jail was in the basement of the county sheriff's offices, and was across the street from the courthouse, across another street from the parking lot of a Holiday Inn. If you stood on the steps of the elegant Victorian that housed the jail, you could see our public library and a government office building where people made arrangements for food stamps. It seemed like a rather large town, but it was really a very small city, the smallest in the state. In order to qualify for state aid in repairing the streets, our city had to file its street plan. We were found to have too few streets, according to a government rule, so we renamed certain avenues at either end. West Broughton had run, in two blocks, across the main street (a state two-lane) into (unsurprisingly) East Broughton. The town fathers renamed them, and the unsuspecting motorist now drove from West Broughton, across Route 12, and up a street called Samson Drive, never encountering East Broughton or any other Broughton. I nipped the yellow light and drove across 12 onto Samson, which was in the general direction of the jail, but which wouldn't bring me directly there.

Samson ended at a narrow lane that went up a steep hill

toward a small municipal swimming pool named for a phys
ed teacher who'd been thought to die in Korea. But he'd
come back. The town was embarrassed by its own emotion,
I suppose, and the poor fellow was punished—though everyone treated him well in person—by the neglect his pool received—clogged pool drains and a torn umbrella for the life-
guard. The road needed repaving and its potholes were his
payment for the municipal embarrassment. My son had
worked there in the summer of his sixteenth year. I walked
around the pool and looked down into its gray slush growing like a fungus in the shaded end. I climbed up onto the
chair where he'd sat and I sat in the cold air and crossed my
legs, leaned forward against the weight of my overcoat as if
I might declaim. There was nothing, though, to say there,
just as there was little to say in jail. As the afternoon dark-
ened, I went there.

At the desk, near the wooden staircase with the tops of its
newel posts carved into giant acorns, a deputy sat to log me
in and reach to pat my shoulder. I knew where to go—
through the heavy wooden door beneath the stairs, and then,
on metal rungs, down. Another deputy waited for me and
opened the heavy barred gate so that I stood at the open end
of a U made of cells. A television set high on the wall
showed the cable sports channel. A local physician who
doubled as the county's jail doctor was examining an Oriental man. The doctor, who smiled at me over the new prisoner's shoulder, said, "You may *think* a thing like that just
heals. Let me tell you: very little 'just heals.' You get help,
or you get sick. Understand?"

The deputy, who'd come in with me, was carrying his
magazine as he escorted me to the cell. I said, "Bobby, I didn't

know they were allowed to sell magazines like that."

He said, "Oh, yeah. The first amendment covers crotches now."

He opened the door and I went in. The smell of the disinfectant wasn't unpleasant. I discovered that each time I was there. I put my briefcase on his bunk, and then I looked at him. I think my body was confused about drawing careful breath, lest I smell something awful, and looking through hooded eyes, lest I see something cruel. I winced when our eyes met. But he was just a boy, a very tall and muscular sixteen-year-old boy who should have been attending his junior year in high school but who waited trial for vandalism. He had broken into the high school computer room twice. He'd done damage. And we all agreed, after the counseling and the tests, after the generous leniency of the school board, and after my wife and I had posted bail the first time, for larcenous behavior and several varieties of felony, that this time, awaiting hearings, Charlie—Chilly to his friends—would spend the dozen days in jail.

He was larger than I, and his hand, when I pulled at it, seemed to weigh more than I remembered hands weighing. Everything about him was large, and too big for me to move easily. His face was the same clenched thickening face of a boy I remembered as pretty. He looked at me with sharp-eyed disgust.

But I asked it anyway. "Charlie, you okay?"

His expression remained. He gestured at the one-piece toilet and the bunk bed and the metal bureau built into the wall.

"Nine days to go," I said.

He sat down on the bunk and looked away from me. I

opened my coat and sat beside him. He wore a light gray one-piece boiler suit. It was unbuttoned almost to the belt line, and I saw how little hair he had on his chest, or on the arms I saw in his rolled-up sleeves, or on the smooth, hard face. I was sweating in the heat of the jail, but I wore my coat anyway. His skin looked dry.

"Mom's—"

"I don't want to talk about Mom, please."

I nodded. I was going to say *crazy* or *dying* or *praying*, and none would have been right, and none would have been fair. She was doing what I was doing: hating the decision, hating its occasion, hating our life, and hating the government that had jailed our son. She was also, as I was, approving the decision, cooperating with the sheriff and the board of education, and we were hating *us*. While we mourned our living son, we ground our teeth while we slept and in the morning shared our nightmares about punishing him.

I put my hand on his long, heavy leg, and he twitched away. I said, as he must have known I would, and as I knew he loathed hearing, "We love you, Charlie."

But he tamely nodded. So I pressed.

"You know that?"

He nodded again. He said, "Can I ever come home?"

I said, still looking ahead, "I think they want to bring it to trial."

"Prison farm," he said.

"For juveniles."

"I don't think it's as little as that word."

"No," I said. "They're tough bastards there. It's a mean, bad place. We're trying to keep you out."

"The lawyer was here," he said.

"I know. We talked to him afterward."

"He must be expensive. His suit was very far out."

"He's got a closetful. Yes."

"Does he think—"

"I don't know, honey." He looked up. I looked over. Neither of us had called him *honey* since he was small. Now, it seemed to me, in his long and heavy age, looking at his life taking shapes he had never imagined, he was small. "But we'll do everything, *everything*, we can."

"Except let me come home."

I focused on my slush-dampened shoes.

"I know," he said. "Reality."

"I didn't use that word with you, did I?"

"Isn't that what this is supposed to be about?"

"It's what it *is* about, hon."

"I know. But I wish I could come home again."

"Honey, you'll come home again. That isn't—"

"Won't they take me straight from here to the prison farm after the trial?"

I couldn't look at him, because I couldn't admit to him that I had never considered his not, eventually, being home. "Reality," he'd said. I reached to throw the overcoat off my shoulders, but it felt too heavy for my hands. My chest and stomach were soaking through my shirt, but I wouldn't have been surprised to shiver.

"Here," he said. He stood, and I did too, and he went behind me and reached around, and he pulled the coat back and off.

"Thank you," I said. "I don't—"

"Yeah," he said. "That's what happens to me."

"It does?"

"A lot. All the time. That's all that happens here, except food and the bathroom, and the lights going off. TV."

"It does?"

"You want to see my homework, Dad?"

"You did it?"

"I had the time."

He handed me several sheets of the rough paper I had left with him. His handwriting, slanted acutely, yet rounded at the tops of looped letters, capitals especially, looked as it had looked when he was in the sixth or seventh grade. I was afraid to read his work. I was afraid that he had written about himself, or us. And I was afraid that he had not. "Great," I said. "Should I read this at home? Why don't I do that."

"Okay," he said. "I don't care. You can bring it tomorrow. You coming tomorrow?"

"Of course I am," I said. "That's what I do."

"Okay. How about economics? The chapter quiz on inflation and unemployment, all of that."

He took a sheet from the looseleaf notebook I'd left with him, and he examined it before passing it over. I opened his text to the end-of-chapter test, and I read the questions about lowered market demands for labor in an inflationary society. I kept looking at the graphs, and at the circles with their colored pie slices.

"You gonna grade it at home?"

I thought of sitting in our kitchen and drinking coffee and reading Charlie's quiz. I could see myself checking his answers: DOWN. UP. MARKETPLACE. SPIRAL. I saw his answers as if pressed, with Leslie's leadless pencil, onto Leslie's Invisible Pad. I saw myself standing soon, as I would. I saw myself waving from the door of Charlie's cell as I had waved to Myrna from the cab of my truck. Where we live is named for someplace else. How we live is named for something else. I saw myself, the traveling teacher, sitting in our kitchen with my pale wife. I would work at my exam. The question would ask me: Name the name for what we're living now. LOVE U Leslie had written. BOLOGNA. Charlie said, "Dad?" Name the name.

❧ To the Hoop

DUANE AND I didn't talk about how she killed herself or where. With us, it was as if anything to do with mothers or wives had begun two years ago. I had never told him in the first place that Jackie packed not only every suitcase she could find in the house, but cardboard boxes, brown paper bags, and plastic carryalls. It was as though we'd decided to move, and Jackie had left without me. In the bedroom was everything she'd owned—souvenir stones, creased postcards, old photo albums, discarded reading glasses, and out-of-date clothes she hadn't worn for many years. There were thirty-five shoes. I looked for half an hour for a missing stack-heeled cordovan pump that would have slid onto Jackie's left foot.

She had taken a room at the Howard Johnson's, not ten minutes from where I worked. She had eaten enough com-

plimentary capsules, spansules, and tablets, manufactured by
my firm, and had washed them down with enough compli-
mentary cough suppressant and her own dark rum, to do the
job, and stop her heart.

Nor did we discuss the women I sometimes brought home
after about a year had passed. The women were good sports,
and so was Duane. I would introduce them, and he would
duck his head and step forward, blushing, and would shake
their hand in his big fingers, then escape. He smiled at them,
but not at me. And even after Cheryl stayed some months
with me—with us, you'd have to say—we didn't speak too
much of her. She was the last. After Cheryl, it was Duane
and me.

And I stopped telling him stories of how at fifteen I had
been strong and tall, though smaller than he was, and able
to run all day in two- and three-man half-court games in
Brooklyn's summer heat at Wingate Field. I wanted to tell
him that I'd finally figured out why boys would play on
blacktop courts from eight in the morning until the sun went
down. It was because the other teams who challenged us
would not only win the game: they'd win the court. It was
winner-take-all, I wanted to say. Of course, he knew that.

I was careful to be silent about Duane's own play. I
watched him, though, as he practiced outside our house in
the country hills. In cold autumn winds, in thick winter
snow—he'd use a shovel and a push broom to clear the old
dairy ramp outside the barn on which his backboard was
mounted—Duane made lay-ups, sank his smooth jump shot
from fifteen feet out, leaped again and again to cradle the
rebounded ball so that his feet didn't touch the ground until

he'd rolled the ball over the rim. In games at his high school, against less muscular boys with fewer skills and less flexible bodies, he grew gawky, he—who could practice in a snowstorm all of an afternoon—became breathless, and then he ran with stiffening thighs and locked elbows; he would forget to set a screen for the shooting guard, he would neglect to block out opposing forwards and would yield up rebounds, he would panic when passed the ball and would shoot from too far out. And I, forgetting myself, would cry from the bleachers, *"Power* move!" I would bellow, "To the hoop! Take it to the *hoop!"*

In game after game I saw his coach let him play fewer minutes. He came to sit on the bench more bunchily, hunched in upon himself as if hiding. At home he insisted on more silence about his play, and his grades began to slide—not enough to provoke a call from school, but enough for me to notice. I saw problems coming. They were the weather I watched for as if I farmed for a living, instead of running communications at the corporate offices they'd shipped me to from headquarters in Cincinnati. During the day, I ran our house organ, writing articles on management shifts and new products, consulting about publicity and community relations, lying for a living, trying hard to make it sound as if I told pure truth about stomach settlers and decongestants and the people who lived here in the center of New York State, with its harsh long winters and splendid, suddenly concluded summers, manufacturing pharmaceuticals and mourning for the Cincinnati symphony and civic theater, the movie houses and bus lines of a *real* city, as they called it. I watched with a cruel contentment as my colleagues drew their pleasure from tales of each other's failures and malfeasances. I was a New Yorker. If I wasn't *there*, then almost anywhere would do.

I called him Dude because that is what his teammates called him, slapping high-fives with the lazy slow-motion casualness they saw among black players on television. These boys were white, and their bodies knew, if their minds didn't, or their tongues wouldn't say so, that the dark grace they imitated was the standard for the toughness of their practice habits and the courage of their play.

In the car after a Tuesday night scrimmage, as I drove us home, I yawned and made a joke of my fatigue by stretching my jaws immensely and offering the noise of what I told him was an aging hippo in heat. On the unlit snowy country roads which glowed beneath our lights, then disappeared into the general dark behind us, he turned to me and said, in a low, controlled, and sullen voice, "Would you mind not shouting at me during the game?"

"Oh. Hey, I was shouting *to* you. You know, cheering for you."

"I know. I kept looking at you. Did you see me?"

"I did. I thought you might be glad to know I was there."

"It made me nervous. I played lousy. All six minutes he had me in there."

"You looked a little tight."

"I looked a little lousy."

"Tentative, maybe."

He didn't answer.

"I meant, you didn't seem to—"

"I know what tentative means."

"Sorry. I will shut up. As long as you don't think I was *scolding* you. I hate it when parents scold their kids on the court."

"I think I'm screwing up because you're there."

I turned in at our short driveway. "You don't want me to come, Dude?"

"And would you call me Duane, please?"

"I will. And I'll stay away from games for a while. Right?"

"Thank you," he said as formally as if I'd picked up his athletic bag and handed it to him.

"You're welcome," I said.

In the cold kitchen, while Duane turned that morning's approximation of order into something shaggier, I lit a fire in the wood stove and made us sandwiches. We always ate some snack before he yawned his way through homework before going to bed. Seeing me slice ham, he said, "Nothing for me, thanks. I'm keeping my weight down."

He was on the stairs, and something like "Good night" trailed his slow and heavy-footed climb. So I was alone, with ham and good intentions, and the usual fears that ranged from drugs to teenage schizophrenia. Jackie had died alone, and in silence. She had left us no word.

I put more wood into the stove, closed its damper, took off my jacket and tie, and sat with the day's mail. Letters still, though rarely, came for Jackie and me, mostly flyers and occasional cards from people I'd forgotten. I sometimes thought of our lovemaking, or afternoons in shopping malls. But mostly, these days, I remembered Jackie's rage. Once, when she was saying she hated having to love me, she had snarled—I'd seen her even teeth. With her face red and her teeth showing, she had sat before me. And then she had walked to the stove, bearing our cups, and had poured us more coffee. And then she had taken both our cups away, before we'd sipped, before she sat again, and had emptied them into the sink. She'd stood over it, with her back to me, and had said, "When I went to bed with you on Friday nights back then, this was not my idea of Saturday mornings." She had left her Coach bags, and her printed personal stationery, and a basketball player who, when the ball was in his hands, grew wide of eye, twisted at the mouth, and leaden of limb.

I fell asleep in the kitchen, listening to the split cherry-wood sizzle and pop. It filled the air with sweetness. I could almost taste the wood, and it made me wish that Duane could. When I woke, the kitchen was cold. Duane and I were in the house, but that didn't help either of us.

The next afternoon, late, when Duane met me in the school parking lot after practice, he threw his gym bag into the back of the car, dropped into his seat as if he'd been slung there, and he said, "I want to quit."

"The team?"

He nodded.

"Why?"

"It isn't any fun anymore."

I drove us up into the hills. The sun was down, the sky was low and dirty-looking. It would snow, and the snow would stick, and in the morning we would have to dig the car out.

"We'll need firewood brought in tonight," I said.

"Will you let me?"

"Quit the team?"

"Yeah."

He was big and handsome, my gaunt boy. His hair grew
low on his forehead, and it was curly, and he hated it. He was
always plucking at it, as if he could force it to straighten. I
noticed him doing that on the court one night, before he told
me not to come anymore. I saw that the worse he failed to
set a screen or pass the ball off, the more he smoothed the
hair on his neck, or pushed it alongside his temples, or re-
peatedly pulled at the ripples of his curls. Cheryl, who was
ten years younger than I, and maybe ten years tougher, had
said, "He's as pretty as your wife must have been. He's got
a woo-woo body like you, but he's as pretty as you are plain.
Matter of fact, when I compare him to you, I wonder what
it is you *do* have. You got legs," she'd said. And when I'd
looked down at my feet, Cheryl had said, "I mean *legs*. You
keep on going. You last. You aren't flashy, but you last. You
know?"

I didn't, because I hadn't. She'd gone too, and I had heard
she lived with the manager of a big sporting goods store. He
drove a car that was famous among the younger chemists and
junior executives at the firm because it was as tastelessly
painted as any car they'd seen. Cheryl was almost stocky, but
not fat, and she loved clothes too tight for her powerful
thighs and thick waist. Her hair was bright blond, and she'd
look you in the eye and talk to you hard, but rarely mean. She
had made me feel optimistic. She had left because the feeling
was a lie. "I just hate sitting around being pale," she said,
"you know?"

I said to Duane in the car as the first flakes fell on the
windshield, "No. You stay. You fight it."

"Fight what?"

"Whatever's getting at you. Was practice bad?"

"The two minutes I scrimmaged weren't bad."

"Are you convincing him you lost it, or did he think so in the first place?"

"I didn't lose it."

"You can play basketball?"

He nodded his head.

"So go play basketball. You don't quit."

"How can I play basketball on the bench?"

"Sit up extra straight."

I insisted that we eat together that night, and I forced him to help me cook. He carefully planted his elbows on the table and let his mouth grow slack. I heard his food grow pulpy in his teeth. I refused to react. In Brooklyn, we had called it a game face: the stony eyes and unexpressive mouth with which you showed your opponent on the court that you knew no fear, could run forever without panting, and hadn't worried about *anything* for over a year. Duane wore his, and I wore mine. We choked down our overcooked hamburgers in silence, and I washed the same six dishes over slowly, until he went up to his homework.

It was, for an instant that night, as if Jackie were away but in reach. I wanted to call her and ask what she would do if she lived with a troubled son as so many mothers do. I wanted to ask her what we, as parents, *really* thought. I'd often not known until she'd told me. Cheryl always had an opinion, and Duane had always known it, resented it, fought it, but had always been impressed. When I'd admitted to him, one weekend, that Cheryl and I were apart, he'd said, "Now you'll have to figure out my curfew on your own."

I went upstairs now to his room and I knocked. He mumbled something, and I opened his door into the hot, heavy air of caged adolescent. U-2 sang songs of social concern he played loudly, and a lifetime of underwear and long-legged jeans lay on the rug. I thought of photographs of airplane crash sites. He was on his bed, looking at a textbook page covered with diagrams. Then, as if he were timing himself, he slowly turned his head and raised his brows.

I didn't throw his jeans at him or shriek about attitudes or the impossibility of studying with such music on. I spoke softly, and he turned the tape player down and asked me to repeat myself. I did. "I said I wanted to apologize for that crack about sitting up straight. You can't play ball while you're on the bench and it feels lousy. I'm sorry you're not playing a lot. I think you're tensing up, psyching yourself out. I think it's your mother, maybe me. You can play yourself out of that, I think. You can get your form back. You want me to talk to your coach?"

"No."

"Because I will, Duane. I'll do—"

"No, thanks."

"—anything I can."

"No thanks."

I stood there and I nodded my head a lot. I said, "Well," and nodded again. He had gone back to looking at the page. His hand reached out for the volume control and I did not speak of it. I backed up, and the door swung shut, as if his thoughts had gently closed it with a slow motion, a single click.

Downstairs, I did what I always do when I have a problem to solve: I forced it into words. On a legal pad I took from my briefcase, I wrote his name at the top in capitals: DUANE. Then, beneath it, along the left-hand margin ruled in two red vertical lines, I wrote, in my finest, firmest hand:

DRUGS?

ILLNESS?

JACKIE?

CHERYL?

ME?

TEAMMATES?

BEING 15?

SEX?

COACHING?

CLASSMATES?

LIFE.

I balled the list and I fed it to the wood stove. And so much for words.

Cheryl had said, "You're my first boyfriend who always wears a suit to work. Some guys wear sports jackets, you know, some kind of tweed or corduroy. But they can decide to wear a crewneck, or a sleeveless pullover. But you wear a whole suit, every day. I'm gonna be measuring people's wardrobes against you from now on."

A year before, we'd been lying in bed, wearing my pajamas. Jackie had given them to me—navy blue with red piping, shipped upstate by Brooks Brothers. Duane had gone for the weekend to a friend's house, probably to watch R-rated movies on the VCR. And Cheryl and I were drinking the wine she had brought and were talking about her favorite topic: Cheryl's future. "I'm just gathering myself," she loved to say. On the little TV screen in the bedroom, a late Friday night basketball game from L.A. was showing, and the slow motion replay of James Worthy exploding into a killer jam for two points plus the foul shot prompted Cheryl to point a stubby white finger at the black man panthering the ball. "I'm like him," she'd said. "I'm gathering myself for something like that. One of these days, brother, *wham*!" I all but tore my pajama coat off her after that. And we were together for a strong, friendly several months.

"I can't be anybody's medicine," Cheryl had finally said.

"Maybe you're mine, though," I'd told her.

"Then maybe I don't want to be. I don't like sickness."

So I couldn't call Jackie, and I couldn't call Cheryl, and what I'd called to Duane hadn't worked. It left me with myself, one-on-one.

I quit work at midday, canceling a lunch date and a conference about the new German contraceptive foam we were marketing. I asked my assistant to deliver the Christmas issue of our magazine to the printer, and I went shopping. Past ski costumes and NFL shirts, in the back, near cardiac fitness machines and free-weight rigs, I found the backboard, basket, and pole I was looking for.

Cheryl was there. I had known she would be. I told her, "I didn't come in here to pester you, Cheryl."

She shook her head and her long hair swung. "I know that. You see? You're putting yourself down. Still."

"I don't mean to."

"I guess you don't. But you do it. You're so fuckin *sad*, dammit. Now you, suppose you tell me what you want and I'll see if I can sell it to you and let's us not have this discussion ever again in our lives. All right?"

"A backboard and hoop to go on a metal pole," I said.

She pointed. "This one you were looking at already. You losing weight?"

"Nope."

"My sweet ass you're not. Are you sick? Are you in love?"

She was wearing a black turtleneck, black shorts over black tights, low, soft white boots. I didn't want to look like a man looking over a woman. So I studied the metal frame of the outdoor backboard, and I said, "No. No more love these days, Cheryl."

"You old bore. This one's got fiberglass on one side, metal on the other. It goes on this two-piece pole, which is the full ten feet, Duane'll love it for Christmas, and he deserves it, so you buy it for him. Is your life all right?"

"I hear that yours is."

"Oh, Dave? We're doing some kind of collision trip. He thinks we're heading for marriage, and I know we aren't, and he's gonna bang smack into what's what, and what's not, and then we'll be through."

"You don't make it easy," I said.

She shook her head. "Nope. I never did."

When she looked at me again, I said, "You were always very nice to me, Cheryl. You were a pal."

"A pal," she said. She inspected the cord of the basketball net. "How's the Dude doing on the team? JV, is it?"

"To tell you the truth, he wants to quit."

"Are they sitting him down, or is he playing bad? You tell him for me that coming up to JV at his age is a tough transition. He might do better on the freshman team."

"I don't think he'd hear me if I told him."

"He does sound like a teenaged boy. You won't let him quit?"

"No."

"No, you wouldn't. It must be tough at home, though, after practice and all. After the games."

"No more than any other undeclared war," I said.

She looked at me angrily. "That boy isn't in a war, and you know it. He's in his life. And that's worse, I don't wonder."

"Sure. It just makes some evenings very long."

She slapped her order pad onto the carton in which the backboard came. Then she lined her pen up alongside it. She put her hands on her waist, and then she sighed. For an instant she was silent, and then she asked, "Who do you talk about it with? You know, at the office and all."

"Nobody. You'd have guessed that."

"Well, I did," she said.

"Yes."

"Yes, yourself." She looked up, as if at the sun, or at a clock. She crossed her strong wrists in front of her and asked, "Would you like me to visit you guys sometime?"

She was looking at me, and I couldn't look anyplace else except her broad, cheerful, muscular face with its two horizontal lines scored onto her brow that told how hard she had to work, sometimes, to smile. "I'll take the set," I said to her. "Pole, backboard, hoop. Is that a collapsible hoop? With those pins that release the hoop from the backboard if you get caught on it dunking or something?"

She looked at me a little longer, then she said, "That's right. What'd you do, get strong or something?"

I said, "Anything but that, and you know it."

She was writing down the stock numbers of the display models. "You going to hire somebody with a backhoe to come on up after Christmas and plant that pole in the hard ground?"

"You use a pickax," I said. "You keep hacking with it, and you sweat like hell, I guess, and you do it. The ground's not really frozen yet."

She looked into my eyes again. She said, "I can still make you blush."

On Christmas morning, I woke up early. I always do. I went downstairs and made a pot of coffee. I lit the bulbs on the tree that I'd brought in on Christmas Eve to decorate alone. Duane had offered to help, and the cartons of balls and hangings, and our silence, had almost defeated me. I had forgotten how much we'd bought for Christmas, the silly spidery drawings that Duane had made in class to hang on the tree, and the little dolls from her childhood that Jackie had insisted, every year, we use. I omitted them. Duane remembered them and hung each one. On Christmas morning, I declared to the tree and the dolls, "I am getting better." Then I lit the tree and called upstairs to Duane, and he came down with a sheepish expression. Anticipation, and childhood's habitual Christmas Day gladness, the pleasure of greed fulfilled—all were eroding his set, stern face. He grinned at me, and I grinned back. "Merry Christmas, Duane," I said. He stooped to lay his head near mine so I could kiss him. And from his bathrobe pocket, his gluey breath enveloping us, he took a little package and wordlessly bestowed it on me.

While I unwrapped the cassette of Linda Ronstadt singing blues songs—the card, in Duane's stringy hand, said, *For a horny old guy*—he tore open the three cartons containing his pole and backboard and hoop, as well as his lesser gifts (a Stephen King horror story, a poster of Julius Erving, a sports watch it would take a technician to start, a sultry aftershave, a Genesis tape, a terry-cloth sweatband). I went up to him, and he straightened and regarded me. I hugged him hard. He didn't hug me back, but he rested his hands on my hips and let me squeeze his ribs. "Duane, I love you," I said. I said my prayer: "We're gonna be all right."

He nodded.

I said, "You want some breakfast?"

He shook his head. "I want to practice free throws," he said. "Maybe he'll play me if I get myself fouled a lot and make my free throws."

Duane, then, was outside on his cold stone court, practicing basketball while wearing gloves and a heavy sweatshirt and a woolen watch cap, looking to me like someone else's child, a stevedore, a boxer in training, some *man*, and not my former baby. I sat inside, sneaking glimpses of him from the kitchen window when I went to fill my coffee cup.

Up the packed dirt road from the south came a long white Trans Am with purple and black stripes that ran its length. It was the ultimate expression of tastelessness in cars. It went very slowly, and I could see, as it passed the house and went in the direction of our roadside barn, that Cheryl sat in the passenger seat, pointing.

The car pulled in at the side of the road, and Cheryl emerged. The driver sat behind the wheel, and I could almost feel the motor throb over the side lawn, the cold air.

She removed a postholer and a pickax from the trunk. They looked too heavy for her, but she marched with a springy step. She wore a man's oversized jacket that said *Yankees* across the back. She went up to Duane and tugged his head down to her. I watched him allow her to kiss him. Then she talked about her plans, I guess, pointing at the edge of the ramp, and Duane shrugged, then nodded. Cheryl swung the pickax, and it bit. The ground wasn't solid yet, so I knew she'd get into the earth. She did. That chunky body swung and swung, regularly, evenly, with strength I knew well. When she'd pulverized the rocky soil, she used the scissor-handled postholer to scoop up dirt. I stood near the wood stove, in my bathrobe, and watched her work away.

Duane went to help her several times, but she shook him off and, after a while, he went to stand beneath his old hoop, holding the ball against his hip. She worked at wedging some heavy rocks from the hole with the postholer. Her boyfriend sat in his idling car, and I stood in my kitchen. After a while, she had a hole I could pour cement into, then stand the pole in, propping it in place with two-by-fours until it set.

Cheryl stood by her Christmas present, leaning the head of her pickax on the pile of earth she'd made. She panted and wiped at her brow with its parallel lines. She always did know how to sweat. She wore a dark stocking cap, and her bright hair stood out around it. Then she turned to Duane, who was watching her.

I said, in my kitchen, "Oh, Duane."

As if she had said that to him, in the way I heard myself say it, he dropped his basketball, and he went to her, and he stopped to seize her clumsily by the waist, then wrap his arms around her back, then hug. He bent his face down and kissed her on the cheek. I would have bet that he closed his eyes. He stepped back. Cheryl reached up and rubbed at his cheek. He nodded, then stepped back farther. As she turned and walked toward the waiting car, Duane went to retrieve his ball. Cheryl turned her head to the kitchen window and she stared at me. I believe that she knew I'd be looking. She'd supplied the hole. I could supply the pole. "I can still make you blush."

The Trans Am pulled away, and Duane watched it go. He bounced the ball once, hard, and he caught it on the rise. He dribbled slowly from the mound of dirt that Cheryl had left to the far end of the cattle ramp, where the old backboard was bolted to the barn. He stood beneath the basket, slowly bouncing the ball. I waited for him to lay it in, or step back and shoot.

My legs tensed with a boy's thoughtless strength against a concrete court at Wingate Field. Looking at Duane, I thought: Up! Take it up! And I felt him yearn vertically.

But he stopped dribbling. He held the ball. He stared up at the old backboard and he gripped the ball as though it were almost too heavy to hold at his waist, much less toss through the air, ten feet of cold, resistant air, to the hoop.

Frederick Busch was born in Brooklyn, New York, in 1941, and educated at Muhlenberg College and Columbia University. He is Fairchild Professor of Literature at Colgate University, where he has taught since 1966. He has held a National Endowment for the Arts Fellowship, a Guggenheim Fellowship, and an Ingram Merrill Fellowship. He was awarded the National Jewish Book Award for *Invisible Mending*, and in 1986 he was given an award in literature by the American Academy and Institute of Arts and Letters. He and his wife, Judy, live with their two sons in Sherburne, New York.

A NOTE ON THE TYPE

This book was set on the Linotype in Janson, a recutting
made direct from type cast from matrices long thought
to have been made by the Dutchman Anton Janson, who
was a practicing type founder in Leipzig during the
years 1668–1687. However, it has been conclusively
demonstrated that these types are actually the work of
Nicholas Kis (1650–1702), a Hungarian, who most
probably learned his trade from the master Dutch type
founder Dirk Voskens. The type is an excellent example
of the influential and sturdy Dutch types that prevailed
in England up to the time William Caslon developed his
own incomparable designs from them.

Composition by Heritage Printers, Inc.,
Charlotte, North Carolina
Printed and bound by The Haddon Craftsmen, Inc.,
Scranton, Pennsylvania
Designed by Harry Ford